AN EMPIRE LOST

Berengaria of Navarre
Book Three

Austin Hernon

SAPERE
BOOKS

AN EMPIRE LOST

Published by Sapere Books.

24 Trafalgar Road, Ilkley, LS29 8HH

saperebooks.com

ISBN: 978-0-85495-279-3

This story in dedicated to the memory of Queen Berengaria — a brave lady indeed. God bless her.

CHAPTER ONE

November 1192

I had been in Rome for little more than a day, and already I had been granted an audience with Pope Celestine. Along with Joan, my sister-in-law, I had described what I had seen and experienced during my time on Crusade with my husband, King Richard of England. His Holiness had seemed charmed by us both, and by the time Joan and I left his presence, we both felt we had secured a new ally.

Not for the first time in my marriage, my husband was absent. Having defeated the Saracen forces in Jaffa, Richard had sent Joan and I a message to say he had further business elsewhere. What or where this might be, we had no idea. We could only occupy ourselves as best we could while we waited for Richard to join us in Rome. Fortunately, the Church had put a villa at our disposal, so we could at least spend our days in luxury. We were now on our way back to our temporary abode after our meeting with the Pope.

We were welcomed back to the villa by a throng in the grand hall. There was much excitement surrounding our papal audience, since so few people ever got to meet His Holiness.

When it calmed down, I had the opportunity to talk with Stephen of Turnham, one of Richard's advisors who was now part of my household.

'Come, Stephen; we will find our new priest and have something to eat. It must be past noon. We will discuss matters of concern.'

'Yes,' said Joan, 'this encountering Popes is quite a hungry task.'

Joan and I sat down with Stephen. Two other knights who were employed to protect us — Guy de Bernez and Stephen Longchamp — were also at the table, along with Father Edwin, an English priest who was acting as an intermediary between us and the cardinals who had welcomed us to Rome, Cardinals Melior and Benedetto.

'We only arrived yesterday, but welcome to Rome, everyone,' I began. 'Tell me, are you and our knights comfortable in your quarters, Stephen?'

'Apart from the horses farting? Yes, we are in the hayloft and have all we need.'

'Are you getting along with the Italian guards?'

'Yes. There's a little difficulty with language, but we'll get there. They are taking us to have a look around the vicinity. All the villas are within walls and guarded; any strangers will be regarded with suspicion, so we need to become known. We're going to visit a church nearby so that you may attend for prayers, Your Highness.'

'Yes, that's the Basilica di Santa Maria Maggiore,' added Father Edwin. 'It is very beautiful, and you will be welcomed there.'

'What else can we see?' asked Joan.

'The gardens are nice, but it is the end of the year,' said Stephen.

'The Colosseum is nearby,' added Father Edwin. 'You have time, and I can escort you.'

'Is that where they martyred all those Christians years ago?' asked Joan.

'Unfortunately, yes.'

'Then we shall go there and pray. But regarding our next move, Father…?' I asked, uncertain.

'It is near the end of November. If King Richard does not turn up soon, you may as well stay through the Christmas period — it is marvellous here — and then decide what to do after that.'

'And markets, Father?' pressed Joan.

'Markets aplenty.'

'Markets and marble, Joan; we can find new gowns and visit churches and palaces.'

'We will come along, Your Highness?' asked Stephen, a question I sensed was for form only.

'We wouldn't move without you, rest assured,' I replied.

'You must not, Your Highness. There are thieves and vagabonds, and you'd make a pretty hostage for evil men.'

'Should we not dress as queens or ladies, Father?' asked Joan.

'Dress for the occasion, Lady Joan; you will know more about that than I.'

'And you, Father? What can you tell us about you, an Englishman in Rome?'

'There are many of us, and you will no doubt meet others; rest assured they will come calling. As for me, I am here on the instructions of the late Archbishop Roger de Pont L'Évêque. Geoffrey Plantagenet is the nominated replacement Archbishop of York. I am learning to teach Latin among other duties.'

'Nominated?' I asked.

'The king has nominated him, but His Holiness has not allowed him to be consecrated yet. He is the half-brother of your husband.'

'Really? I'm growing a family. Pay attention, Joan — a history lesson.'

Father Edwin laughed. 'We'll take our time. There is much to learn about: Cuthbert, Bede, Columba, Alban and many more. The history of my homeland — your realm, Your Highness — holds many tales.'

'Are you my chaplain, Father?'

'I am nothing unless you agree to appoint me, Your Highness.'

'I see,' I said, thinking.

Then Hortensia, the housekeeper, came in with her serving girls and set food and drink upon the table, which was attacked with gusto, and we settled down to an afternoon's trivial chatter. I was sparing with the wine and not slow to see the interaction between my two young knights and the serving girls. *I'll need to be attentive. We don't want any complications before we leave.* So I decided to break up our meeting by going for a walk.

'Take us to that *basilica* you mentioned, Father. I should like to see the neighbourhood.'

'Of course. It is not far, and hereabouts are perfectly safe for you; all of the villas have guards at the gates and in the grounds. I fear that the poor do not come near here, not even to visit the *basilica* of Santa Maria Maggiore.'

'How sad. The poor have souls too; of that I am certain,' I mumbled disconsolately.

The walk was a revelation. From close to the villa we could see over the city, and it did seem all crowded together, with splendid buildings poking their tops out: a mixture of the cruel grandeur that was ancient Rome, and the huddled streets of today.

The *basilica* was splendid. We were met at the door by a priest, but while he was introducing himself my eyes were dragged further in by the overwhelming multicoloured ceilings and walls. I heard his name.

'I am Father Bernard, Your Highness, and because I am English I have been chosen to guide you around this magnificent church.'

'Oh, I see. Do you know Father Edwin?'

'Of course. Welcome, Edwin.'

'Are you in charge here, Father?' asked Joan.

'Not at all, *signora*. I am studying Latin. The *basilica* is a patriarchal establishment, one of four in Rome, and is used by His Holiness for ceremonial occasions. The Pope is the archpriest.'

'Oh, it is very colourful! May we go in?'

It was a fascinating tour. The church had been there since the fifth century, and many of its features were original. I was especially impressed by some of the mosaic ceilings, already over seven hundred years old, and the carvings.

'Fabulous,' I whispered, feeling small.

'God's glory, truly.'

Being there brought some peace to my mind, and when we were offered a place to kneel before the altar I spent some time in contemplation before a polite cough brought me back to the here and now.

'The light is fading, Your Highness. Time to walk back.'

We wandered along the darkening streets back to our villa in silence — no one wanted to break the mood of reflection — then sat quietly at our table while Hortensia guided her serving girls to provide us with some light refreshments.

'You enjoy your visit, *altezza*?' asked Hortensia.

'It has moved me, Signora Hortensia; that is true.'

'I think that everyone feels the same, *altezza*. The place is God's, is it not?'

'That is the truth,' agreed Father Edwin.

I began to feel the call of bed, and I noticed Joan's closing eyelids. She would not need much persuasion to climb the marble stairway.

'Father Edwin, we'll take another walk around the vicinity in the morning. Perhaps you can come with us, and we'll pray at the *basilica*?'

'It would be a privilege, Your Highness. I have a list of those who wish to come and pay you a visit, and perhaps we can sort them into priorities.'

'The curious and the useful,' commented Joan, ever the pragmatist.

'Quite, my lady, as you say.' Edwin grinned and stood. 'God bless you and sleep well, Your Highness.'

Joan and I walked to my privy chambers, both wishing to dissect the day. We then undressed and sat down on my bed.

'Are you content that you have cut your ties with Sicily?' I asked. Joan had once been Queen of Sicily through her marriage to its king, William II. When he'd died, William's bastard cousin, Tancred, had seized the realm and placed Joan under house arrest. Richard had rescued her, and she had since decided to give up any claim to her previous title. Princess Constance, as a descendant of the kings of Sicily, also had a claim to Sicily's throne. Her husband, Heinrich VI — Holy Roman Emperor and king of the Germans — was now aiming to exploit her claim, but the Pope did not wish to have a German royal family so close to the mainland of Italy. It was therefore most convenient for His Holiness to support Tancred as the *de facto* King of Sicily, thereby thwarting Heinrich's demands for Constance to become the queen regent on the island.

'It isn't worth the struggle,' said Joan with a sigh. 'I found little joy in it, and Mother Church has more need of Sicily than

I. Besides, being here with you I have rediscovered peace, and I like it better than war.'

Not many days later we received a note from Isaac, one of Richard's shipmasters. It read:

No sign of the king. Robert of Turnham and the scribe Hugo are close by me in Robert's ship. He has the king's chests but not the king. He sends his regards. We are moored off Ostia and will sail together to Barfleur as soon as we are ready to face the Pillars of Hercules off the Spanish coast. Send for your belongings when you are next at home.

'Oh, that's it then. No chests, no king, no ship,' said Joan.

'But I suppose Stephen will be glad to hear news of his brother,' I said, referring to Robert of Turnham. 'We came a long way on a horse; we can return on one.' I tried to remain cheerful, but somehow I felt that things had changed, and I wasn't sure why. 'We need to go and question Robert. Father Edwin, can you obtain horses for us?'

'Surely — I'll speak to Hortensia. Not a carriage?'

'Definitely not.'

The next morning we were lined up outside the villa, Hortensia looking on anxiously as I arranged my gown around me astride a skittish mare, which knew not Basque, Spanish or English, as Stephen discovered on his gelding. Prodding the beast in the side, I set off behind the escorting Roman *cavalieri*, with Stephen and our two knights behind on either side of Joan. To help make sure that we maintained a good speed, we left behind our ladies, Alazne, Pavot and Torène.

A swift fifteen-mile ride saw us at the jetty by midafternoon, our target ships clearly visible.

'We have caught them before they sail, Joan,' I said, pausing to point out to sea. The two ships were at anchor but moving about on the restless water, ruffled by a fitful wind.

'Your Highness! Brother!' someone called from a small boat lying alongside the jetty.

'Robert!' shouted Stephen as he jumped off his horse and ran along the wooden structure.

'We'll dismount ourselves, Joan. We've lost our guardian,' I said, just as I felt a firm hand take hold of my reins.

'Worry not, Your Highness,' said Guy de Bernez, smiling up at me. 'I'll hand you down, if you'll permit.'

'Catch me,' I replied, swinging a leg over the saddle and sliding down the side of my mount.

He caught me and let me down.

I decided to walk slowly along to join them, and was intercepted along the way by Hugo, Richard's scribe and our good friend. 'Your Highness!' he called from amid the press of the curious and the busy on the jetty.

'Hugo,' I responded as he came to me. 'We have missed you. No king?'

'Sadly, Your Highness, no king. You can greet Robert next. He brought me here in his ship.'

'Let Robert and Stephen enjoy their brotherly reunion; we have time. Do you want to join us in Rome?'

'Lord Robert thinks that I should stay with him until the king's intentions are clear. But I would, Your Highness, gladly.'

I took him by the hand and planted a kiss on one cheek, much to his discomfort. Joan did the same.

'We'll meet with Robert of Turnham now,' she said, grinning at him. Blushing, he led us over.

Robert released his brother to greet me. 'Your Highness,' he said, eyeing me up and down. 'What a splendid sight; you are a vison for sore eyes — you too, Queen Joan.'

Stephen coughed and looked at Joan, waiting for her to say something.

'Robert, you are behind the times,' said Joan, causing Robert's smile to become a frown.

'How so, Your Highness?'

'I am "Your Highness" no longer; I am the Lady Joan. I have given up the title of dowager queen and am a rejuvenated person for it.'

'Where is my husband, Robert?' I asked, before he could respond.

'Last seen in Cyprus. He sent me ahead with his baggage.'

'So he left the Holy Land with his mission unfulfilled?'

'On October the fourteenth. He has a treaty with Saladin allowing pilgrim's access to Jerusalem, and the castles along the coast are to remain as places of rest for them.'

'As long as Saladin lives. But he is not a young man.'

'True, and we must wait to see God's will in the matter.'

'What is Richard's intention when he leaves Cyprus, Robert?'

'He was undecided over which side of Italy to travel up; he is wary of Rome on this side, unwilling to face His Holiness over the bartered bride.' He grinned at Joan and got a sniff in return. Saladin's brother had taken a fancy to Joan, and Richard had seriously considered an alliance through marriage as part of his negotiations — much to Joan's and the Pope's dismay. 'Richard made so many enemies in Outremer. His endeavours have angered many jealous lords, especially those whose men left their lords to join Richard. Besides, coming around the Italian coast might put him in the grasp of the Spanish if he heads for Navarre on land. To try the Pillars of

Hercules did not appeal to him, the lands to both sides of the sea being in the hands of Saracens. He sees enemies all around him, and I know not which passage he will choose.'

'Nor I, Robert, nor I.'

'No your Highness, that is for the future. Can I give you a hug? I am so pleased to see you safe.'

I didn't answer, so flummoxed was I and he stepped forward and held me. It felt good until Stephen coughed and we parted.

'We will be leaving when the wind changes, Your Highness,' said Robert. 'Do you want to join us?'

Flummoxed again, I looked at Joan. She was as surprised as me; it would be another voyage through strange waters, and I knew that the seas off Navarre could be quite wild at this time of year.

'That is an idea, Robert, but we have unfinished business here,' I replied. 'I will wait a while longer for Richard, and we have been promised another audience with His Holiness. There are many who we must thank and say goodbye to, and I do not fancy a passage through the Pillars of Hercules at this time of year, and…'

'Enough, enough, Your Highness — you mean that the answer is no?'

'I'm sure that you can manage without us. But do come and see us when we are settled somewhere nearer to your home. I know not where that will be.'

'The king favours Angers, Your Highness.'

'Well, for all I know, Angers it will be,' I said.

'Is that it, Berengaria? We stay?' said Joan.

I nodded, hiding a tear.

Joan continued. 'Rome is very interesting, and we have not yet attacked all of the markets. With regret, Robert, you must journey without us.' She smiled her sweetest smile and his legs buckled, but he managed a stiff smile back.

'Oh well,' he said. 'I shall await the day when we meet again. You came here to learn about Richard and now you know as much as I do. Sorry.'

Stephen stepped in to ask a question. 'Do you want to remain here in Ostia for a while longer, Your Highness? I can arrange food and beds.'

'Will you join us, Robert?' I asked, reaching out a hand.

Without hesitation he accepted. 'My pleasure and my privilege, Your Highness. Where will you take us, Stephen?'

'The horses can stay in yonder cavalry barracks, and we can go to the hostelry over there by the church of Santa Aurea; it is a *diocesi* of Rome, a guest house for visitors. It grows gloomy now, and we would be wise not to take to the roads in the dark.'

The hostelry was basic but clean, and we were attended to by servants under the guidance of a pair of priests, yet conversation was a little stilted. Robert and Stephen were most concerned about their families back home in England. I listened eagerly to them to learn more about life in England, which left Joan a bit disconnected. Our evening was also overshadowed by Robert's imminent departure and my husband's non-appearance. After a while I became tired and wilted a little. Robert, ever attentive, saw this and stood to announce his departure.

'Your Highness, I should not linger much longer; if the wind shifts during the night, we should be prepared to leave at first light. Will you excuse me if I re-join my ship?'

'Of course, dear friend.' I stood. 'We have endured much, Robert, and have been much supported by you. Thank you, and be safe; we will pray for your smooth voyage. We'll meet again when I have endured the sight of the back of a horse's ears for a while longer and arrived in my new domains. Perhaps that will be England one day.'

He laughed, I shed a tear, and Stephen dragged him out to see him down to the jetty. There was a silence. Joan gazed at me, her eyes glistening.

'Well,' she said, 'another goodbye. How many more?'

The final sight was Hugo, standing near the steersman next to Robert and waving unenthusiastically.

'Life is full of goodbyes, Joan. Let's to bed.'

The next morning, Stephen had our horses ready.

'Which market shall we try next?' asked Joan, avoiding Stephen's helpful hand as she mounted up.

'Markets?' echoed Stephen.

'Quite, Stephen,' said Joan. 'Markets and churches until my brother reappears.'

'Stephen,' I clucked, 'be kind. Find something to take back to your family.'

'How many more?' complained Joan one evening in the middle of December, having seen yet more visitors off.

'There can't be many English left in Rome to see, and there were all those bishops and Italian *contest* and *contessas*. We seem to be this year's prime exhibit.'

'*Circus maximus*,' she giggled. 'Do you think that we should keep Father Edwin as our chaplain, Berri?'

'Perhaps, but I'm not certain that he is only here to improve his Latin. He seems to write something every day.'

'I've seen it; it's not Latin.'

'English?'

'Probably. I wonder if he reports our goings-on to Archbishop Geoffrey?'

'An intelligencer? What if Geoffrey Plantagenet does not keep his position?'

'What indeed? But you'll be in Edwin's writings whoever they go to, Queen of England.'

'Then I should influence what he writes. I'll ask Cardinal Benedetto to appoint him next time we meet. Now, where is that list of services we should attend? We should give up expecting to meet His Holiness until after Christmas; he will be far too busy.'

'Agreed. We are to see the seamstress for our new gown fittings today.'

'And those fur-lined capes. I do not want to trip over on the hems; they're far too long for me.'

Cardinal Benedetto came to see me before Christmas Day. He was led in by Father Edwin. Both seemed uncheerful for such a joyous season.

'Greetings,' I said, descending the stairs into the hall. 'Not so cheery, Your Eminence?'

'*Altezza*,' he said as Joan came down behind me, 'we have some reports.'

'Oh, let's sit.'

Hortensia appeared with a carafe of lemon juice and commenced pouring it into goblets.

'Reports, Your Eminence?'

'Indeed, Your Highness,' said Edwin. 'You told me about the storm you endured on your way to Italy.'

'The one Master Isaac skilfully navigated?'

'Indeed, Your Highness.'

'Not all who followed you were so fortunate,' the cardinal added. 'There are reports of Crusader ships taking shelter all along the eastern coast, off Brindisi and Bari, and perhaps further up the Adriatic Sea.'

'The *Trenche de Mar*, the king's ship; what of her?' Joan asked.

'Alas,' replied the cardinal, 'nothing so specific is reported.'

'We must pray, Your Highness,' added Father Edwin. 'Wait and pray.'

'Indeed; we will relay any news as soon as possible.'

'Yes, Joan. What else? Can we add our prayers to those for Christmas, Your Eminence?'

'Indeed. We will pray for all our returning Crusaders, and Father Edwin will lead you in privy prayer if you wish.'

'We would appreciate that.'

So there were two kings on our minds during the Christmas festivities: the King of our souls and the King of England, wherever he might be.

That mystery was solved well after Christmas Day, when Father Edwin came back from a meeting at the Basilica di San Giovanni in Laterano with Pope Celestine.

'What is it, Father?'

'Not good news, I fear,' said Joan.

'It may be good, or not so bad,' he answered. 'The king sailed up the east side of Italy, but his ship was driven ashore between Aquileia and Venezia. It avoided rocks but could not be re-floated, so all the people on board left it there and went off on foot.'

'That's typical of my brother; he couldn't take shelter like the other vessels, but drove onward before the wind.' Joan was furious and stamped her way around the hall.

'Is that all we have, Father? I wonder if he was heading for Venezia?'

'Let us pray so, Your Highness. We will hear soon enough. He may well choose to cross Italy in front of the Alps. He will not be able to cross, of course, the passes being closed in the winter.'

'If he crosses Italy south of the Alps, he will no doubt want to cross by Toulouse to Aquitaine or Navarre,' said Joan. 'Raymond of Toulouse does not like Richard; he sides with King Philip over the matter of Richard's choice of brides, so his attitude will be interesting.' Before our marriage, Richard had repudiated his previous fiancée, Alys, Countess of Vexin — the sister of King Philip II of France — after finding out she had had an affair with his father. In doing so, Richard had damaged his relationship with Philip and his allies.

'My husband is a Crusader; he has the protection of the Church,' I pointed out, not liking the implication that I might be a second choice, or a convenient one.

'We pray so, Your Highness,' said Edwin.

CHAPTER TWO

1193

It was now the middle of January 1193, and we'd still had no word of Richard.

My bedchamber was full, with all my ladies lounging around in their finery. Joan and I were joined not only by Alazne, Pavot and Torène, but also by Princess Eirini of Cyprus, who had joined my entourage after Richard had captured her father — Isaac Comnenus, former ruler of Cyprus — during his conquest of her homeland. I now believed it was my duty to protect her. Beside her were Nabila and Alya, two Arabian girls who acted as her companions, and Amynta, a Griffon widow who watched over them all.

Hortensia had placed wine and sweetmeats on a buffet at my request; this evening was for ladies only. I knew that Stephen and the two young knights were roistering with the Italian guards in their barracks. Father Edwin had been sent for to visit Cardinals Melior and Benedetto. I knew why but I said naught. He was about to become our new chaplain; I prayed that he would agree.

'Are there any more services or visits, Berri?' asked Joan.

'I'll consult my list.' I glanced at it, then scrunched it into a ball and flung it towards the door as Father Edwin knocked and poked his head in.

'Lists, Father. No more lists for a while; let's be ourselves, and not exhibits,' I said.

'As you wish, Your Highness, as you wish.'

That met with universal approval, and Amynta allowed herself a small goblet of wine.

'A libation,' she said, 'to a quiet January.'

'Amen to that,' we chorused.

After a few moments I came to the real reason for this gathering: how to move on.

'Any news, Father?' He shook his head, so I continued. 'As you all know now, I am guessing that the king may not pass through Rome, and we must plan our way out.'

'Where to?' asked Eirini.

'That is what we should decide. I must make my way to England, or at least find Queen Eleanor and consult her on my way forward. Lady Joan will come with me, to return to her mother and plan her own way henceforth. We may have been left to decide our own future. Eirini, we would like you to come with us, and we'll possibly find you a suitable husband. Alazne, Pavot and Torène can remain with us, but I need to know what Amynta, Alya and Nabila want to do.'

Amynta spoke first. 'If I cannot stay here, I would like to find my way back to Cyprus.'

She looked at Alya and Nabila; they understood most of what we said now, even if they were reluctant to speak. They went into a privy conversation, some of which I heard and none of which I understood, and the results surprised me.

They crossed the chamber and stood on either side of our Griffon lady.

'We will stay with Amynta,' Alya said. 'Amynta is good.'

'I see. Amynta, you said that you would stay here; is that your first choice?'

'Yes, I like it here.'

'Alya, Nabila?'

'We will stay with Amynta,' Nabila replied.

I was relieved: the three electing to stay would solve the problem of what to do with them. I didn't think that the climes north of the Pyrenees or that of Outremer would be the best places to ensure a happy future.

'If that is your wish, I'll speak to Hortensia and see if we can find a position for you.'

There were squeals of delight from the trio.

'I hope that we can solve our situation as easily,' said Joan.

'I have asked to see His Holiness. You and I need his guidance, Joan.'

Later Hortensia agreed that she would seek out positions for Amynta and the two girls. A villa nearby had new occupants, and good staff were hard to find in a busy place like Rome. Therefore, this was an ideal solution.

The next morning brought a weak sun. Father Edwin, a thoughtful expression on his normally placid face, came immediately to stand before me, and to my surprise he offered his hands. He was a lot taller than I, but then most people were.

'Your Highness, I have been asked to be your chaplain.'

Taking his hands in mine, I looked up into his blue eyes and answered honestly. 'I asked.'

He knelt and looked up at me. 'I am honoured, Your Highness. It is a privilege to serve such a lovely, pious lady; thank you.'

'Ah, I too consider it a privilege. The next time you kneel, Father, we will do it together, but not now.' I lifted him and parted our hands. 'Does that include Lady Joan?'

He looked over to her. 'If she wishes, I would be twice blessed.'

'As would I,' replied Joan.

'That's settled, then. Will you travel with us when we leave?'

'Of course. I need to return to Winchester one day; we can go together.'

'Good. Now, tell us what news is in the city.'

'Ah!' he said. That wiped the smile off his face. 'We should sit, Your Highness; there is much to tell.'

'Alazne, go and fetch Lord Stephen, and do not flirt with those Roman soldiers.'

'As if,' she laughed. She was not shy of teasing, but she preferred the company of women — Pavot in particular.

'You have news of Richard, Father?' I asked while we waited for Stephen.

'No, I speak of your mother-in-law, Queen Eleanor. There is disturbing news, not least from Winchester.'

'You are in regular correspondence with the Church there?'

'Oh, yes, Your Highness,' he replied, thus innocently confirming that he was in Rome to improve his Latin by acting as an intelligencer for the Church in England.

'Ah, here is Stephen. Join us, Stephen; we are about to hear news from England,' I said.

'Longchamp?' queried Stephen. Longchamp looked taken aback.

'The same,' Edwin said. 'Your brother, William, is Bishop of Ely and Chancellor of England?'

'Just so,' answered Longchamp with a puzzled expression.

'Then this is of interest to you,' said Edwin. 'When Queen Eleanor returned home after she left you with Richard in Messina, Your Highness, she found that back in England, William Longchamp and Prince John had been in dispute and Longchamp had fled for his life to France. As well as Chancellor he was Pope Clement's legate in England, and he is now His Holiness Celestine's. King Richard had suspicions about John and had already despatched Walter de Coutances from Palestine to mediate between them — to no avail, it seems.'

I nodded, trying to take it all in. It had been Eleanor who had arranged the match between Richard and me. After I had agreed to leave my home in Navarre, she had accompanied me across Europe to join Richard as his Crusade progressed. As Queen Dowager of England, I knew she had great influence over certain aspects of politics and her sons. Richard had never trusted his younger brother, John, suspecting that he had designs on the throne of England in his absence. 'This is a tangled plot, Father,' I said eventually.

'There is more to tell, and you should know all, or as much as filters through to us. It's unfortunate that we are not nearer, and we need to wait for reports to wend their way to Rome. Still, we can form our thoughts. It seems that Eleanor gained control of the council of regents in England and is directing them against John. It is rumoured that he is seeking advantage against his brother Richard with Philip of France.'

'God almighty! Why did they ever leave that toad spawn in charge of England?' gasped Stephen.

'Well, they are regretting it now,' said Joan. 'What a midden to go back to.'

Longchamp was looking very uncomfortable; he had become embroiled in something many miles away, concerning his family, but could do naught about it. I wanted to broaden the discussion, so I asked him to leave us.

'If you have no questions, friend?'

'No, Your Highness. I need to think about this. I pray that my brother William survives, but there is nothing I can do. May I stay with your household?'

'Of course. Worry not; your position is safe.'

'Thank you, Your Highness.' He bowed and left us, a frown on his sweet face.

'Should we go to England, or at least as far as Aquitaine, Father?' I thought we would be safe in Aquitaine; Eleanor was its duchess, and it had become an English possession when she had married Richard's late father, King Henry II of England.

'His Holiness urges restraint, Your Highness, until the mists clear regarding Richard. He feels that we should let your mother and brother sort it out, but he is considering you, Your Highness,' he said, gazing at me. 'If Richard does not put in an appearance, what of you? Expect to be sent for soon, to discuss such things.'

'A goodly question,' said Stephen. 'What if England gains another queen dowager?'

'Oh, thank you, Stephen, for reminding me of that possibility,' I muttered. Everything could disappear from my grasp if Richard did not reappear.

Joan stretched out a hand to me, and Father Edwin gave Stephen a most unholy stare.

'Sorry, Your Highness, I did not mean to…'

'Well, you did,' said Joan annoyed. 'Now, be quiet and listen.' Stephen blushed and shuffled in his chair, but fell silent.

I made a decision. 'I shall write to Eleanor offering my support, and to my father to see if he understands the situation. As Father guards Eleanor's southern border, it is in both their interests to cooperate.'

'And you are somewhere in the middle, my sweet,' added Joan unnecessarily — I knew that too well. In a marriage designed to secure the borders of Navarre and Aquitaine — and with a dowager queen to manage this marriage — I was vulnerable. The turbulent relationship between Eleanor and me loomed large once more.

'Then all revolves around the location of Richard,' said Father Edwin. 'He is the key — that much is certain.'

Silence followed that remark, for what else was there to discuss? If Richard were safe, then Prince John would be undone. If he were not, then a bigger game would ensue.

'It might be wise to begin preparations for your onward journey. His Holiness might want you together with Queen Eleanor,' said Father Edwin.

'Suitably escorted, of course,' added Stephen, 'and we three will not be enough overland.'

'Overland?' I queried.

'Not by sea; the weather is not reliable until spring,' he answered.

'Shall we ride, Joan?'

'Are you certain that is what will be required?'

'I know not yet.' I looked hard at Edwin but did not test his knowledge of the Holy Father's mind. 'But if we are to travel onward, we will need money for clothing and horses, and we have little left in the way of funds.'

I was a queen with dowers, but the income from them was where those dowers lay — in the north at present, not where I was.

Father Edwin coughed. 'Perhaps some assistance can be found, Your Highness? Leave it to me. There are many of your supporters in the city, and I'll see if they can help.'

'And what do we do now, Berengaria?' asked Joan.

'Pray, Joan, pray. Every day we will walk along to the Basilica di Santa Maria Maggiore and pray.'

'I'll come with you as much as I can, between walking back and forth to the Laterano,' said Edwin.

'Do you ride, Father?' asked Joan.

'I have journeyed here from England and walked a lot, but I can manage to ride alongside you,' he responded.

'Then we'll see if Hortensia can arrange a gentle palfrey for you.'

CHAPTER THREE

Three days of prayer were all it took before we were answered, and towards the end of January Father Edwin burst into the hall in full voice.

'Your Highness, Your Highness, he is found; the king is found.'

We rushed down from our quarters, where we had been concentrating on stitching clothing for our journey north. There was lots of squealing, though we were three fewer now that Amynta, Alya and Nabila had moved out.

Cardinals Melior and Benedetto were coming up the stairs into the great hall with Father Edwin when we arrived from above; that was ominous.

'Is he safe?' I called before reaching the bottom step.

'Well, sort of,' Father Edwin answered.

'He is confined,' added Melior.

'In an Austrian castle,' said Benedetto.

'Please sit, Your Highnesses,' requested Father Edwin.

'Joan,' I cautioned, 'are you ready for this?'

'Yes, let's hear what madness afflicts my brother now, Your Eminences.'

Benedetto began when we were settled. 'It appears that instead of travelling across northern Italy, which is infested with Germans, Richard chose to cross over into Austria in disguise.'

'Yes,' said Melior, 'as a woman or a monk; it is unclear which at present. There are differing versions, but with his height he hardly fits either part.'

'But tall kings are difficult to disguise, and he was spotted,' Benedetto said.

'By some local lord,' agreed Melior. 'His entourage were too lavish with their spending and suspicions were aroused. This was on the twenty-first of December. He was taken to Duke Leopold, and he is now in Schloss Dürnstein awaiting the pleasure of Leopold's cousin and vassal lord, Heinrich of Germany.'

'Oh,' was all I could say.

'Why would he need to be in disguise? He is a returning Crusader, is he not?' Father Edwin cut to the nub of the matter — and I knew the answer.

'There is bad blood between them; Leopold entered Akko before Richard when they were recapturing the city from Saracen forces.'

'After Richard's siege machines tore the walls apart,' said Joan.

'But Leopold hung his banners on the gate,' I added. 'Then when Richard entered the city, he had the banners torn down and replaced with his own.'

'Leopold took offense and went home, taking his soldiers with him,' said Joan.

'Holy Mary,' exclaimed Melior. 'This is un-Christian revenge.'

'His Holiness does not like this,' said Benedetto. 'He knows that Richard is held at the pleasure of Heinrich; he must release the Crusader king without delay.'

There was a pause while our thoughts tumbled about, then something struck Father Edwin. 'If Heinrich holds the King of England prisoner, what ransom would Queen Berengaria add? We must keep you safe, Your Highness; we cannot move you without a suitable escort.'

'Agreed,' said Melior. 'We must consult His Holiness.'

'Yes,' said Stephen as he entered the hall. 'The guard here should be strengthened, Your Eminences.'

'Agreed,' said Benedetto. 'I'll see to it.'

Father Edwin's journeys betwixt our villa and the pontiff became ever more frequent, sometimes twice a day as plans were formulated and re-formulated when more information drifted into Rome. Then one day towards the end of January, he brought two fellows with him.

Eirini called up the stairs, her youthful voice echoing off the marble.

'There are men with the priest, Your Highness!'

Joan and I dashed to the top of the stairs and were somewhat relieved to see the top of Father Edwin's head. He looked up.

'Good news, Your Highness; come and see.'

We trotted downstairs and looked at his companions, not recognising them.

'These are Adam of Taleworth and John de Tolosa, Canon of Hereford, citizens of yours, Your Highness.' They bowed and I bid them welcome.

'Is it about the king?' I asked.

'No, Your Highness, I'm afraid not.'

'They have gathered funds to finance your journey north, Your Highness. Shall we sit?'

'Of course. Money, Joan; we can pay for all that cloth now.'

She tittered. 'I doubt we would be allowed to leave Rome without paying, Berengaria. I've noticed that the merchants here are very astute. Anyway, it is for our journey, if there is enough.'

'Indeed. How have you come by the money, good fellows?' I asked politely.

'We have gathered together some Englishmen here in Rome, and they are only too happy to help King Richard's queen,' replied Adam.

'And perhaps meet you, Your Highness,' added John of Hereford.

'Where is Hereford?' I asked.

'On the border with Wales, Your Highness,' replied Edwin helpfully.

I nodded, but with only the faintest idea of where he was referring to.

'Who then are my benefactors, Father?'

'I have a list, Your Highness; among them is a certain Stephen of Turnham...'

'Hah! Desperate measures, Berengaria — such a rogue.' Joan tittered, but her eyes fell upon the squirming Stephen with gratitude. 'Thank you,' she mouthed, and he blushed under her gaze.

'He is one of many guarantors, Your Highness,' said Edwin, obviously amused by Stephen's discomfort. 'Here is the list.'

I took it and read through. 'Geoffrey de Vendosm, William de Roches, Rogo de Saceio, Guy de Bernez...' I looked up and gave him a grateful smile. 'All these men are in Rome? And the Bishop of Porto, Roger de Sancto Germano. Then Walter, Archbishop of Rouen as the final guarantor. Good Lord, all these believe me to be a worthy queen?'

'You have met them, or they have witnessed your dignity, Your Highness; they have no doubts,' said Benedetto. Now it was my turn to blush.

'Upon my soul,' exclaimed Joan, 'it is quite warm in here. Shall we call for refreshments, Your Eminences?'

Amid the general discussion that followed, I sat silent, quite humbled. These good folk hardly knew me, yet they viewed me as their queen.

Only two days later, Pope Celestine sent for me.

It was raining as our carriage rattled down the hill and along to the Laterano.

'What does he know, Father?' I asked as we reached the flat ground and settled down for the short journey.

'Nothing that pleases him, Your Highness, since Heinrich has placed such a price on your husband's release.'

'Release! Or?'

'Or nothing. Richard will remain the guest of the Holy Roman Emperor in Germany until England produces the ransom. Here we are. Let me help you dismount, Your Highness.'

I stepped down to some applause; people knew why I was there. Richard's fate was now known for certain. I bowed gracefully to acknowledge my well-wishers and called to them, 'Pray for Richard! Pray for the Crusader king!'

Someone called back, '*Pregate per la regina! Pregate per la Regina Berengaria!*'

This helped a little, and soon we were within the hushed walls of San Giovanni and Pope Celestine's privy office. He walked in through the door opposite as we entered; Cardinals Melior and Benedetto were there waiting. Celestine crossed straight over to me, and as I bowed to the pontiff, he took hold of my hands and raised me up.

'*Regina*, let us talk. It is not about your husband; it is about the treaty he and the Islamist Saladin signed.'

I nodded; I knew that Saladin was the leader of the Saracen forces with whom Richard had been both fighting and negotiating. 'It guaranteed access for pilgrims to the Holy Land?'

'Yes, but Saladin is dead; he died on the fourth of March. What now of the treaty that Richard fought so hard for? What is your view of the issue?'

The cardinals faded into the background as His Holiness explained the situation as he saw it. The only other noise was that of his clerk as he scribbled down every word.

I left some hours later, leaving His Holiness deep in thought. So Saladin was dead, but what would his emirs do? Leopold had been excommunicated for dishonouring the Truce of God, which should protect Crusader travellers. Philip of France had also been warned about attempting to grab the lands of a Crusader, but that mattered not to Prince John in England, who had been visiting Philip and promising much, including giving away Plantagenet lands that bordered Philip's, and which did not belong to him. These included Normandy, of which I was duchess. In addition, John would accept Philip as his overlord if he supported him in his bid to succeed Richard as King of England. He also wondered if the deceased Saladin's emirs would honour Richard and Saladin's treaty; the omens were not good, with factions splitting the Saracen world apart.

'A mess, Berengaria,' were Pope Celestine's parting words. 'A mess which is mine to solve. Richard is not to come here, so perhaps you should as we discussed go to join Queen Eleanor and see what she has in mind? She seems to be the one best placed to find the ransom, if Heinrich will not obey my commands. We will do all that we can to aid your onward journey. God bless you, *Regina*. With God's help, I will solve this riddle.'

Joan frowned as I repeated His Holiness's words to her back at the villa.

'Homeward bound? Can't say that I'm sorry.'

'Everyone has gone home, except my husband,' I complained.

'We'll go and find Eleanor, as His Holiness seems to believe that she is the one to straighten this mess,' I concluded.

Joan thought for a moment. 'Mother seems to be pivotal in this. We might find her in Aquitaine, if my brother John hasn't sold it. She has an attachment to Fontevraud Abbey.'

'John only wants England,' I said glumly. 'The rest of the Plantagenet lands he'll give to Philip in order to besport himself at home. It seems that John has found himself a playground; God knows what the English think.'

'They're not amused, I should think,' Joan replied.

'Are we going to England?' asked Eirini.

'Does it matter?' I asked, looking at her. 'Wherever *you* go, there will be a queue of suitors.' She was an impressive sixteen-year-old.

'I want to go walking; who will come with me?' she asked.

'Run round to the stables and tell Stephen we are going out, Eirini. We cannot walk without our escort.'

As soon as Stephen and his two knights appeared, we set off to walk among the leafless trees, forgetting the chaos piling up in the Laterano. We counted stray cats and searched out daffodils and said hello to the many others wandering around in the cold sun of early spring.

'It's nice here, is it not?' Joan said.

'Should we visit Amynta?' suggested Eirini. 'There her villa.'

'Good idea. We'll see how they like their new employers,' said Joan.

The afternoon passed amicably, for who would refuse hospitality to a queen, a lady and a princess?

The walk and the visit had helped me to concentrate and prepare to move. If His Holiness found his way through the mess, things should move on apace. Now I wanted no delay in setting off for the north.

As we walked towards the villa, I asked Stephen to gather our people for a meeting to discuss the necessary arrangements. Hortensia was asked to bring sweetmeats and wine, and we settled in for the rest of the day.

First I listed the priorities and explained the situation as I saw it. Everyone was horrified at the treatment of Richard by the German emperor. But away from Rome, especially in the dark forests of Germany, perhaps His Holiness was too distant from his flock.

'Heinrich is damned, surely, if he continues to hold hostage returning Crusaders, a king and a warrior. What ails the German?' said Alazne.

'I know not, but as Duke Leopold is already excommunicated he should consider his next step carefully. That aside, we should be ready to move as soon as we are able,' I said.

Stephen added, 'Then we will be prepared to go when instructed. Have our travel plans been agreed, Your Highness?'

'Not in detail, but I expect that it will be a combination of ships and horses, so we have clothing now for all occasions.'

'Then we shall ready our arms and armour. Our hosts will provide the transport, whatever that is?'

'Father Edwin will make the arrangements with the cardinals; we are in their hands. Joan?'

'Nothing to add — another adventure, Berengaria. Life is never simple around you, is it?'

'Wake up every morning and wonder,' I laughed. Somehow I was enjoying this; we had something to do at last.

As there were no objections, the rest of the evening was spent listing those places in Rome that we had not yet visited, and how many we would try to cross off the list before we left. We had been assured that things were now in motion, as Father Edwin reported his news daily.

'All is well; we have despatched instructions and requests all along your path to ensure your safety. You'll be at sea, then you'll travel into Toulouse and Aquitaine. We expect an escort from Navarre to meet you as you go north, and we trust that Eleanor will make arrangements for you when you reach Plantagenet soil.'

'Is that when things become uncertain, Father?' I asked.

'Letters tell us some things; it may be different on the ground at the time of your arrival,' he replied.

'Into the unknown, again,' snorted Joan.

'Yes, Joan. But be certain of one thing: whenever I reach these new lands of mine, I will not be blown by the winds of chance. I'll have a say in my future, husband or not.'

Joan looked at me curiously. 'Just remember your limits, Berengaria. Mother was entertained in the Tower of London for making her feelings known to a king.'

'Yes, but she is still here, and I intend to survive too.'

Preparations took some weeks, with messengers sent ahead to prepare for our passage through different lands — some not entirely friendly with my husband, he not being the most diplomatic of kings. Thus the month of May had passed before we were in all respects ready to leave.

CHAPTER FOUR

Cardinals Benedetto and Melior arrived at the villa together in June, and I wondered if it would be too hot to travel, but Benedetto came to say farewell.

'I am sorry to see you go, *altezza*,' he said.

I wondered if embracing a cardinal was suitable. Then I remembered that I might not see him again, and held out my hands. 'Parting seems to be the way of life for a queen, Your Eminence.'

'And cardinals,' he responded sadly. 'I have but recently returned from Constantinople. It was sad leaving new friends, but that is my life, I'm afraid. As Cardinal Nuncio, I go wherever I am sent. But this, this is special; I will do my best to be sent to Angers, where you can greet me, or even London.'

I put my arms around him briefly and thought that I heard a sob before turning away and searching out Cardinal Melior, my eyes full of tears. Melior was to be our escort as far as the port of Livorno, near Pisa, where a ship awaited us for the onward sea journey to Marseilles.

'Oh, *altezza*,' he whispered, 'all will be well. Shed your tears later, with Lady Joan, perhaps.'

Stephen coughed to hurry us along, spoiling our privy moment.

Now I watched from the back of my steed as Eirini appeared. I was astonished: I knew that she and Gabrielle, the seamstress, had been working together on her clothing, but this peacock apparition was unexpected. I looked to see Joan's reaction: she was sitting open-mouthed. We were in our travelling, sea-going clothes, and Eirini had followed the same pattern, but with distinctly Eastern Byzantine embellishments. Her balloon pantaloons, gaudy colours and gold rings and bangles were startling. Now I knew where the money I had given her had been spent.

'Holy Mother,' said Father Edwin.

'Good Lord,' added Stephen.

'Why do we ride so far?' the gaudy creature called out.

'Because there is a shortage of suitable ships, Princess,' answered Stephen. 'All are bringing Crusaders and pilgrims home.'

'Oh,' she answered, seeing the law of unintended consequences in play.

She was going to mount her palfrey using the block, but the soldiers of the escort brought to us by Melior were all determined to help the beauty up. They were repelled by a withering look as she leaped astride the beast unaided. She settled into the saddle and looked around, grinning, her raven hair wild.

The disappointed soldiers retired to mount up and be ready to keep us safe on the long journey ahead.

Nudging my mount forward, I looked down once more at Benedetto. My eyes were dry now, so I could see his kindly face clearly.

'Your Eminence, time moves on. We thank you for your attention; God bless you for all your support.'

'Not at all, *altezza*. It has been my pleasure. His Holiness sends his regards, and we pray for you and your ladies, and some peace in the land.'

'Time to go,' called Stephen, signalling to the captain of the escort. Cardinal Melior waved his consent, and the gathered horsemen formed up, ready to leave.

'*Addio*, Hortensia; *addio, Tua Grazia*!' I called as Benedetto let go of my reins. *Goodbye is merely another name for sadness*, I thought, as Stephen, Longchamp and Bernez closed in around me and we set off after the leading escort. I looked behind me and saw that Joan and Eirini were in conversation.

On the second day on the road, I motioned Joan to ride forward with me and catch up with Cardinal Melior; I had some questions.

'Your Eminence.'

'*Altezza*,' he replied, acknowledging our presence. 'Stephen,' he added, casting a glance at our shadow.

'Do you believe that Prince John will find the ransom money, or is he happy to leave Richard stuck in Germany?'

'As long as Eleanor controls the council, the money will be found,' he replied, 'but one hundred thousand silver marks will not be gathered in a week, I fear.'

'Or a month,' added Joan. 'And how much will come from your domains in England, Berengaria?' she asked, something which I had pondered over too.

'The money is not the only thing to concern His Holiness,' said Melior. 'If Prince John believes that Pope Celestine will grant him a divorce from Isabella of Gloucester in order to marry Philip's sister, Alys, he will wait a long time.'

'Poor Alys,' said Alazne, 'being passed around like a pot of ale.'

'Have no concern for Alys,' Joan responded pithily. 'She has carved out her own destiny; my father took advantage of a willing companion, and Mother spent many months in London's grim tower for her protests.'

Behind me, Stephen asked, 'What's in it for John, Your Highness? Dipping in where his father has been?'

'And where Richard refused to go,' said Joan with a sniff.

Melior answered that question. 'John is playing a long game, Stephen, giving Philip what he wants in return for England. And do not forget this: if Heinrich receives all of his ransom demand, he may have in mind taking territory off Philip.'

'If Eleanor uses money from my dowers in England to get Richard back, he will soon fettle his chancing brother, I pray,' I remarked with some spirit.

'That's the thing, *altezza*; that'll do it,' said Melior.

I'd never met John, but already I disliked him intensely.

'How much longer?' Joan moaned. 'I've seen enough of the sea and mountains from up here, and I ache.'

Even with our silk underwear to prevent chafing, our bodies soon tired of the bouncing up and down.

'One more day, Your Highness; nearly there,' called Stephen as we mounted in the early morning sunshine.

'That's eight days on this thing,' replied Joan.

'I like this,' said Eirini. 'It's all new here.'

I supposed, having been confined on an island all of her life, the length of Italy was something new for her. But seven beds in seven nights, in castles and monasteries and hostelries, was probably enough for most people, including queens.

With our rising anticipation, we had trouble sleeping that night in a hostelry, and welcomed first light and something to drink. Stephen was waiting downstairs.

'We should see Livorno before midday,' he said. 'It's where the Pisan fleet harbours.'

'A ship for us, I pray,' I said.

'Hopefully they won't miss one,' he replied, smiling.

We were quite close to Livorno when I spied the first masts. The road was very close to the sea, and we had no height advantage. I saw the leading riders of the escort pointing, and soon what looked like a forest of leafless branches came into view, a small harbour full of them.

Officials were waiting for us, and after some consultation Stephen came back and invited us to move forward.

Cardinal Melior, riding next to me, said, 'It seems that we will be on the sea soon, *altezza*.'

'Which is our ship, Berengaria?' called Joan from behind.

'Keep moving — we'll find out shortly.'

There was a line of soldiers leading from the end of the harbour wall out towards a ship moored alongside. Stephen sprang off his horse and held up a hand to assist me down; it was a long way for me. Neither Joan nor Eirini needed any help, not that they would have accepted any.

'This is the harbour master, Your Highness.' He introduced me to a bearded individual who smelled a bit. I brushed his proffered hand with the merest touch, a kiss being out of the question.

'*Altezza*,' he said, bowing.

'*Grazie*,' I returned and gazed along the quay.

'We'll bring your chests, Your Highness,' said Stephen. 'Let's see the ship.'

'Yes, let's,' agreed Melior, who had joined us.

The harbour master danced ahead, turning frequently to see if we had become lost somehow along the quay, and then stopped by what I supposed would be our next mode of transport.

It was a dromon with two masts and a bank of oars. It had a name painted crudely on its bows, *Il Maiale Volante*. 'Someone's got a sense of humour, Stephen.'

'Does that say what I think it says?' he replied.

'*The Flying Pig*, is that it?' asked Joan.

'It probably rolls a lot,' said Stephen.

'*Santa Madre!*' exclaimed Father Edwin.

'Are we going on that?' asked Eirini.

'Come aboard, *altezza*,' called a tall, well-dressed man from the steering position. 'We will help you board.'

The deck was below the level of the quay, but there was a ladder on the side of the quay wall. Stephen went over the side of the wall and tried to find the first foothold.

'It's only three steps, Your Highness, then you're on the ship.'

Giving thanks that we were in riding clothes, I did what I was told and found the first step, then Stephen had a hold of my hips and I slid down onto the deck and into his arms.

'You can let go now, bold lord,' I scolded, 'and do not tarry with Eirini.'

'Or me,' came Joan's voice, some way above with her foot on the steps.

Stephen caught Joan, Eirini, and then Father Edwin. He did not hold onto my priest for as long as he had her.

'Thank you, Stephen,' said Father Edwin. 'Very kind.'

'Welcome aboard, Your Highnesses,' said the well-dressed figure. 'I am the knight Paolo of Pisa, and I am charged with your safekeeping to Marseilles.'

Benedetto landed with a bump alongside me. '*Grazie, il cavaliere Paolo, bene, bene.* May I introduce Queen Berengaria of England, and Lady Joan, formerly of Sicily.'

'I am honoured. We have prepared the ship for your comfort. You have sailed before?'

'To Outremer and back, Cavaliere Paolo, thank you.'

'Ah, you did not enjoy it?'

'Some parts we did, and some parts we did not,' I replied, remembering storms, falling bodies, bloody seas and buckets.

'We'll make you happy; come see our ship.'

'Why is it named *The Flying Pig*, Paolo?' asked Joan.

'Because it rolls a lot and smells when it does,' he smiled, obviously proud of the thing, and the foul water to be found swishing about in the bilges.

'We have learned a lot about ships in the past two years, Paolo; we know about bilges,' informed Joan.

'Ah,' he said knowingly. 'Here is the steersman, Luigi of Livorno.'

We met other sailors of note, and eventually stood admiring the shelter that had been rigged up for us at the stern. It hung out over the sea.

'Better than a bucket,' I whispered to Joan.

'A bit windier, I think,' she replied, looking down at the water through the gap.

'How long will it take to get to Marseilles, Paolo?' I asked.

'Two or three days; it depends on the wind. If it's very windy, it will take two days and it will be uncomfortable. If it's not windy, it will be very comfortable and maybe take a week.'

'When our chests come on board, can they be kept dry? There's new clothing in them,' said Joan.

'Surely, Your Highness. We'll wrap them up in canvas for you.'

'When do we sail?' she asked.

Paolo looked up at the masts, felt the wind with a wet finger, grinned, and replied, 'Now!' Then he shouted, '*Partiamo; salpate, timoniere!*'

Men appeared from all over the ship and began to pull at the ropes holding the sails, then untied the ones holding the vessel against the quay. The ship began to move away into the middle of the harbour, then picked up speed as the wind filled the sails. Soon we were through the harbour entrance, passing by the Pharos.

'Built many years since,' informed Paolo, 'by *la Gran Contessa*, Matilda. A very famous lady.'

'Who are we to meet at Marseilles, Your Eminence?' I asked Melior as first the harbour and then the land began to fade on the horizon.

'If all is as planned, an escort has been requested from your father, and then a king and a count, Alfonso of Aragon and Count Raymond of Toulouse.'

'Aragon? How so?'

'His Holiness insisted you have the same protections as any pilgrim to the Holy Land. They dare not let harm befall you, and besides, Alfonso is a great friend of Richard.'

'Oh,' said Joan in disappointment, 'not Alfonso of Castile?'

'No, Lady Joan, not Alfonso VIII. Nor his wife, Eleanor of England, your younger sister who you might have been looking forward to seeing.'

Alfonso of Aragon, known as 'the Chaste', had long dreamed of uniting all the Pyrenean lands, which was not what his cousin Alfonso of Castile wanted; he wished for the uniting of all Iberian lands against the Almohad Moors to the south. Suffice to say they did not see eye to eye in the matter, but with the county of Toulouse to his south and Navarre and Aquitaine to his north, it was not surprising that Alfonso of Aragon was a *friend* of my husband. What plots had Henry and Eleanor crafted when they married their twelve-year-old daughter, Eleanor, into the Castilian family? And now Richard and Eleanor had worked to marry me into a dynasty that might have pan-Pyrenean ambitions — and extend the Angevin empire. Was I too suspicious? Time would tell.

'And Raymond?' asked Joan, bringing me back from my musings. 'I hear that he is a keen advocate of marriage.' She said this with feeling, not needing to be reminded of husbands with an excess of lust.

'Ah, yes,' responded Melior. 'Everyone knows he is looking for a third wife. If nothing has happened to her of late; Bourguigne de Lusignan is the current candidate for Contessa.'

'What happened to numbers one and two?' Joan asked, noting the introduction of a Lusignan.

'One died, one divorced,' replied Father Edwin. 'And do not forget that the present Raymond is likely to be a supporter of King Richard. He is a direct descendant of the first Raymond of Toulouse, who took part in the very first Crusade all those years ago.'

'I have met Raymond,' I said.

'How?' demanded Joan.

'On my way to Messina, when I was travelling across Europe with Eleanor. They have splendid Roman baths in his château.'

'What is he like?' asked Joan.

'In his forties, and always with a roving eye. His next wife might inherit the title sooner than later,' I added, to Father Edwin's dismay.

'Your Highness, that is unworthy.'

'I know, but worth a mention,' I laughed.

At the end of the second day the peaks of the *Alpes Maritimes* came into view. I think that we had by-passed Corsica during the night, but as Paolo had been pressing on with a favourable wind, we had been clinging on too tightly to notice.

Sight of land brought a blessed relief as the wind dropped, and we mostly slept propped up against a rail for the remainder of the voyage — wet, salty, and not hungry — this condition was quite normal while at sea.

Evading many dangerous-looking islets and rocks, we entered the long harbour and could see a line of soldiers drawn up at one of the berthing quays. The flags of Aragon and Navarre were on prominent display.

'It seems that your organising skills have borne fruit, Your Eminence,' I said, smiling. 'How do they know it is us?'

'A great relief, *altezza*; one always wonders if people will do what they promise. As for knowing...' He grinned and pointed up at the masts, one flying the red crusader cross on a white background, the other the red cross on a black background.

Then the ship descended into pandemonium as the sails came down. The oars slid out and the vessel was guided alongside by well-practised commands.

Among the gaily dressed crowd of dignitaries I saw the banner of King Alfonso of Aragon, a noted friend of my husband, together with those of various counts. The banners of Toulouse were prominent. Then, with harbour officials and as many folk as could find a place behind the lines of soldiers, came a voice I recognised immediately.

'*Printzesa, Berengaria, erregina.*' It was Captain Javier, an old friend who had formed part of my original escort when I had left Navarre to marry Richard.

I waved enthusiastically. 'Where is Arrosa?' I called hopefully. Along with Alazne and Maîtresse Karmele — who had returned to Navarre long ago — Arrosa had been one of my ladies in waiting. During our travels, she had married Javier and they had left my service when they'd discovered that Arrosa was with child.

'Arrosa is with child again!' Javier shouted over the tumult. 'Our second.'

I was hanging over the rail by now and Joan pulled me back.

'Dignity, Berri — they have come to see a queen, not a family reunion.'

'Curmudgeon,' I retorted, and then called out, 'I'll see you on the quay, Javier.'

He grinned and waved.

'Let us get off this flying pig, Joan. There are many miles before us on land.'

Alfonso was friendly and polite and asked if he could do more. Raymond of Toulouse, when introduced, was equally effusive and keen to help, but he stared at Joan and Eirini while talking to me.

I turned away from him and searched out Javier. He was standing nearby, and we grasped each other gladly.

'How are you? How is Arrosa and your child?'

'Our boy is well. I pray that a girl is on her way. Who have you brought with you? Who is the young woman in that unusual garb?'

'That is Princess Eirini of Cyprus. She is sixteen.'

'Jesu! Does she get many marriage proposals?'

'None. Nobody dares to ask, and with the Queen of England and Richard's sister Lady Joan defending her honour, none are likely to get near.'

'I see,' he said. 'She will break free one day. I thought that Lady Joan was a queen?'

'She has given up her title; enough is enough for her. I'll explain more later. Come, we'll rescue her and Eirini from Raymond; he has already stripped them bare with his eyes. How is it that you are on the quayside to greet us, Javier? It must be five hundred miles to Navarre.'

'Probably more, and we only arrived yesterday. There was not much time between receiving notice of your intended journey and setting off.'

'Thank you. Are you tired?'

'No, Your Highness. I am a soldier; we do not allow tiredness.'

Father Edwin appeared at my side. He had enjoyed none of the sea voyage; in fact, he had looked ill before setting foot on the ship. Stephen, Longchamp and Bernez were again back in armour, which they had stripped off for the voyage in case they fell over the side and drowned. I looked about for Cardinal Melior. He was conversing with King Alfonso and an assortment of bishops and priests as I made my way through the crowd to speak with him.

'Your Eminence,' I whispered, 'we were not expecting all this attention, and we're anxious to get away. My escort from Navarre is here.'

'Yes, but let us spend a little more time with King Alfonso. Anything to keep you talking, *altezza*; I will miss you terribly.'

'Oh, Your Eminence, thank you, and we will miss you. Come and see us when things settle down.'

'I will. Ah, King Alfonso, here is your charge. Her Highness is eager to travel onward, I believe.'

Alfonso II, a man renowned for his desire to unite the Pyrenean lands, something of interest to Basques on either side of the mountain range, smiled gracefully. I was wary of him, as Father had often said, 'Beware of big kingdoms, for they gobble up small ones.' But I was under the protection of Mother Church, and I did not think that this king wished me harm.

'Then what is to stop us? With your permission, Berengaria, we will signal the start of our journey.'

'You are kind, Alfonso, and understanding. All these good folk have come to wish us well, but there are great things afoot, and I should not tarry.'

'Of course.' He raised an eyebrow at someone and the soldiers sprang into action, clearing away the throng and preparing horses for our journey.

'How did you know that we preferred to ride, Alfonso?'

'We have been properly briefed.' He looked at Melior, who I saw had a tear in his eye.

'Oh, Your Eminence,' I said, holding out my hands, 'be not sad; we all must follow our paths, and we may meet again. God bless you, and thank you for your help and support.'

He planted a kiss on my head — quite like old times with Richard, I thought. Then he reluctantly let go and embraced Father Edwin, who received a godly kiss too. I was guided to my horse, not looking back until I was mounted, and by then I couldn't make him out clearly for the tears in my eyes.

I cheered up a little when I realised that I had called a king by his name, and he had named me. That was a privilege of equals.

'Shall we ride together, Berengaria?' asked Alfonso. 'There is much to discuss, and I have word from the north.'

'I would be delighted. A moment, please.' I turned my horse, thankfully an obedient beast, and signalled Javier over. Speaking quietly, I gave him some instructions.

'Go and ride with Lady Joan; do not leave her alone with Count Raymond, and keep the Cypriot princess in view at all times. Stephen and his men will support you as needed. And talk to my priest Father Edwin now and then; he is keeping a diary.'

Javier looked a bit flummoxed but went off anyway. I watched as he approached Joan and waved when she found my gaze; she knew my purpose, and the pair sidled alongside each other with Eirini behind and Raymond sticking to her other side. That would be an interesting tussle: a count and a captain, with Stephen and his men riding closely behind.

'I'm ready, Alfonso.'

'You know of Raymond's history, Berengaria? He is looking for a new wife.' He smiled; he knew of my concerns too.

'More detail would be useful.' I smiled back as we set off.

'He was married to Beatrice of Beziers, but she converted, becoming a Cathar, and they divorced, but she was with child at the time — very awkward. The child is named Constance, but Beatrice died in 1189, which was very convenient.'

That was noteworthy: a divorced count with a daughter, now looking for a wife, with both Joan and Eirini being examined for the position. We needed to keep our wits about us. My unease was not helped by Alfonso's next remark.

'One hears rumours, Berengaria,' he said. 'Raymond has developed some odd friendships and habits, but it is only rumour; he is nice enough otherwise.' He left that hanging in the air. Then I remembered the name people used to refer to Alfonso: 'The Chaste'. He probably disapproved of Raymond if he formed loose relationships while searching for a wife. I decided I'd discuss this with Joan if Raymond's eye settled upon her.

For the rest of the day we only managed twenty miles, but I was enjoying the views, with the sea on our left and the mountains to our right. I vaguely remembered coming along here on our journey south with Eleanor — even from afar she seemed to be directing my life for me. Then I remembered Captain Javier and excused myself to Alfonso to drop back and talk to him. 'Now, Javier,' I said, reining in alongside him, 'we will talk. How is Arrosa?'

The answer to that question filled in a few miles before we got to my father's health and my brother Sancho. That was when Javier became a bit reticent.

'Just tell me, Javier. I don't do mummery anymore.'

'Your brother is coming to realise that it might not be long before he is king.'

'Is Father ill?' I asked with alarm.

'He is past sixty years, Your Highness.'

I was silent for a while as the truth hit me: there were other matters to think about as well as my own. I said that we would chat again and went back to ride alongside Alfonso.

He interrupted my thoughts after few miles. 'You are pensive, Berengaria — nervous, perhaps?'

'Perhaps. You are taking us as far as Toulouse?'

'I will take you that far, if only to get more detail about how Raymond is doing in his marriage attempts.'

'Oh, is that interesting?'

'As an observer, always. You are bound for Aquitaine, or further?'

'I should meet up with my mother-by-law, Eleanor. We will combine to raise Richard's ransom, if the Church hasn't gained his freedom yet. Then we shall see. England is my target.'

'Of course. Eleanor is a formidable woman; my latest information has her in England, giving young John a buffet around the head, no doubt. Have you met your brother-by-law, John?'

'No.'

'You would remember if you had — he is unforgettable.'

'Are you being polite, Alfonso?'

'I try to be.' He smiled.

'Try being rude for once.'

'He is odious. He is trying a double-deal with Philip. His ambition outstrips his wit, I fear.'

'I'd heard something like that; you have confirmed his behaviour for me. I need to be careful until Richard returns.'

'Yes, you must.'

In the evening we rode into a large encampment where all the necessities for weary yet regal travellers were available. Large pavilions for we ladies, separate from the king's entourage and our escort, bathing tents, and an invitation to eat with Alfonso made the site complete. Raymond spoiled that by plonking himself next to Joan and ogling Eirini all night. Later, I questioned Joan. 'What does Raymond talk about, Joan?'

'Himself, mostly.'

'Boring.'

'No, I find him quite interesting.'

'You know he is looking for a new wife, a third marriage?'

'Yes, he explained all that.'

'Bad choices, eh?'

'He didn't choose them — his mother did.'

'That sounds familiar.'

She laughed and hugged me. 'Be not so suspicious, Berri; he is entertaining.'

'As you say, but keep him away from Eirini. She hasn't got the experience to spot a chancer, and she is enjoying her allure. She will find that beauty has a cost one day.'

'I will do so; do not concern yourself. How do you find Alfonso?'

'Pleasant and informative — good company on this long ride.'

'Good. Goodnight, dear sister.'

'Goodnight, Joan.'

CHAPTER FIVE

I was more than pleased when Toulouse came into view, after six days on the road. There was still a few more days to go before we could leave Alfonso and Raymond behind. This evening, we would be staying at Count Raymond's Château Narbonnais, and I was looking forward to the comfort of a night indoors.

The courtyard seethed with welcoming folk — some grand, others not, but we needed to be rescued by officials and escorted through the door into the great hall, where the hubbub continued.

'That was quite a welcome home for Raymond,' I said to Alfonso, who had been propelled into the hall along with my ladies. Javier and Stephen delivered them all safely.

'Raymond?' he replied, laughing. 'It has more to do with the presence of the Queen of England, Berengaria; all Europe wants to know your next move.'

'Oh, my move? I would like to know that too.'

Alfonso laughed. Then I saw Raymond carving his way towards us, his court parting for him as he moved.

'Welcome to Château Narbonnais,' boomed the mighty count. 'My seneschal thought that we may be tired after our journey, so he has not prepared a feast. Instead, Your Highnesses are welcome to come through to my privy hall, where there is a buffet prepared, and your privy chambers are all ready for you whenever you desire.'

'Thank you, Raymond; that is much appreciated. Berengaria?' responded Alfonso.

'I agree,' I said gratefully. 'I would enjoy a little something to eat and perhaps a drink or two with my ladies before we retire.'

Raymond swept us through into his privy chamber, looking behind to see if we were all following him.

The food was excellent, but I was too tired to enjoy it or to stay for very long. I waited a decent interval before making my excuses and leaving for my bedchamber.

Alazne, attentive as usual, began to ask questions. 'I heard some of your conversation, Your Highness,' she said as she unfurled my braids. 'Where *are* we going to?'

'I really don't know. If John is trying to give away my duchy of Normandy to Philip, then should I aim for my county of Aquitaine and Eleanor? If this is out of the question, I need to consider one of my minor counties — Poitou, perhaps — and maybe bypass Eleanor and go straight to England.'

'Not without the king, Your Highness, surely?'

'No, you are right — I must wait. Eleanor is the key.'

'Would you like me to sleep in here tonight, Your Highness? There is a truckle bed over there.'

'Would you? I'd like that. Lady Joan has gone with her ladies; we can talk until dawn.'

We did talk, but dawn was still a long way off when the chamber fell silent.

I awoke to the curses of Alazne as she wrestled her feet free of some clingy covers, then left the chamber to prepare for the day.

Joan walked in. 'Morning, Berri. Sleep well? What're we going to do today?'

'Have a rest.'

'Good. We can go for a walk along the river; it looks very nice.'

'It's the river Garonne,' I said. 'First we'll eat, then Stephen can escort us.'

The river was not far off and presented a very pleasant prospect. It was pointed out that the Garonne had split into two streams at this point, creating an island in the middle, Île du Ramier, it was named. Outside the castle, the city was also walled, and seemed to be in a good defensive state.

Raymond spent most of the day with King Alfonso, discussing matters military and politic. I was sure to hear later from Alfonso about anything important. In the afternoon we amused ourselves exploring Toulouse. Although it was impressive in parts, Stephen became increasingly uncomfortable when we strayed away from the buildings surrounding Raymond's castle. The unpleasant lives of the peasants became obvious: they dwelled in miserable huts, their children without shoes and in some cases not fully clothed. I worried about it and thought that if I came across this in the future, I should do something about it.

Upon our return, Alfonso greeted me with a letter from my mother-by-law, Eleanor.

'Just arrived by courier, Berengaria. Eleanor has found you,' he laughed.

I unrolled it immediately; it was short and to the point:

Come to Poitiers. Do not venture further north. Richard has enemies who would prevent his return. I am in England collecting our dear Richard's ransom. I will see you in Fontevraud when I return; you may wish to help when you are settled.

'We should move on, Alfonso; I should be where I can support Eleanor.' I handed the scroll to him, and he studied it before agreeing.

'Yes, perhaps you should set off in the morning. I'll leave you in the hands of Captain Javier and Turnham's men. Combined, they will keep you safe.'

'How far to Poitiers, Stephen?' I asked my guardian.

'Oh, perhaps two hundred and eighty miles, Your Highness.'

'There'll be no tented encampments, Berengaria,' said Alfonso. 'I'll be heading back south after you set off, but I can send messengers on ahead to make arrangements for you, if you wish?'

'That would be good, Your Highness,' said Stephen. 'Very kind — we've barely enough men to send ahead like that. We'll send yours back as soon as we can.'

'So where will we stay?' asked Joan. 'Monasteries, castles, abbeys and the occasional flea-ridden hostelry?'

'For three weeks only,' grinned Javier. I was pleased to see the two men at ease with each other.

'You have the reckoning of it, Stephen,' said Longchamp.

'We should manage that; we rode further to get here,' added Javier.

'Just so,' added Stephen. 'We'll have Alfonso's scouts but no wagons; we'll need some baggage animals to transport the queen's belongings.'

'Is there much?'

Stephen raised his eyes to heaven. 'Javier, your ladies have been investigating the markets of Rome for six months; three horses might do.'

Alfonso looked at me, grinning. 'A wardrobe for a queen, Berengaria?'

'One queen, a princess, a lady and our companions,' I said, waving a hand in the direction of Eirini, lost as usual in a crowd of admirers.

'Jesu,' said Alfonso, 'she's a vision.'

'How will you part with Count Raymond, Lady Joan?' asked Stephen, rarely one to mince words. 'He seemed very interested in you.'

'Me? Huh!' she responded. 'He couldn't take his eyes off Eirini; I doubt if he would swap her for me.'

'A lonely bed is a lonely bed,' I said unhelpfully, speaking from experience.

'Thank you, Berengaria. I'm a bed-warmer, am I?'

As it transpired, Raymond behaved himself at the farewell, though he only attended Joan as she made ready to mount up. He seemed to have formed the idea that Joan might be more amenable to a proposal than the glorious Byzantine princess. I did not wish him success, and waved him goodbye with less fervour than I accorded King Alfonso.

CHAPTER SIX

With Alfonso's scouts, six in total, always out of sight ahead of us, Javier in the vanguard, Stephen guarding our rear, and Father Edwin behind, leading the three baggage animals, our cavalcade stretched quite a way along the road. Our first target was to be Cognac, well on the way to Poitiers.

I carried only hazy memories of the towns we left behind each morning. I spent most of the time in conversation with Javier to wring out every last snippet of information about the goings-on in Navarre. Alazne sometimes asked questions, and sometimes I asked about the courts, the palaces of Pamplona and Olite, and whether they were still the centres of arts, music and philosophy much beloved by Father and myself, and sometimes about other friends I had left behind.

As we approached Cognac Stephen rode alongside, a worried expression on his face. 'Another three days to go,' he murmured, looking concerned.

'Just tell us, Stephen,' I said, looking across at Joan. 'Something is bothering you.'

'I can see,' said Joan with a smile.

'Money, Your Highness, or the lack of it.'

'Oh. What's in our purse?'

He tugged at the thing suspended from his saddle; it rattled. 'Not a lot,' he replied.

'Joan?'

'Torène carries a little of mine.'

I looked at Eirini, her armlets and earrings glinting in the sunlight. *No, leave her for an emergency.*

'Guy and Longchamp?' I looked at Stephen.

'Enough for two more nights. As we're heading for Poitiers, Queen Eleanor's town...'

'Does it have a sheriff, and a treasury?'

'Yes.'

'Have we enough to get there without sleeping under the stars, Stephen?'

'Just. No banquets, though — *soupe du jour.*'

That raised a laugh, but I wondered if he was serious.

'Worry not, dear Berengaria. We'll survive — we always have. Do you speak French?' asked Joan, changing the subject.

'Of course, I can manage. Which dialect?'

'Occitan.'

'I'll struggle for a while. Can you help?'

'Of course; it'll be fun.'

We rode gaily on, much relieved, but I would have a word with Stephen in privy. I needed to know these things before they were upon us; it was no way to manage a court.

Joan and I often shared beds along the way; it depended on who had the best bed, or whether there were any creatures in the mattress. Tonight we had ended up together, mostly because we couldn't sleep, the destination of our new home coming ever closer. Alazne and Pavot always shared a bed; their sapphic love was none of my concern as long as they were happy and served me well, then Eirini and Torène in their chamber in separate beds. I knew not what Stephen and the men did; I suspected that there were village maids in the offing some nights, but I didn't ask.

'Can you remember Cognac, Joan?' I asked.

'Vaguely. I have been there more than once, although I was born in Anjou.'

'Are you going to stay with me when we reach Poitiers?'

'I will, until Mother appears, I suppose. Her favourite place is Fontevraud.'

'The fame of the abbey is well known.'

At the end of the second day Cognac came into view, set amid a flat yet verdant landscape with many vine fields on either side of the track.

'The castle is on this side of the river Charente. The town is on the opposite side, protected by a wall and a gate on the other side of the bridge,' informed Joan.

'I suppose that Alfonso's scouts have arrived there; we can expect a welcome,' said Stephen hopefully.

He was right: half a mile from the river, people had begun to gather. I was to be exhibit of the day once more, and I sighed.

'Yes, Berengaria, on display again. And us in our scruffy riding clothes.'

'Well, I'm not changing at the roadside. We'll make a dash for the castle gate,' I said.

'Right,' answered Joan. 'Stephen, up the pace when we near the castle; we'll enter at the gallop.'

He laughed. 'As you will, Your Highness, as you will. I'm going to enjoy this. Longchamp, Bernez, Javier — tighten your straps. We're going to assault yonder castle. The Queen of England is about to make an entrance.'

Javier shouted, 'I must see this! The Queen of England, *en tourney.*'

'Oh dear,' added Father Edwin. 'Oh dear.'

I had an idea — a bit late, but it was still the best I could come up with. 'Stephen, wait. Have you got any of my banners in your saddle bags?'

'Bernez and Longchamp have Crusader flags; will that suffice?'

'And I have a banner from Navarre, Your Highness,' added Javier.

'Perfect. Get them out; we'll fly them through the gates.'

'Happier now, Father Edwin?' Stephen asked.

'If they divert a crossbow bolt or a rock, then I am much happier. I'll stay at the rear while you and your madmen charge at the castle gate.'

Joan giggled, but Edwin was right. I needed to be safe as much as Stephen needed to be brave, and there had been little cause for that over the past few weeks, thank God.

'Go on, Stephen,' I said when all was ready, 'but back off quickly if they seem hostile.'

'I promise to do so, Your Highness. Stay well back,' he called. He gave the command, and he and his men set off with we ladies getting ready to bring up the rear.

I smiled, waved and dug in my heels, and we set off at a trot after my flying knights.

It felt good to do something unexpected; perhaps men had it right when they flew in the face of the enemy. This was exciting, and I was surprised when Joan, with a squeal, galloped past me. Not to be left behind, I kicked into my palfrey's side and sped after her.

With my hair flying and my clothes dishevelled, I raised dust all down the hill until we were through the gates. I was greeted by much consternation and men shouting of an invasion. Philip really ought to have drilled his guard better, for we had passed them before they thought about closing the gate.

Once inside, I pulled up alongside Stephen. 'We'll do that again — how exciting!' I gasped.

'Try doing it into a shower of arrows; now that *is* exciting. Here's the guard commander — late.'

We were in a courtyard, with no escape except the way we had entered. An older man ran out from the main door of the castle, carrying a sword and in a state of alarm. When he saw how many of us were women, he slowed, but, watching Stephen and the others, he called out, 'Are you the queens?'

Not the most observant of castellans, I thought, as Stephen spoke up.

'I am Stephen of Turnham, a Crusader, and this is Her Highness the Queen of England with a princess and a lady.'

Taking the initiative, I moved my palfrey toward him and asked, 'Is Count Aymer at home?'

'No, Your Highness, he is visiting King Philip, but until your scouts arrived we had expected you at Angoulême.'

'Ah,' I said, 'have you not quarters for us here?'

'Certainly, Your Highness. We only had news of your impending arrival when your scouts turned up, but we will do our best to accommodate you.'

'The horses needed some exercise. Where are King Alfonso's men?'

'Your scouts are in the hall, eating. I am Seneschal Albert. Who is that?' He had spied our princess.

'Princess Eirini of Cyprus,' said Joan. 'I was the Queen of Sicily; what I am now is uncertain.'

'Are you going to show us around your castle, Albert?' demanded Stephen.

'Of course.' He looked at my companions. 'There is plenty of room; come with me.'

The castle was in need of repair, but Albert seemed unaware of how shabby it was and proudly presented us with chambers. They were damp-smelling and next to the river, which was now nearing its summer low water with all its bad smells. But the fare was edible if limited, and being hungry we gave it good attention. Albert was very considerate and wanted to hear all about the Crusade. We were too tired to oblige but promised to continue in the morning.

So, not a moment too soon, I collapsed on my bed, exhausted, and did not stir until the morning sun brightened the chamber.

Birds were singing, and Alazne, to my surprise, was on a truckle bed in the corner, snoring. I supposed that beds were in short supply, but I decided to sort out the bedchambers sometime today. She could share hers with whomever she chose, though it would not be me.

I heard someone softly singing and went to look out of the window. There was a good view of the riverbed with a sluggish stream in the middle, but the singing was coming from the chamber next to mine.

'Joan,' I hissed, 'is that you?'

Her head poked out of her window, and she grinned at me. 'Yes. Did you sleep well?'

'Mostly, until Alazne woke me up with her snoring. Apart from that, it is a beautiful morning.'

'Pavot was in full voice too. Eirini has stomped off somewhere; I know not where. I'll send Pavot and Torène off to find her.'

'Today's task is something I woke up thinking about, and which we must discuss. Get dressed — we will inspect the town from the battlements.'

I got ready and went to find Stephen. He was in the great hall with all the men who were already up; they had seemingly spent the night there.

'Accompany me up to the battlements, Stephen. I will meet Lady Joan there; we have certain delicate things to discuss… Perhaps you can stay out of earshot.'

'Whatever you wish, Your Highness.'

'How long has Albert been seneschal here?' I asked Stephen as we crossed the bailey to a stairway.

'Since the first brick was laid, I suspect,' he replied with a sigh.

'It was too easy to gain entry; have a word with him and see if you can liven things up.'

'Your Highness.'

We had reached the top of the battlement, and the town of Cognac lay before us. It was surrounded by many miles of verdant vineyards.

'It should be prosperous, Stephen. See if they can spend some money on their protection.'

My attention was drawn to a discussion down in the bailey: Joan and Javier were arguing about who should climb the steps first.

'Joan,' I said, 'does my captain not please you?' I was in a mischievous mood.

'As long as he keeps his eyes off my rear and his hands to himself, I'll be content. What is it that you want to talk about?'

'Where is Torène?'

'With Alazne and Pavot, trying to find Eirini. Pavot kept her awake until she went off to find some peace.'

'Good, for it is those two whom we need to discuss. Stephen, go and observe the views with Javier over there —' I pointed to the watchtower at the end of the wall — 'while we have a little chat.' When they were out of earshot, I turned to Joan. 'In four days we will be at my first target, Poitiers, where your mother instructed me to wait, and then you are going on to Fontevraud.'

'Yes,' she said, a bit puzzled until it struck her too. 'Oh, Alazne and Pavot.'

'A parting of the ways.'

'Oh dear, that would be cruel.'

'Yes. Think about it while we make ready to depart.'

Later, on the road, Joan came alongside and we shared our thoughts.

'So I'll remain at Poitiers — it must be safe there — until your mother arrives at Fontevraud.'

'You won't try to bring that meeting forward?'

'No, I'm not looking forward to coming under your mother's control.'

'And what will staying in Poitou and Poitiers gain you, save putting off the inevitable?' asked Joan.

'Time to demonstrate, time to recover my reputation. I have had no say in my life for nearly three years. Putting things into proper order in my new county will reach Eleanor's ears and remind her that I will be the only Queen of England one day.'

Joan reached across from her steed and our hands touched briefly. 'Berri, that's some idea — one to ponder.'

'Now, how should we divide our ladies?'

'You like Alazne too much, and I Torène.'

'Can I take Pavot with me? We will not be that far apart, and when Richard returns things will settle down, surely.'

Although Joan did not immediately agree, she seemed to be wrestling with the idea. Then she said, 'I'll take Eirini with me — two each. Agreed?'

Although Richard had charged me with Eirini's care, he could not complain about his sister having care of the princess, surely.

'Agreed — and write often when you get to the abbey.'

CHAPTER SEVEN

Later that day we arrived at a castle in Tours. Alazne was helping me to settle when Joan walked in.

'Should I leave, Your Highness?' asked Alazne.

'In a while,' said Joan. 'We want to ask you something.'

I sank back against the embroidered pillows and waited while Joan sat next to me. It was still light, but it had been a long day and I was tired, although the birds outside were in full song.

'Alazne, do you and Pavot wish to stay together?'

'Yes,' was the response, accompanied by a wash of tears.

'Should I ask Pavot the same question?' asked Joan.

'Oh, Lady Joan, would you?'

'I would. Will you accept her response?'

'Yes,' she said, wiping her eyes on her sleeve.

'Very well,' said Joan, 'but there will be some changes for you to consider.' She turned towards the door. 'Pavot, I can hear you breathing; come in, please.'

Pavot appeared suddenly in the doorway. I could see Torène's hand on her back. Alazne gasped and Pavot could not take her eyes off her, the couple obviously fearing the worst. It was my turn to speak.

'We have discussed this, Lady Joan and me, and we can see a solution, but we all need to give something up in order to gain something else. Do you see?' By this time Pavot had crossed the chamber and the pair were holding hands. I continued, 'Pavot, if you want to stay with Alazne, then you must come with me.'

That statement led to a silence while the implications sank in. Pavot looked at Joan. She nodded her head, and soon our lady companions were locked in each other's arms, crying.

Torène remained open-mouthed in the doorway until Eirini shoved past her from the corridor to see what was going on.

'I will explain,' I began. 'I have been advised to remain south of Angers until Queen Eleanor has judged it safe for me to proceed further north. She is expected to travel to Fontevraud Abbey from England very soon. Lady Joan will go there and wait for her, so we must split up. Do you see that?'

They all nodded.

'So, if Pavot will attend me for a while with Alazne, the matter will be settled. And if you, Torène, will stay with your lady, that also will be settled. Then, if Princess Eirini would also go with Lady Joan, that will make things even, and we can all get back together later. Are you content?'

There were more tears and hugs before Pavot and Alazne were dismissed.

The birds were still singing when I awoke the next morning. I saw that Alazne had settled on a chair in the corner.

'Alazne, wake up. Did you sleep there all night?'

'No, Your Highness. I was with Pavot, but when I came in you were still soundly asleep.'

'Thank you. Let's get dressed.'

'I am, Your Highness.'

'So you are; let's dress me, then.'

While we prepared for the day, Alazne coughed and said, 'Arrosa and Javier, Your Highness. Every step of our travels moves them further apart.'

'Ah, how could I forget? Shall we send him home?'

'We are safe here, surrounded by men.'

'I have observed. Fetch him and we'll make him happy.'

The good fellow was more than delighted. 'You are most gracious, Your Highness. Arrosa will be delighted to see me … I trust.'

'Of course she will, and we will be sad to see you go, but there is a time for everything. Go with my blessing and we will see you again, if you want.'

'Oh, yes, it is a delight to serve you. I hope to present my new child when next we meet.'

We all went down to the hall to breakfast together, joining Stephen and the rest of our entourage.

'I have something to tell you: Captain Javier is leaving us,' I said to the group. 'His wife pines for him, so I am sending him home.'

Javier was a very popular man, and so he was immediately swamped by well-wishers.

'We'll see him off,' I said, chomping on some very passable cheese. Then I looked for Father Edwin. 'Are your writing implements to hand, Father?'

'Yes, yes, in my bag, Your Highness.'

'We'll write to your mother, Joan, and let her know where we are and what we're doing,' I said. 'Father, do the Benedictine messengers pass through here?'

'Probably. I'll ask to add your documents to their load.'

'Thank you,' I replied, pleased that the old Roman courier service was still in action.

Javier's departure was another of those all-too-frequent farewells. I did not want to prolong this one, so with a formal kiss on my hand he mounted up, and he and his troop set off back to Navarre.

Two more castles and three more days saw us to the outskirts of Poitiers, where we paused to inspect the town.

'A river, a Roman wall with a castle built into it, and many churches,' said Father Edwin.

'Where's the castle, Joan?' I asked.

'Over the river Charente and up the hill. Richard told me that Mother was rebuilding parts of it,' said Joan.

'We will be expected. I suppose that we should send King Alfonso's men back to him,' I said, looking at Stephen.

'Yes, they've done well, but we shall be safe here. Will you reward them?'

'Reward? Have we got any such thing?' I asked, remembering how empty our purses were.

'We'll pool what we've got left; you won't need money once you are in your new castle, Berengaria. It'll have an income,' said Joan.

Her remark startled me; I had nearly forgotten. 'Of course; I am Countess of Poitou. The town and county are my responsibility.'

'Another new beginning?' she said.

'As long as there are more beginnings than endings, I shall be content,' I responded. 'Shall we inspect my castle?'

'And your treasury, Your Highness,' laughed Stephen of Turnham.

CHAPTER EIGHT

Poitiers was pleasant, and we felt safe within the walls of this complex building. In the palace, we were housed in a tower known as the Tour Maubergeon, named after Eleanor's grandmother, who was the mistress of Duke William XI at the turn of the century. She was known as Amauberge the Dangerous. She must have been an interesting woman, and I had seen some dangerous parts of Eleanor — what a strange family I had married into. These facts I had gleaned from the seneschal, but neither he nor Joan was willing to go into much depth concerning Eleanor's grandparent.

As soon as Joan was content regarding my comfort, we had a tearful farewell. Joan and I clung to each other and Pavot laid her hand on her shoulder while Alazne watched from the doorway with Father Edwin. Eirini, Torène, already mounted, sat quietly, waiting until we'd finished our declarations of enduring affection.

Longchamp coughed. 'It's only fifty miles, Your Highness.' He was to be Joan's escort from Poitiers to Fontevraud.

'Time to go. I'll write and visit whenever I can,' she said, wiping her eyes with her sleeve.

Longchamp helped her to mount up. She almost walked her steed into the wall as she peered backwards, waving.

A second later she was gone, and a silence fell upon the courtyard.

The next day I lay in bed as dawn broke, pondering my fate. Alazne tapped at my door.

'Your Highness, are you awake?' she asked.

'Yes, come on in.' I was pleased to see her, for the daylight had brought with it the seed of an idea.

'Can Pavot come in?' she asked.

'Of course; I will expect you to be together henceforth. Alazne, get me dressed. Pavot, find the seneschal, and we will start the day with something to eat, then tour the town.'

When we were ready, we walked into the privy refectory for some food.

'Good morrow, Your Highness,' Seneschal Pierre of Poitiers greeted me.

'Good morrow, Pierre. Is my escort, Stephen, here?'

'Lord Stephen has eaten and gone to the horse lines to inspect his steeds, Your Highness.'

'Good. Inform him that I shall be riding out to inspect the town later. Could you provide a guide?'

'My pleasure, Your Highness; I shall accompany you myself.'

'Do you know where my chaplain Father Edwin is?'

'Indeed, Your Highness; he is staying with the garrison chaplain. There is accommodation for visiting Church officials.'

'Send for him and tell him to meet me at the stables, wherever they may be.'

'Certainly, Your Highness, and I'll take you there when you complete your meal.'

'Thank you. Now, what have we here?' I took a look at the buffet. The table was well laden, and all seemed fresh; I thought that I might enjoy my time in Poitiers.

'Are we all going to view the town, Your Highness?' asked Alazne.

'Not unless you want to. Perhaps our quarters could be improved a little to suit our needs.'

Alazne quickly took the chance to seek some improvements and looked at Pavot, who nodded. Satisfied that we had allocated the day to the best effect, we turned our attention to food.

The stables were as impressive as the rest of this complex building. Pierre was very proud of them, and the money lavished upon the castle's construction seemed to have had no bounds. Stephen met me in the stable yard and pointed at a fine palfrey.

'Will that suit you, Your Highness?'

Despite the thing being caparisoned with all manner of heraldry, I thought it would, and managed to clamber without difficulty onto its colourful back, aided by a stool. Not so Father Edwin, who needed a shove-up to get into the saddle of a similar mount.

'I've instructed Longchamp to remain and take a look around, to see how things are managed here, Your Highness,' said Stephen.

'Good,' I responded. 'It seems very relaxed to me — not many clunky soldiers about the place.'

'Probably rotting in the desert somewhere.'

'If they were to return, they must be back by now; we spent six months in Rome.'

'I'll pray for their souls,' said Father Edwin helpfully.

'Our guides are over there,' said Stephen, pointing along the length of the stables.

I spied Pierre of Poitiers mounting his steed, and soon he trotted along to greet me.

'We'll show you our town, if you're ready. We'll have an escort of twelve.'

'Are we in danger?' I looked at Stephen and his men.

'Of course not, Your Highness, but it is not every day that we have the new Queen of England visit. It may be a little crowded once we leave here.'

I nodded. 'Lead on, Pierre.' He set off at the head of his troop. 'Stay close, Stephen; I don't want to be lost in a crowd.'

Stephen grinned, pulling alongside me as we set off behind Pierre's grand cavalcade. Then our presence was announced to all of the county of Poitou by a trumpet blast from above the castle gates. *So much for a quiet tour*, I thought. Stephen, I saw, was enjoying this, grinning and waving.

The tour turned out to be a tour of churches, so many in number were they. The main one was the cathedral of Sainte-Pierre, recently rebuilt by Henry and Eleanor. The amount of money lavished on grand buildings in this town by the pair was astonishing, and it set me thinking. My thoughts were reinforced as we progressed through the cheering crowds and from time to time peered up alleyways and through gaps in the crowd. Groups of poor men and some women could be seen crouching in the shadows — the contrast was startling, and I felt quite uncomfortable.

I was deep in thought when we halted outside Sainte-Pierre's, and the archbishop, Guillaume Tempier, gazed at me from a small wooden stage erected outside, a curious expression on his face.

'Your Highness?' he ventured. 'Shall we assist you?'

'No, Your Grace, but thank you,' I gasped as I slid off onto the stage.

'Welcome, Your Highness. This is a privilege. Let me conduct you into our splendid new cathedral.'

He went to great lengths to explain the whys and wherefores of how my mother-in-law and her errant husband, Henry, had spent so much money on this splendid building. There was a break in his flow when we approached the splendid altar, and he asked if we could stop to offer up a prayer. When he pronounced the amen and we rose from the prie-dieux, I said to him, 'I prayed for the poor outside, Your Grace; there seem to be many.'

Looking directly at me, he responded, 'Ah, yes, the poor. We too pray for them and feed the destitute.' Then he continued with his guided tour through the opulent cathedral. *Is this splendour for God, or archbishops?* I wondered. I could not rid myself of this thought.

I was pleased to find fresh air outside once more. Archbishop Guillaume pressed me to stay for a while, but I politely refused.

'We have much more to see on our first tour. But be assured, Your Grace, we shall return in due course and have a much longer conversation.'

When we were moving again, I motioned for Pierre to ride alongside me and asked him, 'What provision is there for the poor? I saw men missing arms, and blinded, and some coughing fit to die. How many returning Crusaders are there in the town? And why are there women in the gutters carrying children in rags?'

He seemed astonished, as if I had asked him to jump into the river. He eventually made an embarrassed confession. 'I know not, Your Highness; it has not concerned me. But there are those who may help you in that regard.'

'Who? Where?'

'The church of Sainte-Radegonde, near the riverbank. There is some kind of hospice there.'

'Take me there. Who was Radegonde?'

We set off in the direction of the river and Pierre explained the church's history as we walked the horses, acknowledging the waves of the crowd as we went.

'Radegonde was a saint, a Frankish queen in the sixth century. She built the first church on the ground. It is a collegiate church, not within the authority of Archbishop Guillaume, but in the charge of an abbess who appoints canons to govern it. It provides its own funds and owns land, some of which may interest you, Your Highness.'

'Will we be welcome? Are they expecting us, Pierre?'

'Not officially, but the noise of the crowd should have alerted them. Everyone in the county knows of your presence in Poitiers, Your Highness.'

Merchants and beggars, men and women with children — some clean, others in rags — lined the short ride, and there was a gathering outside the church of Sainte-Radegonde.

'It seems the abbess and her canons are expecting you, Your Highness.' Pierre stated the obvious.

'What's her name, Pierre?'

'Abbess Bernadette of Angers.'

I slid off my steed to be greeted with a kiss on the cheek from the abbess. She grasped my hands.

'God bless you, Your Highness. We did not expect a visit, but we are truly honoured.'

'God bless you, Abbess Bernadette. I heard about you from my guide, Seneschal Pierre, and decided to visit.'

'Then let me take you into our church; it has been here for many hundreds of years. You must tell me about Outremer. We hear tales from returning Crusaders, but it is not certain what is true and what is imagination.'

'It is returning Crusaders and the poor who have brought me here. I am concerned about their welfare.'

'Ah, you have noticed. God bless you, Your Highness. Shall we pray for a while? Then I have something to show you.'

I agreed. Stephen relieved himself of his weapons, and he and Pierre followed without the men as Bernadette led me to the altar, where a priest waited to lead us in prayer.

When he was finished, Bernardette laid a gentle hand on my arm.

'Your Highness, we can go now.'

'Of course.' I rose and we set off out of the church. 'Where are you taking us?' I looked behind to see my entourage following closely.

'A hospital of the Knights of Saint John. We gifted them some land down by the river, and they care for returning Crusaders and some poor of the town.'

'Knights Hospitaller, so far from the Holy Land?'

'They have come up from Montpellier, where they established a hospital. These are the ones who follow the statutes of Roger de Moulins, which he recently established — that is, to care for the wounded and sick. This hospital is in the care of a knight's chaplain, and he has a dozen brother knight infirmarians to assist him. His name is Brother Walther of Canterbury.'

'English?'

'Indeed, and difficult to understand.'

I looked back to see if Father Edwin was still following, and gave him a wave. 'I know someone else who will be pleased to see Brother Walther — my chaplain is English.'

Walther was the size of an ox, with huge hands. 'Your Highness, we prayed that you would pay us a visit,' he said.

'Then your prayers have been answered, Walther of Canterbury. Here is my chaplain, Father Edwin. You may understand him better than I do,' I jested.

Edwin came forth, and the pair engaged in an exuberant brotherly hug.

'Show us your hospital, Walther, and put my chaplain down, if you please.'

The tugs of home never leave us, I thought.

Walther led us into the hospital. A few of the infirmarians were lined up to greet us, and I had a chat with them as I was introduced.

'What ailments are common, Brother?' was my main enquiry.

'Those of the mind, Your Highness,' one of the infirmarians replied, and the others agreed.

'What meaning hath this, Walther? Are there no limbs missing?' I asked.

'Plenty, as you can see.' He waved his arm at the rows of truckle beds. 'But it is not just the hurt that one can see, but that which is hidden. Some have missing limbs, eyes, and barely healed wounds, but the worst have scars of the mind, and their behaviour is the damage. Those with missing parts survive to reach their homes here, but those without visible injury are the ones who need help most.'

This statement came as no surprise. I still had terrible dreams about what I had witnessed on Crusade: heads rolling about on the bloody sands; legless, armless bodies screaming; and children butchered before their mothers' eyes.

'I have suffered such restless nights, Brother Walther. I am no stranger to disturbing visions.'

'You were with the king.'

'We were. We were not on the field of battle, but nevertheless we witnessed such unimaginable things.'

'Bless you, Your Highness; you do understand.'

'I do. So how do you support all these poor souls?'

'We are self-sufficient: we have land with tenants, we make and sell things, and we have benefactors. We manage, Your Highness, I'm not asking for money, but if…?'

I smiled. 'I'll see what I can do. How do you treat these lost men, Walther?' I was gazing at a fellow who looked very young, hardly out of his teens. He was slumped against a wall, rocking back and forth, staring at a statue of the Blessed Mary set high on a wall, but with little life in his eyes.

'His friends brought him back from Outremer. At least, they brought his body back; I know not where his wits are. We treat them kindly, feed and house them. Some return to us in mind as well as body, but others have left us for good, and all we can do is pray.'

Many of the patients had empty eyes. Some leered at me in a most disturbing way, some drooled and others stayed facing the wall. I prayed that the devil would not enter their unwary minds.

A sniffling noise reached my ears.

Walther peered over my shoulder to see Father Edwin weeping. He looked at me with hurt in his eyes and I had no response that I could voice. This was a lingering price that some had to pay for Richard's obsession and the Church's demand for a Crusade; what God Himself thought I could not imagine.

'Thank you, Walther. We must move on, but I will return. Come, Pierre, Stephen.' I put an arm around Edwin's shoulder. 'Pray, Father, pray, and we will find some practical ways to help these lost souls.'

On the way back I had decided on a course of action, and summoned Pierre to my side.

'In the morning, Pierre, attend me with your accountings. Bring with you the treasurer and the larderer and ensure that they too bring their accounts. We will see what's what in this town.' My request was met with silence until I asked, 'You heard?'

'Yes, Your Highness, as you wish.'

Pierre retired to ride behind me, and I was joined by Stephen to receive the cheers of the crowd as we returned to the comfort of the palace of Poitiers.

There was a letter from Joan when I returned. It confirmed that Eleanor was in Normandy raising money for Richard's ransom, but I knew that, and there were other matters to attend to here. I invited Alazne and Pavot into the privy solar and waited for Edwin to appear. I had sent for him earlier and wanted to discuss certain matters before my palace officials appeared before me the following morning.

When they were settled, I began.

'What did you notice when you left the confines of the palace, my friends? Tell Alazne and Pavot.'

'Noise,' said Stephen, 'lots of noise.'

'Father Edwin?'

'Poor, lots of poor.'

'Ah, yes, beggars on the streets,' agreed Stephen.

'Good,' I said, 'you noticed.'

Alazne and Pavot shuffled in their chairs, not knowing what was coming next.

'Yes: beggars, children in rags and brazen women outside their hovels. They cheered me, I am ashamed to say. In this prosperous town no one should be without food or clothing. Children should not beg, nor women cheapen themselves for coin.'

'Prostitutes?' exclaimed Alazne.

'Oh dear,' said Father Edwin.

'Absorb that, then tell me what you find within this palace.'

'A palace of plenty,' said Longchamp, who had just walked in.

'Food and wine,' said Edwin.

'Nice beds,' said Pavot.

'Quite,' I said. 'Have you seen any starving servants, or men-at-arms, or badly dressed women?'

There was no answer.

'We went to a Saint John's hospital today, Alazne, Longchamp; it was full of men damaged in their heads by war. Some might not recover their wits. Some will not return because they are rotting in the bloody sands, and some who are here are not fit to work. So before you judge harlots —' I looked at poor Edwin — 'consider how else they can provide for themselves and the children left behind when their fathers left for Outremer, on Crusade for Mother Church.' I almost spat that last remark out. 'Time for change, my friends, time for change. On the morrow I shall meet with the seneschal, the treasurer and the larderer, and I shall inspect their accountings. What should I look for and what are my priorities? I invite you to consider and speak.'

Stephen was the first to give his views. 'I am not an expert in accounting, but the returning Crusaders need caring for, Your Highness.'

'If I may, Your Highness?' Longchamp put in. I nodded my approval for him to speak. 'The garrison has many returning Crusaders among its ranks, and some are no longer fit to fight. They make good sentries, but I fear that if the town came under attack they would not be capable of defending it for very long.'

'Stephen?' I looked to him for guidance.

'I'll discuss the matter with Pierre and see if we can improve things.'

'Thank you. Anything else?'

'The poor,' chorused Alazne and Pavot.

'The poor,' echoed Father Edwin.

They looked at me, and I surprised them.

'The king, my husband's ransom is still being gathered. So when I see what money is available, we will meet again and decide on our priorities. Stephen and Father Edwin, please attend me when I meet with my officials.'

The steward brought in refreshments and the meeting broke up. Then my ladies invited me to inspect the improvements they had made to our accommodation, so we left Stephen and Edwin in conversation and I followed as bidden. It was pleasant, and we were now in bedchambers with a connecting door. I praised them for their efforts, but my mind was not on comforts at the moment, and my tumbling thoughts denied me sleep that night until the last candle had guttered out.

I was brighter in the morning. We ate in the solar, although Pierre had asked if we might take our meals in the hall so as to be seen by the palace staff and officials. I agreed to take the evening meal there, but this morning I wanted to concentrate on my meeting. Then, having an idea, I instructed Pierre to prepare the hall for that meeting. It would be held in public with nothing disguised.

When Pierre sent word that all was ready, we swept into the hall, clothed in our best, and surveyed the arrangements.

Pierre had done well: there were three trestles lined up in a row, each with parchments laid out on them. Behind each stood the architect of their works, Pierre in the centre with his co-clerks, one on each side. I stopped before him and asked, 'Who will be first, Pierre?'

'Larderer Garnier, Your Highness.'

A fellow with a prominent nose and girth bowed and greeted me. 'Your Highness.'

'Explain your rolls, Garnier, if you please.'

With a nervous glance at my entourage lined up behind me, he began.

'There is one roll for each year, Your Highness; they are marked. Which one would you select?'

I pointed at the one marked 1192, and he rolled it out across the table. 'The last completed one, Your Highness.' He looked at me, knowing now that I knew what I was seeking.

'When do you usually complete these, Garnier?'

'I hope to have them ready before the end of January, Your Highness. I keep them up to date and they are only held up by late payers.'

'Good; I saw to that in Navarre too.'

I spent some time examining his work and asking questions, and I received satisfactory replies. I then looked up at Pierre, who was fidgeting next to Garnier.

'Pierre, you next, if you please.'

His accounting was also meticulous, but it revealed the extent of the palace's indulgent expenditure — a cause for concern.

We moved to the next table, behind which stood a sharp-looking middle-aged man, a minor noble by his appearance.

'Treasurer Roland, Your Highness.' The introduction was followed by a graceful bow.

'How did you come by this appointment, Roland?' I asked.

'I was appointed by Queen Eleanor, Your Highness.'

Marvellous, I thought, *she will not have picked any nitwits.*

'Tell me about our treasury, income and outgoings.'

They largely mirrored Pierre and Garnier's where expected, but not when it came to one particular item.

'What's this, Roland: Angers? It swallows up most of the surplus.'

'Queen Eleanor's instructions, Your Highness. It is the king's treasury in Angers. She expects all of her holdings to remit their surpluses to the king's treasury.'

'I see, and are these accounts checked by anyone?'

'Every year, Your Highness. In February I travel to Angers with my rolls and with a treasure chest. She has asked that I travel every month now, for the king, you understand?'

'Indeed.' I pondered for a moment before thanking Pierre and the others. 'We will attend supper tonight in the hall, Pierre. Thank you for the invitation.'

'Our pleasure, Your Highness. Are there no further questions?' He seemed both puzzled and relieved.

'Yes, I will see you later.' I had seen enough and led my people back into our solar in the tower.

'What did you glean from that, Your Highness?' asked Stephen when we had settled.

'A prosperous place with good accounting, and they are far too comfortable in here with beggars at the door. Then there is my mother-by-law.'

'She has her hand in your purse, Your Highness,' chuckled Father Edwin.

'She has indeed. That will be a matter for discussion. However, as it concerns the king's ransom at the moment, there is little to be done, but when he returns I will examine the matter.'

'The poor?' asked Pavot.

'The larderer will give out spare comestibles, and the seneschal shall find savings from his household spendings to give to the Church to care for the destitute. Stephen, there is money in the accounts for the garrison and defence; find out how they are spending it and see if you can put it to better use. We may not be here long, but I intend to set a pattern of management for all my possessions when we are settled.'

'God bless you, Your Highness. You are a paragon of virtue,' said Father Edwin with a tear in his eye.

'Steady yourself, Father. Let's get ready for supper. Ladies, circulate among the court women; Stephen, get to know the sheriff and the garrison commander. I want to know everything about the palace of Poitiers and the town.'

'What about me?' asked Father Edwin, feeling left out.

'Stay by me and watch. Make notes on anything of interest. I want to know what undercurrents flow in this well-fed world.'

'We've found out something,' said Stephen, looking conspiratorial. 'It concerns Duke William IX of Aquitaine. He had a court of earthly pleasures here, no moral standing and lots of lost women.'

Without exception eyebrows were raised at Stephen's revelation, and there were some gasps.

Satisfied that he had our attention, he continued, 'William was a noted troubadour, but composed songs and poetry of a bawdy nature. One day he met his match in addictions of the flesh: the woman named Amauberge. Disgusted and humiliated, William's wife, Philippa, fled to a convent, and Amauberge kept possession of William's bed without opposition. Once he had experienced her wild desires he would not give her up, thus offending all the other women who had happily attended to his pleasures. Need I say more, Your Highness?'

'No further detail is required, Stephen. Whence did you glean this salacious stuff?'

'It is common knowledge. Some of the older soldiery tell tales of Duke William's goings-on.'

I thought about this for a few moments. 'If this wild woman is the grandmother of Eleanor, then she is the great-grandmother of my husband.'

'God preserve us,' gasped Edwin, making the sign of the cross.

I went to lie down to contemplate the nature of the family into which I had married. It was not a restful period, and I was pleased when Alazne came to ready me for supper.

CHAPTER NINE

As much as I wanted to move further north, even as far as Normandy, and one day on to my realm of England, we were constrained to stay out of harm's way, as Eleanor saw it.

Joan's letters had become ever more pessimistic with news about Richard and John. John, it seemed, had become good friends with Philip of France. This report I viewed with extreme suspicion, for Richard and Philip had parted in Outremer as mutually hostile partners in their mission. Sometimes Joan turned up at the palace unannounced, as the journey was hardly worth despatching messengers to warn us, so I took to welcoming her when she arrived and making the most of her visits.

As time went by, my control of Poitiers spread into the county of Poitou, and I made certain that Eleanor knew about it through Joan.

Since the distance between Poitiers and Fontevraud was only fifty miles, Joan usually managed it in two days. She said that she enjoyed the ride, but I thought that it might be some relief to be away from her mother now and then. Today we were blessed with another visit and Joan arrived on a horse, fully caparisoned as would befit a queen. Eirini was not to be outdone: a vision on a white palfrey. They were accompanied by an escort of twenty, flying the banners of the Crusade and Aquitaine.

Their scouts had arrived to warn us a few moments before, and we wandered along to the gate to wait. I was always happy when Joan came calling.

'Berengaria!' called Joan, spurring her horse, then sliding off as she reached me.

'Joan, we have missed you this past month. Let me see.' I stood back and cast my eyes over her elaborate riding outfit.

'See,' she said, pulling at her kirtle, 'a split skirt for riding and striding.'

I hugged her. 'Come in. We have made some more improvements and Stephen has tidied up my soldiers. We have some funds now and uniforms for them.'

'I see; very nice. Do you see how many are looking at Eirini?'

'I do. Come here, Eirini; you are a spectacle. Let me embrace you.'

Eirini sparkled and rattled with all the jewellery she wore, and gave me a dazzling smile.

'Come, let's go to the hall. We will hear your news. Are you ready with your quill, Father Edwin?'

'I am. Speak, Lady Joan.'

'The first bit of news concerns my brother, your brother-in-law, John. He is now self-proclaimed King of England.'

'What does Eleanor name him?' I asked.

'A treacherous rat, but he hides in Normandy while she is raiding England's coin and Angevin treasuries — including that of Normandy. Even Church silver is not exempt; tenants and tithes have all fallen before the steady advance of Eleanor.'

'Why has John chosen Normandy? He can't hide forever,' said Stephen.

'Because he has been trying to cultivate King Philip. They pooled their resources and asked Heinrich to keep Richard in Germany if they matched Eleanor's ransom.'

That remark fell into a stunned silence.

'Philip would also gain Normandy,' Joan continued. 'John would not resist if Philip invaded your duchy, Berengaria.'

'Holy Mother.' Father Edwin's quill stopped scratching.

'I'm doing well,' I sighed. 'Lady of Cyprus — sold. Duchess of Normandy — sold. Do I still hold this castle?'

'Queen of Sicily — the king died,' Joan responded, and we laughed.

'But you are still a princess, and Queen Dowager of Sicily?' asked Longchamp.

I was ready to jump in quickly in case Joan took offence, but she was not bothered. 'I've left the dowager bit behind, Longchamp, but I am still my father's daughter, a princess of England. That did not cease.'

'I do not suppose you've brought us any good news from the north, Joan?' I asked.

'I have news of Richard. I've been saving it to cheer you up.'

'Joan! That should have been first. Tell!'

'Richard has agreed to new terms. Heinrich finds them favourable; His Holiness is giving them some consideration.'

'What are they?'

'An increase in the silver by another fifty thousand marks, plus two hundred hostages in case Richard attacks Heinrich once freed. Richard's niece, Eleanor of Brittany, is to be betrothed to Duke Leopold's son…'

'What does she think of that?' I asked.

'It is not yet known, Berengaria. I expect her reaction will not be favourable.'

'His Holiness will not agree to that, having excommunicated Leopold for the seizing of Richard,' gasped Edwin.

'Anything else?' I asked, seeing a mountain of debt and gross demands pushing my husband's release ever further away.

'Yes,' said Joan looking intently at Eirini. 'He wants Eirini sent to Leopold's court in Austria. It seems that he is her uncle and demands the right to care for her.'

'He says I am family, the jester,' spat our beautiful princess. 'I will not go.' She folded her arms and sat back in her chair.

'No, you will not be sent,' I said, and determined that it would not happen.

'Did Richard agree to all these demands, Joan?'

'We believe that he did, back in June.'

It was now September. Winter was approaching and communications would be slowing down.

'What should I do, Joan?'

'Wait, just wait. I'll keep you informed. Have you collected any more ransom money?'

'Yes, it's coming in. I have a grasp on the accounting now, although your mother had already allocated some before I arrived here. I'll give you some funds to take back and add to the ransom chest.'

'Chest!' she exclaimed. 'There are enough chests in England, waiting to fill a ship.'

'Is that what one hundred and fifty thousand gold coins takes up?' gasped Stephen. 'A whole ship?'

The enormity of Eleanor's quest was made clear in that one statement. But spending a few days in the fading sunshine with Joan was a great relief from daily worries, except of course she had brought new ones with her, which we discussed at length while wandering the fields and forests of my new domain. Her departure came all too soon, and I shed a tear as she disappeared at the head of her escort into the distance, chatting to Eirini, who as usual had left a trail of frustrated suitors behind her.

Joan did not return until November, on a rain-soaked day.

I was stitching with Alazne and Pavot. The days were short and the light poor, but we managed a little each day, leaving

Stephen to get on with watching over Pierre and his day-to-day management of the palace. Not that there was anything to worry about: it was in good hands.

I had Richard on my mind, and I wondered what the ageing Eleanor was doing. I supposed that one day, when she went to her maker, I would be left to pick up the pieces of a fractured Plantagenet dynasty. How would Richard act without his beloved mother, I wondered?

Hearing a commotion in the yard, we dashed down the stairs to find Joan on a soggy mare.

'Joan! You're soaking,' I exclaimed. 'Steward, a hot bath for the lady, quick as you can.'

Joan slid off the steaming mare and fell into my arms. 'Warmth, warmth. Hold me, Berri; this is a journey to forget.'

I saw Torène dismounting behind her and waved. She and Pavot propelled Joan through the door, and I watched as they scampered off towards the bath chamber.

They left two unfamiliar wet ladies standing by their horses, water dripping off the ends of their noses.

Alazne chuckled. 'Pavot hasn't forgotten her former duties, Your Highness.'

'No, but she has forgotten those two. Let's get them inside.'

I approached the pair. 'Welcome to Poitiers. Do you serve Lady Joan?'

'Yes, we are her companions of the bedchamber,' replied one.

'Who was that with her?' asked the other.

'That was her former lady, Pavot; they were together on the Crusade.'

'Pavot. Lady Joan and Torène have spoken many times about her.'

'I am Queen Berengaria.'

'Oh,' said the tall one, wiping her nose on her sleeve. Then she curtsied. 'I am Marie-Louise. This is Amiée, and we are from Normandy, Your Highness.'

'I am the Duchess of Normandy. Where is Princess Eirini?'

'She is being looked after back at Fontevraud,' said Amiée.

'I see. Come, let's get you inside. Alazne, take Lady Joan's companions to their quarters and get them warmed up, then let's find some dry clothing for them.'

Later, when Joan, Pavot and Torène reappeared, we embraced, and I pushed a goblet of wine towards Joan.

'The Germans have been to London and carried off one hundred thousand marks of silver, and yes, it filled a ship,' she said, sipping her drink.

'Jesu,' said Stephen.

'Are they to be trusted?' asked Edwin.

'Probably,' responded Joan. 'His Holiness has made it very clear that if the matter is not settled before Christmas, he will declare Heinrich excommunicated and place Germany under interdict. The outcome is not in doubt. There is something else, Berengaria.'

'What can be worse?'

'One of the hostages nominated by Heinrich is Eirini. The other… Berengaria, it's Sancho.'

'My brother?'

'I fear so.'

'Why? What has he to do with this?'

'He is an ally of the Plantagenets, and a person of sufficient importance to be a hostage to Richard's actions.'

That was a blow. I had never wished for my father's kingdom to be so closely bound with the fortunes of Eleanor and Richard, and now my brother was embroiled.

'What if Richard is released and does attack Germany? I wouldn't rule that out; he is impetuous beyond measure. What next, Joan? Can it get any worse?'

'Worse? I doubt it. But what if Heinrich decides to take the bid from Philip? He and the treacherous John have a stake in this. Mother has set a date to take the remainder of the ransom, fifty thousand marks, to Germany herself. She has chartered ships for the seventeenth of January, which is when they expect to have gathered all the coin. Her fleet will be departing from the ports of Dunwich, Ipswich and Orford. She intends to impress upon Heinrich the sea strength of England and sail up the Rhine. I pray that she reaches Heinrich first.'

'A game,' I said with force, 'a new game. Have we not had enough of these damned games?'

That night I cried in Joan's arms. 'Why has Sancho not written to me to tell me about this? And Father, he must be devastated.'

'Don't fret, my sweet. Heinrich would not dare to harm hostages, not in the way that Richard disposed of them outside Akko. The Church will never let Heinrich rest and he will be condemned to eternal flames.'

The reminder of Richard's disgrace outside Akko did little to ease my fears, but I fell asleep in Joan's arms.

After two days she was off again, back to Fontevraud. She doubted if she would see Eleanor setting off from England, but she would send as much coin as she could across the narrow sea.

Christmas came, and I had become a regular visitor at the Cathedral Sainte-Pierre and the church of Sainte-Radegonde, where my presence had become an extra attraction for folk hereabouts and helped to swell the collections. I sent riders to Barfleur to wait for news as early as it could reach this side of the narrow sea. Other than that, I could do naught but wait and pray.

A cold February kept us largely indoors, which was cold comfort as we waited impatiently for news from Germany. We knew that Eleanor had indeed arrived on the Rhine in time for the due date of the handover, but Heinrich had stalled, hoping that she would be outbid by Philip and John in their quest to keep Richard in Heinrich's custody. At least the emperor had allowed Eleanor to visit Richard in Mainz.

By the end of February the long-awaited news reached us. Further negotiations had taken place, and Richard had accepted Heinrich as his overlord. England was now subservient to the German king-emperor, and a further important hostage was demanded as a surety: Walter de Coutances, Archbishop of Rouen in my Duchy of Normandy, who had only gone to Germany in support of Eleanor but was now detained at the emperor's pleasure.

If Heinrich was set on annoying Pope Celestine, he was going the right way about it.

'I must go now, Berri,' said Joan after the latest batch of news had arrived. 'Mother should return soon with Richard. I'll keep you informed.'

I had been preparing for this, but that did not mean it was welcome. I did not believe that God's love alone would sustain me without Joan.

We wept together in privy, but I needed to ask something.

We were lying in dawn's faint light. I heard Alazne scuffling about in the next chamber and decided to ask before she and Pavot came in.

'Joan, why is Eleanor keen to keep me away from my other possessions, from England? Do you know?'

She sat up on one elbow and looked me in the eye. 'What do you mean, Berri? Why should she be thinking of anything other than keeping you safe?'

'Because I am the Queen of England, yet she charges about the land acting as if it were still her sole domain.'

'She is probably trying to stay in control. What do you want to do?'

'I'm going to see her. And I'm going back with you.'

'Well, Berri, you have Poitiers better placed, better organised. So yes, do come with me. We will be nearer the north coast and the ports.'

Alazne and Pavot came in as we were planning the move.

'Pack your things, ladies; your mistress is leaving,' said Joan.

'How long have you been thinking about that, Your Highness?' gasped Alazne.

'Since my mind woke. What use am I here when soon my husband will be back, and we can try to begin a new life together?'

'Amen to that; I'll pray for you,' said Pavot.

'Let's get dressed and tell the others,' I said, throwing back the covers. Joan returned to her own chamber to allow her ladies to get her ready.

Once dressed, we dashed down to the hall where Joan's escort was waiting to depart, but we delayed that while my household ran off to pack their things.

'Stephen,' I said, 'find Pierre. We must make arrangements. We should leave someone behind as my representative, to show an interest and maintain communications. I am the countess of the county still.'

'Longchamp or Berncz?'

'Bernez will do. I'm going to tell him and the men.'

It was not until the following day that we actually left. After much fuss and bother we got on our palfreys and set off, leaving Pierre to tell the archbishop and the other churches that we had left Poitiers.

'But I shall return when things have settled down — tell them.'

'We will miss you, Your Highness. And be sure to bring the king when next you visit,' Pierre called after us.

'Joan,' I said after a while, 'how far is Le Mans from Fontevraud?'

'About sixty miles. Why?'

'I'm the Countess of Maine, remember?'

'Oh, that as well — yes, I remember. Are you going to bring peace and order to Maine now?'

'I might.'

'It is nearer to Normandy, but it would be best to stay clear until Richard shifts Philip back over the border.'

That was a disturbing thought. If Richard wanted the territories that John had ceded or sold to Philip, there would be conflict.

CHAPTER TEN

1194

The abbey of Fontevraud was indeed a place of retreat, and the final resting place of the Angevins — known as Plantagenets after the flower — including Eleanor's erratic former husband, King Henry II. Both men and women lived here separately. It did not take long for me to feel that I liked it, especially as the whole establishment was in the charge of an abbess.

Currently she was Abbess Mathilde III of Bohemia, a very nice if authoritarian lady. She came to see us as we stretched ourselves after dismounting. Her opening remarks were a bit odd, although delivered with a smile.

'England seems to have more queens than most, Your Highness; one day I might have the pleasure of seeing the two of you together.'

Joan was having none of that. 'Berengaria is England's queen; my mother is the dowager, Abbess, if you will allow the distinction.'

I needed to control my emotions before I burst into an unqueenly giggle. But her remark merely raised the abbess's eyebrows.

'Oh, of course, I did not mean to imply otherwise,' she said. Then she addressed me. 'Queen Berengaria, Queen Dowager Eleanor keeps privy quarters here for when she visits; would you care to make use of them?'

'We would like that, Abbess. How will our ladies be accommodated?'

'And our men,' added Joan, looking at Stephen, who was shuffling uncomfortably in the face of such imposing female authority.

'There is accommodation for your ladies attached to the queen's quarters, and here comes the abbot. He will see to your menfolk.'

Settling into new accommodation had become a simple affair over the past few months of continuous travel before we reached Poitiers, but now that we could deposit all of our belongings into our quarters for an indeterminate stay — without the help of our men — the next few hours proved to be a little frantic. The two novices whom the abbess directed to help were more of a hindrance, and we were pleased when we could dismiss them.

'Well, Joan,' I said, lying back on the bed, 'that's that for a while. I wonder where Eleanor and Richard are now?'

'On the high seas or in England. We'll know in due course, I should think,' she replied, hurling herself onto the bed alongside me.

Alazne and Pavot took a chair each while Marie-Louise and Amiée hovered uncertainly.

'Are your bedchambers comfortable, ladies?' I asked.

'Yes, Your Highness. They're along the corridor.'

'Well, now we are all settled, we'll hold a household conference; that's how we organise things.'

Everyone took seats and I started.

'It is now the end of February and King Richard has been free for almost a month. Our latest intelligence is that far from hurrying back to England, he and his mother are being feted all along the Rhine and into Flanders. I have a list: they started at Köln, which I understand is far from the sea, then went on to

Louvain, Brussels and Antwerp, which is the last place we have had word of.'

'When are they expected to return?' asked Alazne.

'We know not. You will know as soon as I do.'

'Are we allowed to explore?' asked Marie-Louise.

'Of course,' answered Joan. 'We can wander and pray to our heart's content; that's what this place is for.'

When news came at the end of March, it was not what we had been praying for.

A novice sent by Abbess Mathilde found us sitting beneath some trees with bare branches, it being the first warm day of spring. The birds were in full voice — a hint of things to come.

'Please, Your Highness,' said the novice, executing the deepest curtsy I had ever seen, 'Abbess says that I am to tell you that a messenger has arrived from Barfleur, and is asking for you.'

With that, she fled back in the direction of the abbey, holding on to her headdress with one hand.

We found both the messenger and the abbess near the stables, where the messenger's horse was being attended to.

'Your Highness,' Mathilde greeted us, 'this man has come to speak to you. I'll leave you in his company.'

'No, stay, Abbess. This may concern us all.'

'Then we shall retire to the *refectorium*; men and women may meet there.'

Stephen came along as I chatted with the mud-spattered rider. 'You have ridden from Normandy, good fellow?'

'Barfleur, Your Highness.' He reached into his jerkin and pulled out a scroll — a bit squashed, but clean. 'It's from my master, Robert.'

'Robert?' queried Joan.

'Of Turnham, my lady. He guided Queen Eleanor's ship on her voyage into Germany.'

'My brother!' exclaimed Stephen. 'My little brother is still in the thick of it.'

'He has been one of Richard's fleet commanders for as long as I've known him,' I replied. 'Let's see what he has written.'

Everyone drew near as I unfurled the scroll and began to read aloud: '*Greetings, Your Highness, from your most loyal friend, the king's commander. I can inform you that the king and Queen Eleanor landed safely in the port of Sandwich on the twelfth day of March and set off for Canterbury, where they intended to honour and give thanks at the tomb of Thomas Becket for the king's release. The king intends to travel his realm to let all see that he is safe and well. He also intends to hold a meeting of the Grand Council in Nottingham at the end of March to discuss his further action. God bless the king, and God bless Queen Berengaria.*'

'Is that all?' asked Joan.

'Yes.' I almost choked and was near to tears. Joan took the parchment from me and glanced through it.

'Jesu, Robert speaks of Mother as if she were still the queen. There are no references to the king's queen, and no invitation to join him.'

She looked up and then at me, shooing away my household. She held her tongue until they had retired from view, all save Father Edwin.

Only then did she enfold me within her arms. 'Oh, Berri, what perfidy, what thoughtless, unfeeling contempt. I am sorry and I apologise for that brother of mine. I am ashamed.'

Clinging together for a while, our tears mingled, and I could think of naught to say.

Father Edwin came to comfort me, holding me by the shoulders and apologising.

'Forgive me, Your Highnesses. I fear that something may be missing from your letter. Are you certain, Lady Joan, that this is the only missive?'

'Read it,' said Joan, releasing me to pick up the offending note from the ground where she had dropped it. She handed it to Edwin without comment.

'Good Lord, how cold.' He let the document drop. 'We should pray, Your Highness — pray for God's guidance in this matter, pray that some of the king's attention can be diverted to his blessed queen.'

I agreed with that sentiment, but there were more immediate things that I could do. 'Call my household back to me, Joan.'

Soon we were surrounded by caring people, all anxious to know what was to be done. Stephen was the first to speak.

'I was surprised that the first letter after the king's release was from my brother,' said Stephen.

'Yes, I expected it to be from Richard himself. Where is the courier who brought the note?'

The man was soon found and dug out of the kitchen.

'Do you report directly to Lord Robert? What's your name?'

'Aye. It is Will, Your Highness, Will of Dover.'

'Very well, Will. We are going to compose a reply. If we find you accommodation for the night, can you leave in the morning and take my response to your master?'

'That is my purpose in life, Your Highness, and my pleasure.'

'Good, thank you. Father Edwin, quills and parchment. Stephen, we will open communications with your brother and see what we can discover about my husband's doings.'

'Good idea. Can I put a few comments in your note, please?'

'Of course; tell him what we are doing to preserve the king's realm. That must surely interest him.'

Joan laughed. 'I have often wondered what *does* interest my brother, apart from chopping people up.'

The first response from England came as a surprise. It was not from Robert of Turnham as expected, nor from Richard, but from Eleanor.

'Good Lord,' gasped Joan. 'From Mother?'

'Yes. Let's go inside and read it in my bedchamber. Alazne, find Stephen and gather everyone together in the refectory. We'll attend as soon as we have read this.'

'Come on, Berri, stop staring at it. Open it now,' said Joan.

With shaking hands I tugged at the tape and broke the seal. 'Hear this, Joan: *Dearest and most beloved daughter, your letter has reached us and Richard has asked me to reply. You may rely upon me to keep you informed at every opportunity. I realise that we have been quite remiss in this regard and that you deserve better. Please forgive us, but the past few months have been a period of chaos, long journeys, voyages and broken promises. Firstly, pass my love to my dear daughter Joan, whom I love dearly…*'

'And will marry off as soon as I can find someone willing,' interrupted Joan, laughing.

'I'll continue,' I said ignoring her remark. '*At the Grand Council in Nottingham, Prince John was summoned back to England to explain his doings, and Richard has been re-crowned in Winchester.*'

'What about you, Berri? When's your re-crowning?'

'I've been crowned twice already — once for England and once for Cyprus.' We both giggled.

'Take care not to be un-crowned twice, Berri; a second un-crowning can be painful.'

'There's more. Eleanor writes that she is pleased to read that I am managing my counties well and asks that I pay some attention to Maine. Then I should wait until Richard returns to relieve King Philip of possession of Normandy, which his brother has done ill by.'

'He's planning war, Berri; he's hardly off the ship before his obsession surfaces again.'

'Obsession? Normandy is ours by right. At least we know his intentions; our wishes have not concerned him in the past. Why should we expect anything else?'

Joan put an arm around my shoulders.

'He is what he is; I'll pray for him,' I sighed.

'Our households will be waiting. What are we going to tell them?'

'The truth. I am going north to Le Mans, and you are remaining here until you hear from your mother.'

'Yes, no need for me to move. I like it here. At least you will receive news from England sooner than I, the port of Barfleur being closer to you.'

'Yes, I'll set up a courier. How far is Barfleur from Maine?'

'Eighty miles less than from here. Still, you've not seen the sea for a while. Perhaps you can take a ship to England.'

'I'll look forward to that, but I suspect that Richard will be over here first.'

I spent the following week dithering and annoying Joan, who seemed to have something else on her mind.

'When are you leaving, Berri? I'm trying to prepare myself for Mother's return,' complained Joan at table one morning.

'I'm waiting for news from Maine. Stephen has gone to take a look. If Philip *has* seized Normandy, I might be in danger if I go too near my duchy.'

'Danger was all around in Outremer.'

'We only had one enemy there. I don't know who's who here. Will those who backed John so easily resume their loyalty? They may not relish facing Richard's wrath.'

'True. What if Richard chooses to seek out those who abandoned him, or indeed begins hostilities against Philip? We know not yet.'

The courier who arrived the next day informed us further.

Abbess Mathilde brought him along to the *refectorium*. 'Someone for you, Queen Berengaria,' she said, indicating the Benedictine rider behind her.

'Your Highness,' he said. 'I am Brother Luke, from Le Mans.'

'Really? Welcome, Brother Luke; you seek me? Are you from Queen Eleanor?'

'No, Your Highness; I'm from your brother, Prince Sancho. He is in Normandy and sends his love.'

My heart lightened. 'Thank the Lord for that! We must see him,' I cried.

'Thank the Lord, he is released. But what's he doing in Normandy?' asked Stephen.

Brother Luke responded. 'When Heinrich released him, the emperor demanded that an army be sent from Navarre to help defend him against French intentions. This was part of your father's agreement with Queen Eleanor: to defend King Richard's territories while he was on Crusade, and now by implication Heinrich's territories — he being Richard's overlord.'

'This is becoming quite complicated,' I said, trembling inside. Richard had extended opportunities for hostility in Europe in order to secure his release; what a pottage of trouble he had brought upon us.

'Becoming? When was it not? You can travel north now, Berengaria,' said Joan.

'Can I?' I said, looking at Brother Luke.

'As far as Maine, yes. I suspect that there is still danger in Normandy, and some uncertainty in parts. Some lords have not yet decided who to support, but the king is discussing the issue with them and expects them to see sense.'

'Discussing? With a sword in hand?' laughed Joan.

'Brother Luke, are you going back to Le Mans?' I asked.

'No, Your Highness, I am on my way from Canterbury to Rome, travelling south.'

'If I write to Cardinal Benedetto, can you carry my letter for me?'

'It would be my honour, Your Highness. I leave in the morning.'

'Oh, Berengaria, you *are* leaving us now.' Joan stood and wrapped her arms around me. A disapproving cough from the abbess brought that show of emotion to an end, so we went out into the spring sunshine for a walk in the woods, with Stephen following at a distance.

'Joan, this *agreement* between Father and Eleanor puts me in a wider field. Father's game of mutual protection did not envisage this, I'll warrant. What if Richard's promise of fealty to Heinrich was only intended to last until he was freed?'

'It would not surprise me, yet he'll need no promises to a German emperor to confront a French king,' replied Joan.

'So the likely outcome is that Richard sets out to regain the lands lost to Philip through John's machinations, regardless of other considerations?'

'Yes.'

'That didn't require much thought, Joan.'

But what was there to think about? A lion caged was not a lion set free; I thought we had better prepare for claws in the chest of the King of France before long.

'I suppose that I'd better get ready to leave in the morning. These Benedictine couriers do not tarry; they have much travelling to do.'

'What are you going to write?'

'I'll inform the cardinal of what we know. He will keep His Holiness up to date. The better my relationship with Rome, the better I will be viewed from there.'

'True. In this great game, the more allies you have, the better the outcome, I suppose. Will there be somewhere in Maine for you to stay? Will the damage caused by John's occupation of Le Mans be remedied?'

'I suppose so. I'll ask Brother Luke; he will know somewhere.'

The 'somewhere' was about thirty miles away, enough for another day's travel, at the castle of Beaufort-en-Vallée in the valley of the Loire — a Plantagenet stronghold.

Father Edwin had the letter ready for Luke's departure, and he went off with God's blessing.

With Joan, it was a quiet farewell with not much to feel happy about, but I needed to go, and if my brother was active nearby in Normandy I should be able to see him. I decided I'd write when we got to Beaufort.

Now it was early May, the roads would be suitable for travel, and so I set off that day.

Joan held on to my foot when I was settled in the saddle. 'Write often, my sister — we'll pray for you — and take control of that brother of mine.'

'You're in the right place for praying. As for Richard, we'll see what's what.'

I bent down to kiss her, and we parted with a smile.

'Messengers to Beaufort left last evening, Your Highness,' said Father Edwin. 'We shall be properly received when we arrive.'

'Good, thank you. Alazne, Pavot, Stephen, are you ready?'

'Yes, Your Highness,' came the chorus.

'Stephen, lead on.'

The castle of Beaufort-en-Vallée was set high on its motte, on the side of a hill in green and pleasant surroundings. It was not the biggest place that I had stayed in, but as peaceful as any. They were lighting the braziers set upon the battlements as we neared, leaving no doubt as to where we were headed.

The gates opened and the castellan waved us into the bailey, where I was pleased to dismount, aching in the usual places. This was one of Eleanor's castles, built by her late husband Henry and held by the Angevin Plantagenets since King Stephen's reign.

'Welcome, Your Highness. We have been expecting you. I am Denis of Angers.'

'Thank you, Denis. We'll take a glass of wine and then go to bed, if you please.'

'Of course, Your Highness, whatever you wish.' He waved at a couple of sergeants, who immediately began to help my fellow travellers with their baggage and set about attending to the horses.

'Come, come, please follow me. How many ladies?'

As a castle, this place lacked comfort, but as a defensible fort it lacked naught. We settled into draughty chambers with truckle beds and a tiny hall. There was nowhere that did not smell of stables and the garderobe; I suspected that the latter would permeate the whole place when the weather was warmer — but how long would we be here? That question was not answered when messengers turned up two days later and Stephen persuaded me to linger a little longer while the issue of who occupied Normandy was settled.

The following week I found out, when an array of mounted knights presented themselves at the gate.

Hearing the fuss, I went out into the bailey. Seeing me, Denis called down from atop the gatehouse. 'Your Highness, it is someone for you, he says.'

'His name?'

'Something foreign. Sancho or something.'

'Sancho? My brother! Let him in, Denis.'

As soon as the gate swung back, in rode my brother, solemn-faced and covered in dust.

I was in his arms in an eye-blink, anxious to know what ailed him. 'What is wrong, Sancho? Have you lost Normandy?'

'No, dear sister. Richard landed at Barfleur on the thirteenth of May. Normandy will be his soon, but Father is not well, and I am going home to see him.'

I was saddened, deeply saddened. King Sancho, the sixth of that name, was a man of learning and poetry who had kept a joyful court for all to visit. I knew that my brother would not be going to see him if his condition was not serious, but I could not go with him. My husband and the trouble that always attended him was not far away now, and I had to see to our future.

Sancho had read my thoughts. 'You must stay, Berri; stay to greet your husband. This is the most important thing.'

I unwrapped myself from his embrace. 'Come inside, Sancho. Let us feed you.'

'This is small,' he said, gazing about the crowded castle, nothing more than a tower and a bailey set upon a natural motte. 'How are you managing?'

'Fine. There are only a few of us: my two ladies, Lord Stephen, Lord Longchamp and six men. Then there is a dozen of the castle guard and the castellan, Denis. We have three serving maids, a steward and a cook. We are quite cosy.'

'What about money? I have a small treasury with me.'

'All's well. There is a small income from Poitiers which they send, and this place has some income from the village and surrounding lands. There is sufficient for our needs.'

'And Normandy. You will soon be in your duchy.'

'Of course. Now that Richard is there, I will wait for word from him.'

'Are you looking forward to that?'

'Dearly,' I replied, but there was little joy in my heart at the prospect. Why was that? Perhaps because in all the time we had been married, we had never quite got to know each other. The privy times that a man and his wife should share were missing — we needed to start again, from the beginning.

One night and a farewell was all that Sancho could spare, and I was soon alone again. Then after a week, we had a new visitor.

We were in the gatehouse, gazing upon the treetops in the valley of the Loire below. The river was some two miles away and more sand than water in the summer. Still, this small fortress was safe.

'There are riders approaching! Close the gate!' Stephen called to the guard below.

As the riders drew nearer, we saw that they had a Crusader flag held high.

'We'll let them identify themselves first,' said Stephen.

The leader brought his palfrey to a halt below my feet. 'Good morrow, Your Highness. You have forgotten my face?'

'I can't see your face, jester. Kindly remove that metal surround.'

He removed his helm and the mail coif.

'Robert!' exclaimed Stephen. 'Brother, are you lost?'

'Nay,' was the cheery reply, 'but open the gate; I am parched.'

The gate was opened, and Robert and his companions squeezed into our bailey.

We tumbled down the ladder to greet them. A happy reunion resulted, and I called for wine in the hall.

'You are far from the sea, Robert,' I said, after taking a sip of wine.

'I have noticed, and I had become unused to the saddle,' he complained, reluctant to take a seat.

'Is this your destination?' I asked.

'I doubt it, Your Highness. He may be far from the sea, but he is never far from the king's business,' said Stephen.

'And what king's business brings you here, Robert?'

'I am on my way to Poitiers. He has sent me to act as *pro tempore* seneschal of Poitou. His Highness is very impressed with you, Your Highness. It has been reported to him that you have brought order from somnambulance and turned the county around.'

'Oh, he knows where I am!'

'And what you have done.'

'Which is more than I know about him. Where is he, Robert?'

'With his mother. They were waiting for John when I left Angers.'

'I'd like to witness that meeting,' said Stephen.

'There'd be a queue,' I retorted.

'They tend to keep family meetings privy, I have found,' said Robert.

'And I. Richard rarely discusses anything of note, not even with his wife,' I said.

'Well, he wants me to impart this. There are malcontents roaming the country, upset that their support of John has come to naught. They may be harbouring evil thoughts about you.'

I was shocked; I had never been this far north in my life. 'Why me?'

'The capturing and ransoming of kings seems to be fashionable, Your Highness. The king would be most upset if John's former plotters saw an opportunity to capture you.'

'What does he want me to do?'

'You can remain here until you receive word that it is safe to move on to Le Mans.'

'I can do that; worry not.'

'Good. That said, what can you tell me about Poitiers?'

The rest of the evening was spent discussing the issues we had found and solved further south, during which I discovered that Robert was also the seneschal of Anjou. *He groans under the weight of appointments*, I thought. Still, it did not seem to bother him, and he promised to send Guy de Bernez to re-join me as soon as he had taken over the reins at Poitiers.

Denis had brought out plenty of wine, and soon the soldiers of the garrison and Robert's travelling companions were having a jolly time at the far end of the hall. I felt a lot better too.

'You seem happier this evening, Your Highness,' ventured Pavot.

'You see, Your Highness, your actions have been noticed from afar, and seem to be much appreciated by the king,' added Alazne.

'Thank you, ladies. Messages and messengers are fine, but I'd rather have a visit.'

'We should wait until matters settle down,' said Father Edwin. 'Wait until the king has Normandy secure, and then as Robert has said, we can move further north to Le Mans, perhaps.'

'You are right, I know. I'll go to bed now, Robert, but you and your men are welcome to remain. I'll see you in the morning, before you depart.'

'Thank you, Your Highness, it's much appreciated. God bless you.'

I did not need to rise early the next day, most of the men having stayed up long and too near the wine carafes. They were not mounted up until nearly midday.

'There are still seventy-five miles to go from here, Robert. I doubt that you will reach Poitiers before dark,' I said.

'It matters not. It is warm enough to sleep in some thicket. Serves them right, drunken lot,' said Robert. He took my hand and kissed it. 'Listen,' he went on quietly, 'there is something that you should be aware of.'

My heart trembled. 'What?'

'Richard is not well. You remember his fevers in the Holy Land?'

'The bed-drenching sweats and shivers?'

'Those. They have not left him. When he was in Germany, Heinrich's physicians needed to deal with them. The emperor must have feared that Richard might die before he received any ransom, so he was given the best of treatments, but he looks ill. Be prepared, Your Highness.'

'I see. Do these physicians know the reason?'

'They know that the condition is not unknown in the lands of the Mediterranean, but no cure is permanent.'

'Anything else?' I asked.

Robert shuffled and averted his eyes. 'I'll mention it before you hear it from other sources. During the chilly nights when he was shivering, they shoved a woman into his bed to warm him.' Robert blushed. 'Sorry, Your Highness.'

'A particular woman, or any woman?'

'Anonymous, but caring; it depends where he was at the time. There seems to have been a cohort of physicians surrounding him who were like-minded. Have no fear, Your Highness; there is no competition for his love for you.'

'Thank you, Robert. You'd better go before you can dream up any more good news. And do not be a stranger; I want to see you often.'

Reluctantly he mounted his steed and waved his men forward. They soon disappeared into the verdant woods on their way south.

Alone again, my misery soon took over, and I went back to bed to contemplate my life and pray for guidance.

If the king needed the comfort of a woman in his bed, would his wife not suffice?

CHAPTER ELEVEN

1195

Something was wrong in my life, and I knew what it was: rejection. Though he was free, my husband still had not come to my side.

The news we received at the end of June did not help: Father had died, and my brother was now King Sancho VII. Now I would never get the chance to tell Father of the things I loved about him: his bringing of poetry and music to our beloved Navarre; his trust in my ability to manage his court when Mother died; his love for me, my brother and my sisters, Blanca; Constance and Theresa, and whatever the outcome, his efforts to keep our people safe in a turbulent world.

My brother was left with the Plantagenets to deal with. How would he react now he was King Sancho VII? I decided I should write to him and tell him my feelings about Eleanor. She was the force behind Richard, the one who pulled the strings. News of her travels reached me — she had bypassed me on her way to Fontevraud, which I thought was unnecessarily rude. She and Richard had dragged John before them in Angers, where Richard accepted John's plea that he had been ill-advised and forgave him his double-dealing. Eleanor declared herself 'done with the world' and went to contemplate its doings from the abbey, allegedly taking the veil.

Richard, seemingly recovered, was now fully engaged in the business of reoccupying the lands which John had ceded to Philip. Philip was surely regretting his actions: he found out how ruthless my husband could be as Richard declared victory after victory until Normandy was fully recovered.

John had gone to sequester himself out of sight in Normandy. Richard did not want to see him in public — ever. Whether my husband wanted to be seen in public with me was a recurring and unwelcome thought.

'Write to him, Your Highness,' said Edwin. 'We write to everyone else.'

'What would we do without you, Father? Fetch your implements and we shall think of what to say.'

I tried to be pleasant and not ask any awkward questions, except to hint that I would rather be with him than apart, and perhaps I could help him with his night sweats. Then I despatched the thin scroll via a passing Benedictine courier.

It was the end of July before I received a reply. Although signed by Richard, I knew that it had been dictated to his scribe. Even so, it manged to convey Richard's style.

The tone was terse, the dismissal curt. He was too busy chasing out the French, building new castles and forming alliances against Philip wherever he could find them — *to give my queen the secure domains that she deserves*. That was that: I was not wanted in Richard's new warzone.

'What am I to do, Father?' I asked as Edwin dropped Richard's scroll on the table after reading it.

'Do what you did in Poitiers: care for your people,' he replied.

'Father, was I an extra concern to him in Outremer? Was I a hindrance to a successful outcome, an additional worry on top of his fevers?'

Father Edwin looked puzzled. 'No, Your Highness. Others tell me that you were the epitome of loyalty and a reminder of what would be normal when you reached home. This episode with Philip will soon be over, and then you both can turn your attention to what matters: a joyous union.'

'Thank you, Father,' I responded after some consideration. 'The county of Maine is about to receive my full attention.'

My pique was eased by one of Joan's short notes: *Mother has arrived in Fontevraud and sends her love.*

It was a late confirmation of Eleanor's whereabouts, for which I was grateful, though I regretted that Joan had not delivered it herself.

By the autumn of 1195 I had successfully distracted myself by establishing hospitals for returning Crusaders around Beaufort castle. It was not long before some Knights of Saint John appeared and took over the running of them. It was obvious to me that many were in serious need of comfort. As in Poitiers, to stand near these places at night was to listen to men crying out in their sleep and making noises of despair as their tired minds tried to make sense of the death and destruction wrought by both sides in the awful conflict — which they had witnessed first-hand. I wondered at times if Rome, from a distance, fully understood the price these men were paying.

Late one afternoon, a cry from the gate came to me in the hall.

'Messenger!'

'What now?' moaned Alazne.

There was one message from Richard and one from Robert. They conveyed the same thing: I was to be in Poitiers for Christmas, where I would be joined by Richard.

'I have almost three months for three weeks' travel, Father; should I set off in the morning?'

'Certainly, but not this month.' He smiled, calming me, else I should have screamed or hurled pots.

Having the time, I was visiting the main hospital regularly, which I prayed gave some comfort to the stricken men in there. At the same time, on my way to church and back, I could not help but notice the number of poor and homeless people lying about on the streets. Many of them called out for help as I passed by, but as I was well guarded they could not come near me. I resolved to do something to help.

I approached Father Raphaël, the priest of the local church of Notre Dame, and persuaded him to dole out food each day if I arranged to deliver it to his door. Local land tenants were asked to contribute food as a small relief from the rents they owed me and deliver it to the church, which I also allowed a small relief to — 'God's share', as I said, recalling the words of Saint Luke.

As December approached, I was much cheered by two letters: one from Joan at Fontevraud and one from Robert at Poitiers. Robert had taken on the task of rebuilding Poitiers Castle and had included king's and queen's quarters. I had not got as far as wondering how I was going to learn to live with Richard, but I found the idea of having somewhere of my own quite intriguing.

Joan's note, which I read in privy, was full of cheer. Eirini had made her way back to Joan: evidently there was no German fit for her attention, and now that Richard was freed, Leopold could not hold her. Then Joan wrote of the support I would have when I went to Poitiers for Christmas:

I have been preparing two girls for you. You cannot form a queen's household with Alazne and Pavot alone, so I'll send Isabeau and Cateline to Robert, and they can begin the preparations for your arrival.

That was good, but I soon suspected that Eleanor was behind this: two girls or two spies? Reading on, however, dispelled that unkind thought, as Joan had written:

And despite Mother taking an interest, I have chosen them myself, so you will have a full garrison of Robert's men and four ladies to help you when Richard is not by your side.

I re-read the final phrase: *when Richard is not by your side.* I remembered our time in Outremer, when he had been absent more often than not.

'Your Highness?' said Edwin, a question in his voice as I placed the roll upon the table.

'What is it?' asked Alazne, holding hands with Pavot.

'Still Christmas in Poitiers,' I replied.

It was the middle of December when we rode past Fontevraud, returning Eleanor's discourtesy. I saw no reason to be subservient to her: I was Queen of England, and although she held residual power through her position as matriarch of the family, the future was mine. So we went straight on to Poitiers.

It had been altered, but not yet finished, judging by the building activity going on and the poles and platforms surrounding parts of the building.

'Your Highness!' A call from within the dusty castle reached my ears, and I spied Robert waving from atop a platform.

'Robert?' called Stephen.

'Aye, brother, I'm learning building.'

'Uneven walls, more like,' I heard some plaster-stained figure near Robert complain.

'I'll be down in a moment,' responded the would-be builder, 'when I find a ladder.'

He soon reappeared, framed by a doorless aperture, covered in dust and grinning like a fool.

'Having fun?' asked Stephen, smiling at his brother.

'Yes, it's most interesting.' Robert strolled over to greet us. 'Good morrow, Your Highness. How went the journey?'

'It was endless. Have you built a bathhouse into this place?'

'Of course: there's a privy chamber for you, and the fires are burning.'

'Hot water!' Alazne picked up on that part of the conversation. 'Hear that, Pavot? Hot baths.'

'May I help you down, Your Highness?' asked Robert, standing by my palfrey.

'Of course,' I said, then allowed him to lift me down. 'Is Richard here?'

'No, he is still in Normandy, thinking about building a new castle near Les Andelys overlooking the river Seine. It commands the route into Rouen.'

'Is that to annoy Philip? I thought they had agreed to stop that.'

'I believe so, Your Highness.' Robert stood back to look at me. 'That is the problem. They prefer to annoy each other, and to hell with the rest. But seeing you, Your Highness, tells me he has made the wrong choice by staying away.'

I looked around, but everyone else was busy. 'Careful, Robert; unwise words can be misheard.'

'Sorry,' he replied gently. 'There are two ladies waiting for you over there.' He pointed at the pair waiting in the bailey, on the steps up to the grand entrance.

'Isabeau and Cateline?'

'The same. They've been working hard to make your quarters presentable.'

'Good; we'll meet them. Alazne, Pavot, leave that baggage. Come and say hello to your new companions.'

A tense moment followed as the new girls, or rather young women, curtsied and greeted me happily, then both pairs eyed each other.

I made the introductions. 'Alazne and Pavot, meet our new companions.'

'I am Isabeau,' one said.

'And I am Cateline,' said the other.

The four bowed to each other, then my sweet Alazne moved forward, smiling, to embrace the pair one by one, followed by Pavot.

'We could do with some help,' said Alazne. 'The queen is very busy.'

'Oh,' said Isabeau, 'you are foreign.'

'No, from Navarre,' responded Alazne defensively.

'I have heard of Navarre,' said Cateline with a smile. 'You must tell us all about it.'

'And the Crusade,' added Isabeau. 'What was that like?'

'You might not enjoy that,' said Pavot.

They were fine for now. Now all I needed was a husband.

'Do you want to see your quarters?' asked Robert, a bystander to the conversation.

We wandered through the rebuilt or redecorated corridors, Robert shuffling behind, saying naught but coughing a lot.

'Do you have a throat ailment, Robert?' I asked.

'No, Your Highness; it's the dust. I had hoped that the new improvements would meet your approval, but you've said naught.'

I faced him and planted a kiss on his cheek. 'I am overwhelmed. This is as good as our villa in Rome. Is it not, ladies?'

'And it's clean,' said Alazne.

'As good as could be expected,' added Pavot, 'apart from the dust.'

'It'll soon be cleared,' I said, 'and we thank you two, Isabeau and Cateline.'

'Yes,' said Robert, 'they have worked wonders, and we have several serving girls to help.'

We had the whole of one side of the palace; our quarters were up some stairs and all along the second floor. There was one large bedchamber and four smaller ones, a privy *refectorium*, and at one end a garderobe with a water basin.

'This is the queen's privy bedchamber,' said Robert, ushering me into the large chamber. It had a large bed and was better decorated than the others.

'The furnishings are not complete yet,' I said.

'Of course, Your Highness; the finish will be your choice. Just say, and it will be done.'

I spotted a door in one corner. 'Where does that lead, Robert?'

'It's an antechamber that provides passage to the king's chambers,' he replied, leaving the possibilities of such a facility to my imagination.

'Where's the bath, Lord Robert?' asked Alazne. 'I heard a bath mentioned.'

'Down below, Lady Alazne, next to the kitchens, but it can be reached through a privy stairway and passage from here.'

'So that we do not need to be dressed to reach it?' added Cateline.

'As you say, Lady Cateline, and I'll be pleased to escort you if you so wish,' responded my wicked guardian.

Cateline laughed, taking no offence. It seemed that Robert and my new ladies had become friends before my arrival.

'Well,' declared Alazne, 'apart from having to be escorted to the bath naked, there is one other problem, Your Highness.'

'It's not compulsory, Alazne,' I said, trying not to laugh. 'What else bothers you?'

'This chamber is bare. Though I see robe chests and closets everywhere, the walls are bereft of hangings. Everything we say echoes.'

'Sorry, ladies,' said Isabeau. 'Everything was taken down and put into safekeeping. You can have a look and see what you want to retrieve.'

'Let's settle in first,' I said. 'We will bathe, eat some food and make a list of things to do. We can do that at table. Robert, where is Father Edwin?'

'You've brought your priest?'

'Of course, but where he is I know not.'

'Across the inner bailey there is a chapel and the king's receiving hall, and a planning hall which the king asked for. You ladies settle in, and I'll stir up the cooks and find your priest. Then upon my return I'll expect to find you undressed and ready for the baths.' A remark which he cast over his shoulder as he left.

'Lackwit,' teased Alazne, giggling.

It was the twentieth day of December when I received a note from Joan. It read:

Richard is here in Fontevraud, giving his mother all his attention. He wants me to marry Raymond; he says Toulouse will be better than Sicily, and together with Navarre they will safeguard our southern borders. I'm back to being one of Richard's assets, a pawn in his new game. I shall resist, and I will not accompany him to Poitiers for Christmas. God bless you, dear sister, and good fortune with my brother.

Little had changed. I cried into my pillow that night, weeping for Joan and not caring who came to spend Christmas with me. Richard himself never made an appearance; I was not surprised.

CHAPTER TWELVE

1196

It was the second week in January when I awoke in the glum dawn light to hear noises in the next chamber. 'Alazne!' I called in alarm, and she came running in.

'What's that disturbance at this time of day?' I asked, pointing at the door in the corner.

She crossed the chamber floor and threw open the offending door, which led into the antechamber.

'Good Lord, what are you doing here?' I heard her cry. 'It is full of men, Your Highness.'

Leaving the bed, I gathered my nightgown around me and went to see for myself. There were three men, all staring at Alazne.

'Who are you?' I demanded.

'Er, the king's guard ... madam, and you?'

'Queen Berengaria.'

A heavy silence fell upon the trio. Then one spoke. 'Sorry, Your Highness, we did not realise that you were so near.'

'Well, now you know. This is a privy chamber for the use of the king and queen; please leave.'

'Sorry, of course. Where does the king's guard stay?'

'The corridor is wide enough. Off you go.'

Alazne tittered as the men prepared to leave, but the antechamber door leading into the king's bedchamber opened suddenly and there stood Richard. His men all bowed.

'What, what?' he said.

'Good morrow, Richard. You've found your bedchamber,' I spluttered.

'Berengaria, good morrow. What's the fuss?'

I was shocked. The figure before me had aged beyond the few years we had been apart. His face was lined, his hair unkempt and his eyes tired. He was still in his day clothes, although he had clearly just been woken.

'There were men in here.' I pointed at the goblets and carafes on the table. 'This is privy, for us.'

'Oh, yes, of course. We should talk.'

A young man appeared behind him; he was properly dressed, but anxious. 'Your Highness, we heard a to-do. Is all well?'

'Yes, yes. Meet the queen, Reynard. Berengaria, meet my knight, Reynard; he carries my banner and keeps me safe.'

'Good morrow, Your Highness. Have we disturbed you? I am sorry.'

What a polite young man, I thought, as he ogled Alazne. She disappeared back into my chamber.

'Who's that? I remember her, I think,' said Richard.

'Alazne, one of my ladies of the bedchamber. She was with me in Outremer, remember?'

'Yes, yes, of course. Well,' he said, 'this is a reunion of sorts, I suppose.'

'Quite. We expected you for Christmas.'

'Ah! Yes, Christmas. Mother is quite old now; I thought it best to…'

'Stay with her,' I finished, looking at him closely. He was still very tall, and as he moved into the chamber I could see that there was still power in him, despite the lines of age that had settled on his nearly forty-year-old face. I caught a whiff of his body odour. 'There are all the best facilities here, if you intend to stay,' I went on.

'Baths, do you mean?' He managed a smile.

'And new kitchens.'

'Good, good. Did you bring that Syrian cook with you? He was a fine fellow.'

'No, we barely escaped Jaffa with our lives.'

'Ah, you've had some adventures, I hear.'

'Indeed — and I've met the Pope, which is more than you managed.'

'Still a scold, I see. We must sit and talk — much to discuss. We'll get into proper clothes first.'

'Perhaps there's something else first,' I said, moving closer.

'What?'

'A kiss for your queen.'

I received a peck on the head, then Richard disappeared back into his privy chamber. I retreated into mine and found all four of my ladies standing there.

'Well, Your Highness?' asked Alazne.

'He seemed to remember me … and you,' I said, looking at her. 'Get that chamber cleared of the guards' detritus. They are not allowed in there; it is privy for me and the king.'

'It will be done, Your Highness.'

'Should we eat first, Your Highness?' asked Isabeau.

'No, first we find our priest for morning prayers, and then we eat. Perhaps the king will have found the baths by then.'

I did not speak politely — I was not in a polite mood. The day might have brought me my husband, but it had not brought me much joy so far.

When I had calmed down, I sent for the steward and instructed him to have food and drink served in my privy antechamber. My ladies were sent down to the hall to eat, and I sat at the table waiting for Richard to return from his bath.

The noises in the corridor told of his return. Despite the tremors in my stomach, I was going to remain firm.

As the king's party passed by along the corridor, one of his knights poked his head in. I told him to ensure that the king knew I was waiting on his return with his food.

It was not long before that gained a response, and Richard opened his bedchamber door and entered.

'Ah,' he said, eyeing the table. 'Food. I was told you were in here, what, what.'

'We can move down into the great hall, but there might be a few things to discuss before we eat together in public.'

'Ah, of course. You are a very good organiser, Berengaria, very good, yes.'

'I managed a few palaces before I met you. Sit; the bread and pastry are good, and the wine is decent.'

He sat and began to investigate the contents of the table, which had improved since my first visit. 'I heard that you had taken control, and Robert has finished the task of improving the accommodation hereabouts.'

'Nearly, there's some left to complete.'

'Are your quarters suitable?'

'Very. Yours?'

'Good, good.'

'I heard that you were ill again, in Germany.'

'Same again, horrible fevers. It leaves me weak as a kitten — I hate it.'

'Does anything improve matters?' I asked, thinking about the warm women who were allegedly shoved into his bed to combat his shivers.

'Not much. I had some strange dreams. I go to sleep and wake up drenched in sweat. Can't think straight for days after.'

'Perhaps you should avoid making decisions for a few days afterwards?'

'Mmm, interesting. Nobody has said that.'

'Try allowing them.'

'Too many want to advise me. Don't know who to listen to, so I make my own decisions. I've sent for your brother, you know? The new King Sancho.'

'Sancho? Why?'

'Things to talk about, mutual benefit things — we can work together, yes?'

'Yes.' I pecked at my bread and cheese and took a little sip of wine. Mists were clearing, and questions were being answered. 'You are quite content that King Sancho holds your southern borders safe?'

'Yes, yes, and he forays into Maine and Normandy if we ask him to.' He was relaxing now, mellowing.

'Yet you seek further border safety by marrying your sister off to Raymond?'

That stopped him chewing. He took a slurp of wine and looked at me. 'God, you're sharp — got a tongue as well. Mother's idea, that — too clever for me.'

'Joan has not got over your attempt to marry her off to a Saracen.'

'Not got over it, eh? Bad idea. I've apologised for that. But matters move on.'

'But — *Raymond*? How long can your sister last, married to that man? He disposes of wives like chicken bones.'

'He'll not do that to *my* sister; have faith.'

Yet Bourguigne de Lusignan had been married and put aside in the time since we'd seen Raymond last. A new wife would be his fourth.

Richard had cleared his platter by now, and I was wondering how much longer I could pin him down. I decided to do it bit by bit and see how far I could push him.

'The Church hereabouts has been very cooperative, especially in giving funds to help free you, and in giving aid to the poor. I have set up hospitals for retuning Crusaders in Beaufort-en-Vallée, and I would like to assist the Saint John Infirmarians here. Do you approve?'

'Yes, yes, good idea. I heard that you were active in that regard. Pleased to help. I must pay everyone back when I have everything under control. No need to ask me about such matters; I have my own to attend to. You are my queen, after all.'

'You'll come to church with me, then?'

'Of course. Is there a chapel within the palace?'

'Yes, but we should be seen at church together, as king and queen. It will please the people.'

'Yes, the people; those who paid my ransom.'

'And whose men fought and died for you.'

'Ah, yes. Will you show me around the palace?'

'Gladly. I'll send for Robert, and we can go together.'

'King and queen, together. Yes, yes, good.'

'My quarters are through that door.' I pointed to it.

'I see, yes, yes, good.'

'I'll come and collect you when I find Robert.'

So saying, I made my way back to my quarters. Nothing much had changed, really; he remained the Richard of old. I expected that the promises he had made to his new overlord, Heinrich, would soon be cast aside as he regained control of the Angevin territories. I almost felt sorry for Philip; choosing John as an ally was likely to result in pain.

'Alazne, do we have any queenly garments? The king and queen are going to inspect Robert's new build.'

From somewhere within the diverse collection of clothes we had gathered in Rome, Alazne produced a respectable gown and a silver circlet.

As we made our way along the corridor, I motioned for Alazne to rap at the king's door.

It was opened by Reynard, who greeted me with a smile.

'Is that the queen?' Richard's voice echoed along the corridor from within his quarters.

'Yes, Your Highness,' answered Reynard.

'Bring her in; I'm all ready now.'

And he was, nicely done up in colourful clothes.

'Good Lord, you've got a crown on your head,' he said.

'Only a circlet. Where's your crown?'

'Somewhere betwixt here and Cyprus; Robert seems to have lost it.'

'Did you not wear one in Westminster when you were there?'

'They found one for me. It was mere mummery; it let them know that I was back.'

'Well, Richard, your head is crown enough and good enough for church. You'll be fine.' I said that to cheer him. The truth was that his hair had almost disappeared, and what was left was wispy and sparse.

'I suppose they'll know I am the king because I'll be holding your hand.'

'Your being head and shoulders above everyone else would indicate that.'

'Ah, yes, that. We're an odd couple, if ever there was one.' He smiled down at me.

We set off down the steps across the bailey. At the gate I spied Mercadier — a mercenary warrior who now accompanied Richard everywhere. He was silent, bearded and glowering, as usual.

'I wondered where he was,' I remarked.

'Mercadier, inspecting the defences, yes, yes,' Richard replied.

Once out of the palace, we were cheered all along the road to the church. Richard surprised me by sitting still throughout the entire sermon. He seemed to be in another place in his head.

The period that followed was odd. In public we were, to all observers, king and queen. In privy, even in the same space, we were separate. He made efforts to be polite, but always seemed to be elsewhere in his mind, and sometimes he was absent in body too. One morning I woke to find he had disappeared.

'Gone off to see his mother?' asked Alazne.

'Yes, she is getting old,' I said without conviction.

'Still, it's two days there and back, Your Highness,' added Isabeau.

'I'll ask about it when he returns. If you are noticing, it will not be long before tittle-tattle seizes the day. Does he seem ill to you, Alazne?'

'Yes, pale, quivery at times. That illness we witnessed in Outremer still lingers, I believe.'

'He puts on a show, but I can see beyond it,' I said. 'When he is not concentrating I see pain in his eyes.'

'Tell us more about Palestine, Your Highness,' said Cateline. 'There are things we still do not understand.'

'You might never reach a full understanding of the horrors we witnessed. We can only relate them to you, and what you feel may not be what lingers in our hearts,' said Pavot.

It was true: horrors still floated about in my dreams, and at times during the day.

Father Edwin came to see me during one of Richard's absences, cheerful as usual.

'Your Highness, I've been at the church with Father Raphaël.'

'Good; how goes the alms work?'

'We are working on a plan. The king has promised more money, I hear.'

'Yes, he has been persuaded to part with some from his treasury.'

'We can spend it well here. But I wanted to talk about something different.'

'Father?'

He shuffled about a bit and cleared his throat. 'His Eminence, the bishop of Lincoln, Hugh of Avalon…'

'I know him not.' I waited.

'He is concerned, Your Highness, and he asks if all is well.' That came tumbling out in a rush.

'I am fine; how is he concerned? Is he not content with how we are organising Poitiers?'

'Erm, no, Your Highness, it is more a matter of how you and the king are organising…'

'I see,' I said, wondering how to explain that we were sleeping apart. 'Well, as you see, the king is at the palace quite often.'

'Good.' He gazed skywards, and his attention was taken for a moment by some squabbling birds. 'There are those who have your best interests at heart, Your Highness. They do ask about you.'

'Yes, of course. And they are concerned about the welfare of the realm, too?'

'Yes, the peace of the realm is important.'

They wanted confirmation that an heir was likely. I decided to divert that particular query. 'Indeed. My brother King

Sancho will be here soon to discuss issues such as that. Was there anything else, Father Edwin?'

'Er, no, Your Highness. I look forward to seeing King Sancho once more. We will see him in church, I trust.'

'Or our chapel.' I nodded to indicate that he could go. The question of an heir to the Angevin empire was one that concerned me too. It was unlikely to be achieved from a distance.

Richard returned from Fontevraud, and Sancho arrived as predicted. I thought that Sancho wanted to spend some time with me, but Richard took him off to discuss whatever they had agreed to discuss. Richard did not invite me into the meetings of the mighty of his realm, but after a while I walked in, and a place was found for me next to Richard. He said naught and was polite, but clearly he did not know how to manage this, which amused me.

They talked a great deal about our common borders across the Pyrenees, and who could be trusted and who they had concerns about on the southern side of the mountains. I attended their meetings two or three times, but tired of it until what turned out to be the final day of Richard's stay, when I was required to attend.

There were some curious glances from various lords and churchmen, about twelve of them, as I took my place between Richard and Sancho, who grasped my hand in support. I was opposite Robert and Stephen, who were both grinning at me, and I decided to take the initiative.

Richard began to clear his throat, but I put paid to that and addressed the gathering. 'Good morrow, my lords. What fix have you trapped yourselves in that you need my presence?'

Richard banged the table with his hand and burst out laughing. Sancho tightened his grasp. The mood was set and the response was friendly. Then it was my turn to be surprised.

'We need you to carry my responsibilities in the south, my queen,' said Richard in his usual no-nonsense way. 'King Sancho is to maintain our peace and will cross back and forth through the Pyrenees. I must go north and remove Philip's hands from my Normandy, which leaves you to liaise between us. If you could continue to do your good works with the poor, especially those returning Crusaders found in penury, we would count it a great use of your time.'

There was a gentle slapping of the tabletop as Richard's lords showed their approval.

'And no doubt it would please the Lord, Your Highness.' This from Ademar, Bishop of Poitiers, sitting at the far end.

'We know of your actions in Beaufort-en-Vallée, and here in Poitiers, and we are duly rebuked by them,' said Robert, grinning.

'Aye, care for our retuning Crusaders has not been properly considered, Your Highness. You have shown us the way,' added Stephen.

'God's way,' said Ademar, not to be outdone.

'You have been discussing me?' I asked, maybe a little too forcefully.

'Indeed, my queen, and all to the good,' said Richard. 'Is it settled, then?'

'Yes, my lord. I will do my best.' This was all that I could say.

'Good, good, that's it; we'll get on with the business of relieving Philip of my lands.' Then he stood, and that was that; I was the grist to Richard and Sancho's mill. I was pleased, and then scared; this was more than managing my father's palaces. Failure in this matter had consequences.

Richard was off again the following morning. By this time I knew there would be no night-time visit, but I made an effort to be in the bailey when he was ready to set off, with my ladies gathered about me.

'There is much work to be done, Berengaria. Château Gaillard needs my attention — the construction must be right — and I will call in to see Mother on my way, to advise her on our position.'

'So you are left to get on with it, Your Highness?' said Alazne as Richard's cavalcade disappeared through the gateway.

'Nothing strange about that, Alazne. They only want me to be what I am.' I looked at her, my lady and my friend; we had been through much together. 'Richard seems to think that I exist only above the neck.'

She moved as if to hold me, but I backed off.

'Hugs later. I need to think.'

'And to talk. You are missing Lady Joan? You were the best of friends.'

'Apart from you and my other ladies, she is the only friend I can confide in.'

'We will not leave you, Your Highness; count on it.'

'Thank you. Come, we'll tell the rest of our plans for my domains.'

'Let's pray that Richard does not sell them to pay for his confrontation with Philip,' Alazne muttered. She was right — nothing much endured around my husband, except death.

My brother caught me on my way back inside, and we embraced. It was time for another farewell.

'Worry not about Richard's treasury. He tells me that since he and his mother gained control of England, the money is pouring in through new taxes, and some of it is heading our way,' said Sancho.

'Good, I can use it.'

'There is something else that we talked about, or rather listened to, and it concerns your friend Joan.'

'Oh, do tell.'

'I understand that King Alfonso escorted you part of the way here, and that you met Raymond of Toulouse.'

'Yes, Alfonso does not have a high opinion of Raymond. He accuses him of loose morals, of excessive appetite in some mysterious regard.'

'You mean sexual excess?'

'That was implied.'

'Then you should know that Alfonso has been looking for an opportunity to swallow up Toulouse for some time now. His opinion of Raymond should be regarded with suspicion.'

'And Alfonso is the reason that Father made an agreement with Eleanor to safeguard our southern borders?'

'In a word, yes. And now Richard is seeking ways to aid any ideas that Alfonso may have in regard to Toulouse.'

'So how does that affect Joan?'

'I don't know yet, but he has something in mind. Just watch and listen; all information reveals something. I must go now; my men are waiting.'

'I trust that you are aware of the dangers of tying Navarre to the fortunes of the Plantagenets, dear brother?'

His arms tightened around me. 'Aye, sister — a choice of devils, but a choice it must be. The eyes of Leon and Castile are upon us, but we Basques are spread across the Pyrenees, so the north as an ally is as good as the south. I must tell you about Blanca before rumours circulate. There have been — conversations.'

'I suppose they concern marriage? Who is the fortunate one?'

'Someone in the French court has been proposed. I have an envoy there at the moment, negotiating the matter.'

'Philip's court — what will Eleanor do?'

'She can do what she likes. This is a matter between kings.' Sancho looked into my eyes. 'Be not so concerned. It was you who counselled me to be wary of drinking from a Plantagenet cup.'

'True, but neither should you stand with a foot on both sides of a river. Philip hasn't given you a name?'

'Not yet. I'll let you know when it is fixed, and I'll try to see you more often.'

'And write more often.'

We hugged until Alazne gave one of her 'that'll do' coughs, and I was released.

'Farewell, Queen of England,' said Sancho from atop his steed, grinning.

'Farewell, King of Navarre,' I replied, holding back my tears, and waved as he exited the palace gates at the head of his entourage.

The birdsong returned to claim the air.

'What now, Your Highness?' asked Pavot, clinging to Alazne.

'Nothing has changed. I am queen of that which I survey; what is beyond remains a mystery.'

Poitiers, once Eleanor's favourite possession, was mine to control, so I set about it with some dedication and the blessing of God.

A week later I received a letter from Joan.

'She has agreed to marry Raymond,' I said to my ladies, with my stomach churning.

'Something she might regret,' said Alazne, mirroring my thoughts. She and Pavot embraced me as the other pair watched in puzzlement.

'What is wrong with Raymond?' asked Isabeau.

'And Eirini — what about that beauty?' Alazne added.

I consulted Joan's letter. 'They are staying together, and Joan's marriage is to take place in Rouen.'

'Ooh, can we go, Your Highness?' asked Alazne.

'New gowns, ladies,' said Pavot.

'Not until the poor are fed,' I retorted sharply.

The truth was that I was devastated. I felt the controlling hand of Eleanor behind this, and I trembled for Joan. And what about Eirini, more grist to the Plantagenet mill? *Time will tell*, I thought fearfully. *Time will tell.*

CHAPTER THIRTEEN

Another letter from Joan came to me in August while we were in Poitiers. It seemed quite cheery, as if Joan was now settled in her mind.

I called on Alazne to gather the ladies in my solar.

'October, in Rouen, ladies,' I informed them.

'*Will* we get new gowns, Your Highness?' asked Pavot.

'If I am able to afford it. You'll need to wait a few more weeks while I get to grips with our income. This may have once been Eleanor's domain, but she has held it loosely for too long; there are too many gaps in the accounting.'

Later, Isabeau came to see me during a quiet period. I counted her as a friend now. She had chestnut hair and a well-formed face with brown eyes and full lips; I wondered how long I could keep her. So many men were watching the poor girl, for, like Eirini, she had a surfeit of beauty.

'Your Highness, Lady Joan's marriage...'

'Yes?'

'Can we afford new gowns? The others are asking; it is all they talk about, and it's quite boring.'

'I expect that we will; the money from tithes, taxes and rents, and from the king's treasury are reliable sources by now. The demand is changing too. Casualties from the Crusades are falling, we have found employment for more of the poor, and the bishop is being helpful, especially since Richard agreed to begin repaying the money collected for his ransom.'

'It's just as well that they kept proper records, with of all this money moving about.'

'True, and so do we. Stephen is aware of the importance of accurate records and keeps the clerks' heads down.'

'Is that why a king's collector lives here?'

'Yes, I'm keeping him close. I am minded to go and visit Lady Joan before we all depart for Rouen, to see how she is. Would you like to accompany me?'

'Yes, but ... Alazne, she is quite friendly, but she is your closest lady. I would not like to discomfort her.'

'You leave her to me. She will be amenable to a few days here with only Pavot for company.'

'How do you know, Your Highness?'

I grinned. 'Because she will think of it herself.'

A light shone in Isabeau's eyes as she saw my meaning. 'I can see why you are successful at making plans, Your Highness. I shall observe with interest.'

'And learn, dear girl, and learn. The world is a devious place. You should have the answers before it asks the questions.'

She smiled. 'I have already been asked the same question in many disguises.'

'You mean marriage proposals? How old are you?'

'Sixteen.'

I cast my eyes up and down her figure. 'I'd be surprised if you had not been asked. What answers do you give?'

'I always give the same reply to the devil in disguise: *no, thank you.*'

We laughed together, and I knew we would get along quite nicely.

In the event, Alazne did not need much persuasion to remain in Poitiers. When I said that I only wanted two ladies to accompany me, she immediately volunteered Isabeau and Cateline. 'You can't leave those girls here on their own, Your Highness; who knows what might befall them? Besides, they know little about managing a household. Leave Pavot and me; we'll take care of the palace, along with Stephen.'

So, with a show of reluctance I left for Fontevraud with the two girls, Bernez and Longchamp providing our escort.

I was received quite nicely by Eleanor, although I was shocked by her appearance. How long ago on the sands of Italy at Bagnara had we said our farewells? And now she was showing her age, her face lined, her eyes a little dull. She did not move very much and remained seated throughout our meeting.

'I see you are well, Berengaria,' she said. 'I have been following your progress closely. Such adventures! Did you know that I went on the second crusade in 1147?'

'I haven't heard about it in any detail, madam. How did you fare among all that blood and hate?'

Her eyes flashed at the memory. For a moment I saw a young Eleanor.

Joan was standing behind her with a hand on one shoulder.

'What words can describe it?' said Eleanor with venom. 'A shambles, chaos, a badly led rout. I was humiliated and nearly killed.'

'That sounds familiar. How awful. Badly led?'

'By my first husband, Louis VII of France. I got rid of him after that.'

'You got rid of the King of France; that is well known. But how?'

'The creature was a bad jest, and I have friends in Mother Church. But don't get any ideas. Are you not with child yet?'

I supposed that the question would come up. 'No, madam; that would require some effort from Richard.'

That gave her cause to think. If she wanted to be direct, then so be it.

'He has not mounted you?'

'He made an effort in Cyprus but was called away on business before he achieved anything.'

'Cyprus?' She was indignant now. 'But you've been together in Poitiers.'

'In the same building, madam, not the same bedchamber. He is busy with matters to do with France and the damage wrought by his brother, your son John.'

That brought about a silence, and I saw a teardrop fall — not what one would expect from a woman with such a fearsome reputation.

'I'm sorry, madam, but I have followed Richard to hell and back and I remain a virgin. He has other priorities.'

'They are not the priorities of his father; he couldn't keep his hose on.'

'Mother! Please,' gasped Joan.

'It is true. Henry haunts me from beyond the grave. If he hadn't let that strumpet Alys into his bed, all would have been well betwixt Richard and Philip. That would have put you out of the picture, my dear, but fate has a part to play in all our lives.'

'Berengaria has naught to explain, Mother,' said Joan. 'It is my brother who needs pointing in the right direction.'

Eleanor looked me up and down and declared, 'I am weary. I'll take a nap now. Perhaps we can talk later.'

She beckoned two nuns standing in the background with Isabeau and Cateline, and they came to help her to rise and leave the chamber.

'We'll *not* be discussing it again, Joan,' I said. 'We'll talk about you and Raymond now; that's what I want to know about.'

'And that's what I want to tell you about too.'

We embraced. 'Oh, Joan, we have been too long apart,' I said into her ear.

'I know, my sweet, but we are drifting dust in the winds of fate. Let me look at you. Come, there is a privy garden we can sit in.'

It was a cosy place, sheltered and quite warm in the summer sun. Seating had been placed around a fishpond, so we took our place on a bench with my girls sitting nearby. Torène, Joan explained, was unwell and I was sad not to see her.

'There seems to be little peace in this world, Berri. Every time I settle, something arrives to move me on,' said Joan sadly.

'True. None of us are where we started, and you are moving along once more.'

'Toulouse is pleasant enough.'

'And you will become a countess. How were you persuaded?'

'Richard explained the circumstances of Raymond's past — the early death of one wife through illness, the religious differences of another, and his incompatibility with the third.'

'And his plans for the defence of the Plantagenet lands?'

'What plans?'

'Oh, come along, Joan, you can't have missed the common borders. Aquitaine with Toulouse and Navarre; it all intrudes into Castile, Leon, and Aragon. The Plantagenet empire is poised to expand; have you not seen that?'

'I have not. I do not consult maps daily.' She gazed at me. 'Well, what of it?'

'One of the reasons Father dealt with Eleanor and agreed a treaty for the protection of Navarre was to keep the Castilians out, and it will not be long before the Aragonese feel discomforted by your marriage. When the Angevin Plantagenets strike south, it may reap an unwanted reward.'

'You believe me to be naïve, unwise?'

'I love you, dear sister, but beware of glittering coronets; they can tumble.'

'I'll be wary. I've already dropped a crown. You sniff plots everywhere.'

'I have been observing your mother, and I intend to survive.'

Jo's hand tightened around mine. I was not sure that she had considered all aspects of her forthcoming marriage and who might dare to put Richard's sister through the same torment she suffered in Sicily.

'Here comes Eirini; she will be coming to Toulouse with me.'

Eirini, a shining, jangling vision, strode into the garden. Isabeau's jaw dropped and Cateline stared.

'Eirini,' I greeted her.

'Your Highness. It is nice here, yes?'

'It is very nice here. You look splendid. Meet my new ladies.'

She took in Isabeau and Cateline with an imperious look. They were suddenly made quite dull, and I felt the same.

'Lady Joan is to be married, yes?' I said.

'Yes. You and your ladies will come to the wedding?'

I looked at Joan.

'Of course,' she responded. 'Bring them all. I would like to see Pavot again; we shared so much.'

We spent the evening in pleasant conversation. Although the food was plain, the wine was acceptable, and Eleanor stayed away.

In the morning we set off back to Poitiers, with hugs, kisses and declarations of love.

We were not far from Poitiers when we encountered a solitary horseman: Stephen, who had ridden out to meet us. After greetings, he pulled in alongside me.

'Your Highness,' he began, and then favoured me with one of his brightest smiles.

'I recognise that smile. What is it, Stephen?'

'I needed a word in privy, Your Highness, and back at the castle it's not always easy. I wanted to talk about my family in England.'

I had not considered his family, and I felt I should have asked about them. 'We have not mentioned them for a while, so tell me more about them, Stephen. Do you not receive letters from Edeline?'

'Yes, Your Highness, but unlike yours they do not concern affairs of state, and I read them in privy. Edeline is bringing up our three daughters — Alice, Mabel and Beatrice. I would have liked to add a son, but we set off on Crusade. I would like to play some part in my daughters' lives someday.'

'Are they safe?'

'Aye, Your Highness — all safe in Kent.'

'Across the narrow sea. You should tell me about them more often; I want to know. One day, when I cross the narrow sea to England, I will insist on meeting them.'

'I know that you would like to see them, but meanwhile, will you manage without me, Your Highness?'

'Your brother will be close by; you need not worry about me. Go with my blessing and give my love to Edeline.'

'You are very gracious, Your Highness. It will not be easy to leave you.'

'No, it's not something that I look forward to either. We'll make arrangements, and we'll need a new protector.'

'I'll talk to Robert and see who he can appoint.'

'Thank you. Will not Bernez and Longchamp suffice?'

'Perhaps, but the king should have a say, especially when you get to England.'

The rest of the journey went by quickly, and I called Alazne and Pavot into my bedchamber to tell them all about our visit to the abbey.

The next day, in a meeting with Robert, he informed me that he had been ordered back to Anjou, there to maintain his duties as seneschal.

'But who am I to be left with?'

'I have not yet advised the king who to appoint. I would be content with Bernez or Longchamp, or a knight named de Mauléon. They are all pleasant young men, but de Mauléon is Lord of Talmont. Whoever it is, he will be under my control, and I'll hold him responsible for your comfort. We'll send for more soldiers to be installed here for your safety, though the king can hardly spare any while he is hounding the French.'

'So I am losing both of you brothers?'

'No, Your Highness, *we* are losing you. It has been a privilege and a joy to be near you.'

'Am I to remain here?'

'I think it wise, Your Highness. While the king gallops around Normandy, you will be safer here.'

'Ah well, I cannot contest that. When will you leave, Robert?'

'When we are satisfied about your safety. I'll think on it, and we'll decide together.'

With the procedure agreed, I called Father Edwin and my ladies together to explain the future. 'As you are aware, matters are in flux and the king is about his business with the French in the north.'

'Are both Stephen and Robert of Turnham leaving?' asked Alazne.

'Unfortunately, yes. Robert is going only as far as Anjou as seneschal, and Stephen is going to visit his family in England. He has not seen them since he set off on Crusade.'

'So, who is to be the castellan here?' asked Isabeau.

'A fellow named Savery de Mauléon.'

'What about Longchamp or Bernez?' asked Alazne.

'I suspect that Longchamp would rather go back to England, although he will not say so. His uncle, the chancellor, is having some difficulties with the English lords — something to do with excessive tax gathering — and our Longchamp feels that family support might help. Bernez will stay with us.'

'Mauléon's fine by me,' responded Alazne. 'I don't know him, but one man's as good as the next.' As expected, the others agreed.

'Very well, I'll tell him. As for us, we'll continue with our work in the hospital and assistance to the poor. I'll need to expand our household, so there'll be new people coming in; I need reliable envoys to keep me informed about the world. Perhaps we can find a cook to rival the Syrian we had, Ahmed. Alazne, see if you can sniff one out. Ask in the hospital; there may be a Crusader there with some knowledge of herbs and spices. Father Edwin, speak to the Hospitallers. Act as my envoy; see what they need and keep me up to date with the tittle-tattle from the village and the cathedral.'

'Your Highness, That's the best task I've ever been given — tittle-tattle master. Thank you.'

'Can I accompany you, Father?' asked Isabeau. 'I can improve my English.'

'Oh, of course. I'll tell you all about the English saints.'

'Father Edwin, a prayer for success and peace, if you please,' I said, 'and for happiness in the forthcoming marriage of my friend, Joan.'

CHAPTER FOURTEEN

The time to travel to Rouen came soon enough, and Robert joined us to augment our escort. He intimated that *if* Richard attended the wedding, he would seek to have some time with him. I was leaving Savery de Mauléon to govern Poitiers and taking Bernez with me. Savery had been a bit nettled about that, but I made it clear that he would be the sole master of Poitiers during my absence, which mollified him somewhat. Twenty-year-old men could be a bit sensitive at times, that I knew.

So off we went, our best gowns safely packed into chests in a wagon, which followed behind us. The journey from Poitiers to Rouen was two hundred and fifty miles, and I was pleased on the sixth day to see the outline of this Norman stronghold appear on the horizon. It was near midday, and I was feeling hungry and fed up with the sight of my palfrey's ears.

Rouen, chief town of Normandy, one day to be my duchy, welcomed me as Queen of England — even though this was as near to England as I had yet been. At the town gate a captain of the guard introduced himself and asked us to follow him to the ducal palace, once used by William the Conqueror. Into the bailey we progressed, where I saw that Joan was waiting on the doorstep. Then, hardly pausing for an ostler to grab the reins, I slid off to embrace her, then went inside.

'This is nice,' I said, looking up and around at all the flags and banners hanging from the walls. The tables were already groaning beneath the weight of a monstrously long buffet. 'How are you, my sweet?'

'Overwhelmed, Berri. So much to do, then the marriage, and we're hundreds of miles from Toulouse. I'll be glad to get it all over and done with. I'm so pleased that you could come, especially with Mother unable to attend — she lacks the energy now — but Richard is expected.'

I gasped. 'We are expecting Richard?'

'He has sent word that if we are ready we should get on with it, but he will try to attend. This should be the last wedding for me. I can't spend much time with you this day; they want me for this and that. We'll meet in the morning, perhaps, and in here after the ceremony. Eirini is here too; I'll send for her, and you can have a talk. I'll call the steward and he'll take you to your quarters.'

'A nice turn of phrase, *get on with it.* Wait a moment, Joan. You must tell me that this is agreeable to you. Richard is using you again — you know that.'

'I know, but Raymond was pleasant when last we met. I did have a few moments with him in privy in Toulouse. Now, I must prepare for the morning, and so must you.'

'It is in the morning?'

'Yes, Raymond wants to get back to Toulouse. Go and prepare, Berri; we'll talk more after the ceremony.'

I was woken in the morning by Alazne.

'Your Highness, Your Highness, the king is here; he is asking for you.'

'Good Lord — my dress, help me, quick. Where is he?'

'In the great hall, making sure of the arrangements for Lady Joan's marriage.'

'I suppose that he is surrounded by every noble in Anjou. Is Robert about?'

'Yes, in attendance already.'

'Hurry. Cateline, Isabeau, help Pavot and Alazne, please.' They had just arrived, uncertain as to the cause of the commotion. 'The king is here. You must attend me. What time is it, Alazne?'

'Time for something to eat, Your Highness, then the wedding gowns.'

Richard was already holding court in the great hall, but when I entered he broke off his discussions to greet me, waving his audience away. I was treated to a peck on the head, and, to my surprise, an arm around my shoulders.

'It is fine, Berengaria, is it not, to have Joan safely housed once more?' He called across to his waiting officials. 'Done for the day — the wedding is more important. Now then, my queen, a little something to eat, I think. Then we'll dress for the occasion, eh?'

Joan *housed*; I could have put it better. 'Of course,' I replied calmly.

After a light repast and an hour or so spent dressing, we were off to the cathedral.

The *Rouennais* were lining the streets and gave Richard and me a rousing cheer as we walked along. Mercadier was breathing down Richard's neck, and my ladies and Richard's lords were in procession behind us. We must have seemed the very epitome of royalty, although they might not have known who I was had Richard not been holding my hand, and had I not been wearing a crown produced from somewhere within the palace.

Banners and flags were everywhere, and I suspected that the wine had long been flowing by the time we appeared.

I managed a few words as we strode along, but Richard's long legs diminished my attempts to appear regal as I tried to keep pace.

'How is your war against Philip progressing?' I puffed.

'Good, good. Man's an idiot; he knows more about clothing than swords.'

I cast my mind back to the colourful outfit that Richard had worn at our wedding. 'Better to be handy with both clothes and swords, I believe. Can you slow down a bit? This gown is heavy,' I said, looking up at him.

'Ha! Berengaria, you have it right. With my sword in hand, I can wear what I like. Ha! Slow, slow.'

He was dressed to kill, a colourful warrior covered in emblazoned cloth, with a mighty sword sheathed in a tooled leather scabbard at his side and his tabard shining with gold and silver lions. I wondered if ever a bride might be as outdone in costume by her brother as Joan might be today.

I chanced a comment. 'That is almost as gaudy as your wedding dress, Richard.'

'Wedding? Ah, no, you've not lost your humour then?'

'Not as often as I have missed my husband.'

'Missed?' He gave out a great peal of laughter and had hardly settled before we arrived at the *basilica* door.

The *basilica* was in the process of becoming a cathedral under the direction of the grandly named Archbishop Gautier the Magnificent, and one end was still crowded with planks and poles. The archbishop met us at the door.

'Your Highnesses, welcome. Please excuse the dust. Queen Berengaria — a duchess in her own duchy, and a countess too, if my recollection is correct.'

Richard harrumphed and gazed about him as if to remind the archbishop of who was king.

'Your Excellency,' I replied quickly, 'if the dust turns into a building to please God, then so be it. And I have a dizzying number of titles, but one will suffice.'

'Allow me to conduct you to your place, Your Highnesses.'

We were escorted along the centre of the packed nave to arrive before the altar, and there to sit with a prie-dieu before us. Alazne and Isabeau were standing behind me, while Pavot and Cateline were ushered to the front of the standing congregation to our rear. In a line to my left were what I supposed to be the grandees from Toulouse. Glittering in their midst was the resplendent figure of Eirini, dressed to impress. To my right was the seated line of those from Richard's realm — they all stood to acknowledge us, and we sat down.

The area in front of the altar began to fill with clerics, until, with a trumpet blast from behind, the archbishop made his entrance, followed by his acolytes. The place was rapidly filling up with smoke from the many thuribles and censers being wielded with enthusiasm by young priests.

Then, on a signal and another trumpet blast, the choir raised their voices in praise of heaven, and Count Raymond VI of Toulouse, Marquis of Provence marched up the centre of the nave, followed by his escort, to stand before the archbishop.

Joan's entry was more restrained than that — more rustle than stomp as she emerged from a side door, flanked by two of her ladies, and more queen than countess. My heart filled with gladness to see that she was not outshone by her brother. She took her place alongside the mighty Raymond.

Archbishop Gautier bade us stand to pray for peace. I could not have prayed with more fervour than I did for that.

The actual ceremony was over almost before it began. As Joan was Raymond's fourth attempt to enjoy a successful marriage, I thought he might have grown weary of the pomp. The thought did not remove my unease with the situation, and I prayed for Joan like never before.

When the ceremony was concluded, Raymond took Joan by the hand, and they walked down the aisle together. She was almost as tall as him, and they looked good together. I shushed my ill feelings and prayed instead for a happy future for them.

Archbishop Gautier crossed over from the altar behind them and indicated that we should walk with him behind the newly married couple. I heard Richard wish them well as we joined the procession and was very pleased to see that he had a care for Joan, whether she were a hostage to diplomacy and dynasty or not.

Crowds were waiting in the warming sun, and I received as many shouts of good wishes as Joan. I tried hard to smile and not trip over my gown, nor be distracted by the sea of eyes upon me.

There was a line of wagons and two carriages waiting outside, and I watched as Joan and Raymond climbed into the first — an open carriage to be driven off to the palace. A second carriage was waiting with Robert of Turnham standing by it and grinning.

'Your Highness,' he said as he bowed to Richard. 'Queen Berengaria,' he added, turning to me. 'You'll need to suffer this carriage for a while, Your Highness. We can't have you cocking a leg over a horse today.'

'Brazen lord; when did you arrange this?' I asked, trying to suppress a grin.

'When you weren't watching. Now, may I hand you up, Your Highness?' he asked, standing by the steps at the rear.

I held out a hand and climbed in after Richard to sit on a bench set across the width of the carriage. I was pleased that the weather was kindly and dry. My ladies followed, then two of Richard's nobles came on and sat opposite, staring at my companions. Isabeau blushed, but Alazne was stony-faced, offering no encouragement. The short journey went by without conversation until Richard turned to ask a question of one of his men concerning war — he couldn't forget that even at his sister's wedding. There were other wagons behind for the remaining guests.

We passed a noisy press of townsfolk on the journey from the church to the palace, and the bailey was overflowing. What should have taken a few moments was stretched, and it took an age to enter the bailey and climb down. Robert, riding behind, leaped off his palfrey and was standing ready to hand me down as I stepped off.

'Are you well, Robert?' I asked.

'Well, Your Highness, and busy,' he replied.

'My privy chamber, soon as you can, Turnham.' Richard's interest in his sister's wedding was fast diminishing.

'As you command, Your Highness,' acknowledged Robert, but I saw a spark of resentment in his eyes at Richard's rudeness.

'Richard,' I said gently. 'Let Robert have some time to congratulate the bride. It won't take long.'

'Oh, of course. Lead on, Turnham, lead on.'

It being noisier and more crowded than it had been outside, it was difficult to conduct a conversation, but a steward found me and invited me to join Count Raymond and his newest countess in a privy receiving chamber off to one side of the hall. Richard had found his lords once more, and his investment in his sister's great day had waned.

Joan was surrounded by her new family, but when I entered she broke away and enveloped me in a warm hug.

'Come and meet Raymond, Berengaria; his family are here.'

Joan guided me to Raymond, who observed the correct protocol, taking nothing for granted, even though we had met earlier on our way from Rome.

'Your Highness, I was pleased to hear that you had completed your long journey safely, and especially with my dear Joan here, now Countess Joan of Toulouse.'

'It was something of a relief to me also, Raymond. Now, who is this?'

Clinging to his arm was a comely young maiden who somehow reflected Raymond in her looks.

'My daughter, Your Highness. May I introduce Constance; she is the daughter of my second wife, Beatrice of Beziers. She and I had religious differences, and Beatrice is now a nun.'

'Constance,' I said, offering a hand, 'how are you? So many miles from home.'

She smiled sweetly and bobbed. 'Your Highness, Angers is interesting, if a little chilly,' she said pleasantly.

'Ah,' I replied, 'it's quite warm for October. Do not wait for winter if you feel the cold.'

Her father laughed. 'We have snow in the mountains but escape to nearer the sea during wintertime.'

'Then you should make haste to return south; the weather can change quite quickly at this time of the year.'

'We will,' he replied. 'We're off first thing in the morning; our baggage has mostly left already.'

That remark brought it home to me that Joan would be leaving soon, and I might not see her for quite a while. I looked into her eyes, and still there was that sadness.

Then Raymond said, 'Please excuse us, Your Highness; we should be out in the hall with our guests.' He looked at Joan with tenderness. 'My dear, there are more people to meet — your brother in particular.'

'I'll see you later, Joan,' I said, giving her a kiss on the cheek and wishing Raymond good fortune in gaining Richard's ear.

'Yes, later.' And off she went, with Raymond's arm guiding her into the great hall.

I engaged with Constance. She was pleasant and interested in our visit to Rome, but the noise was increasing as the wine continued to flow, and I tired of it all.

I caught Alazne's eye, and we slipped through the crowd and found our way into the quarters allocated to us, leaving Isabeau chatting with Constance; they were the same age and getting along well.

'Oh my word, Alazne, what a commotion,' I said as we settled on the bed. 'What do you think of Raymond?'

'If I were the marrying kind, I would not marry him. He's too old.'

'He's only in his forties,' I said.

'But if Lady Joan wants children, is it not too late?'

'Alazne, what a thing to say! No, it is not too late for a man, and what do you know of such things anyway?'

'Not a lot. I can manage without *that*, Your Highness, thank you.'

The noise from the king's chamber next door increased as he and his companions entered, so I dismissed Alazne, instructing her to leave the door ajar. I lay back against the pillows, worrying about my best friend, but as I was so tired I fell asleep without Richard's attendance.

In the morning I was woken by Alazne and Pavot dashing into the chamber. 'Your Highness, wake up. They've gone; they left just before dawn.'

That was a shock — no fond farewells.

'What do you mean?' I said, realising that I was still fully dressed in my best gown.

'The count and most of his retinue have gone.'

'And it is pouring down,' added Pavot, pointing at a window.

It was then that I realised that the noise in my ears was not from too much wine but from the weather outside.

'Good Lord,' I said. 'Imagine travelling in this! Where is Richard? Go and find Robert, please. Pavot, there are things to discuss. Alazne, help me out of this finery.'

Pavot left then came dashing back. 'They are together in the great hall, Your Highness, and nearly ready to leave.'

Alazne soon had me washing in a cold tub set in the corner; it was a rude start to the day.

'Is there no warm water in this grand establishment?' I moaned.

'Not unless you want to wait until I can grab some servants, Your Highness.'

'Well, I'm not standing about naked while that happens. Pass me that towel, then go and find the others. Where are they?'

'I know not, but they were all very giggly when we left.'

'Get me into a day gown and we'll go and find Richard.'

I was a bit sharp with Alazne, but I was annoyed. I knew that we were here for Joan, but Richard's behaviour I found quite insulting.

I entered the great hall to find it just as busy as when we had left, but this time with servants scurrying about trying to clean up the mess from last night's celebrations.

Robert was standing in the hall, looking at the chaos of the debris and talking to Isabeau and Father Edwin.

'Your Highness, are you well?' he asked.

'Fine. What happened with Joan?'

'I have spoken to the chief steward. It was arranged for her to leave as soon as possible because of the short days. Everything was prepared and Countess Joan was safely loaded into a well-furnished carriage to set off at the first blush of dawn. I'm sorry.'

'Not to fret; it's not your doing. Joan hates wagons. Did Raymond travel with her?'

'Apparently not; he left on a fine palfrey. His daughter was in the wagon with the countess. The captain at the gate informed me that there was some kind of … discussion.'

'Discussion?'

'Between Raymond and his countess. She wanted him with her in the carriage and asked why no horse had been provided for her. But the Cypriot princess travelled with her, and it came to naught. Did you see the king last night?'

I shook my head. Robert did not say more, but I knew his thoughts as well as my own. Joan had done something she would not normally do: obey.

'I've had a privy chamber cleared for you; let's get you and yours fed.'

'Where is Richard now?' I asked.

Robert gazed at me as if I had grown horns. 'Did he not say farewell, Your Highness?' I blushed and he began to hold out a hand, then stopped short. 'I'm sorry, Your Highness. You do not deserve this,' he whispered.

'He's gone?' I murmured.

Robert nodded.

Should I have expected anything else? I asked myself. This was normal for my butterfly husband: lost in his own head without a thought for those around him. But king or not, I thought I must surely enter his thoughts now and again — or had his imprisonment and the recurring illness robbed him of his wits?

Shrugging, I motioned for Robert to lead us, and we followed him. Looking at Isabeau, I demanded, 'Where were you last night?'

'Pavot snores, so I found a vacant chamber. It was very nice, with a huge bed and lots of wall hangings. There was someone else in there, but when she awoke I did not know her.'

'Mmm, you probably spent the night in King William and Queen Matilda's privy bedchamber.'

'Who?'

'I'll tell her later, Your Highness,' said Edwin from behind.

'What's in here? I'm hungry,' said Alazne.

'Come in, ladies,' invited Robert warmly. 'Let's gossip while we eat.'

I wasn't all that hungry, but after a glug of wine I felt a little better and managed some bread and cheese and grapes.

'What do we do now, Robert?' I asked after a while.

'The roads are rivers out there. I don't know how far Raymond's cavalcade will have travelled, but it will be futile trying to catch them up.'

'They would have taken the same road as us?'

'Yes, by coincidence it's the best way. They might call in at Fontevraud to see Countess Joan's mother.'

'Oh, quite. When can *we* leave?'

'I would advise waiting until the rain stops, and then we can see what condition the roads are in.'

'Very well,' I agreed, seeing no reasonable alternative. 'We'll pack and wait for an opportunity. We can talk politics, Robert — see what's what, eh?'

'You'll not be trying to catch up with the king?'

'Do you know where he is bound?'

Robert shook his head. 'No, Your Highness.'

'Then wherever he is bound, ensure that we are ready to travel back to Poitiers, please, Robert.'

'Your Highness. There is something else I should mention. The king has found me a spouse; I need to go back to England to marry her.'

'Found? Are all brides foundlings in Plantagenet eyes?'

'This one was not lost, but she has inherited some land in Yorkshire, and I am nominated to care for her.'

'A reward for loyalty, no doubt? She has a name, this beneficiary?'

'Aye, Isabella of Fossard. She's from a wealthy family. They own Castle Mulgrave near a place called Whitby.'

'Is she comely, Robert?'

'That is something which I will discover in due course.'

'I will pray for you,' I said, but I had difficulty in hiding my grin. Robert had been caught and gutted: the price of serving a Plantagenet. A very similar case to my own.

After two days we were on the road again. I never expected to catch up with Joan, and we never did. At each stopping point, be it hostelry or abbey, they had been and gone. I had thought to call in at Fontevraud to see Eleanor, but as she had not attended Joan's wedding and Richard had spurned the opportunity to converse with me, I was uninterested enough to decide against it.

Now, back in Poitiers, a depressing cloud sat on my shoulders, which not even the sensitive Father Edwin could rid me of.

'You are unhappy, Your Highness,' he stated without preamble, 'and it makes all around you unhappy. Can we not find a way to help you?'

'What could there be to dull the pain of parting from my best friend and an ignorant husband?'

'What did you occupy yourself with before we went to Rouen?'

I looked at him, startled. Of course! 'I worked in the town. I tried to improve the lives of the poor and the disabled Crusaders.' I straightened up. 'I have been blinded by my own selfish wants. Can I be forgiven, Father?'

'I can tell you that you can be, but you must forgive yourself. You have done nothing wrong; your concern for your friend is just and understandable, and Richard's obsessive view of the world is well known. You just need to bring yourself back to the life you have carved out — a life at which you are very good, if I may say so, Your Highness.'

'I will dig out a plain gown and see what is to be done. While kings scatter the entrails of men across the countryside, the poor multiply. May God have mercy on their souls.'

As time went by, it became apparent that the need to care for Crusaders from Richard's war was coming to an end. Some died, some recovered, but until someone else began a new war, the poor were beginning to outnumber the wounded. Therefore, our focus shifted to caring for women in childbirth and the undernourished.

I heard nothing from Toulouse, but because we were so busy, the lack of news hadn't been noticed until almost two months after Joan's wedding, when Father Edwin puffed his way up to the solar with a missive in hand. He seemed pleased.

'You've been questioning the messenger again,' I accused him, wondering how he managed to intercept the various couriers as they turned up at the gate.

'It's from Toulouse, Your Highness,' he said, smiling and ignoring my accusation.

'Ooh, Countess Joan,' cried Alazne. 'Do read it, Your Highness.'

'Yes, how is she?' added Pavot as I tore at the rolled vellum.

I read for a moment. 'She is with child.'

There were various shouts of joy. I read on and felt relieved and happy for my friend; she seemed to be content with her new husband. It seemed that the rumours about his behaviours whispered to me at various times were false. There were some words that troubled me, though.

'Countess Joan writes that Raymond has many enemies, but that she tries her best to support him at all times.'

'Well, Your Highness,' said Father Edwin, 'is that not how it should be, a man and his wife in partnership as the good Lord intended?'

'Indeed,' I said. 'As the good Lord intended: being happy and concerned at the same time.'

'When is the baby due?' asked Isabeau.

I scanned the letter again. 'July next year. He is to be named Raymond.'

'How do they know that it is a boy?' asked Cateline. She received no answer.

'We'll all pray for her. Father Edwin, a special prayer for Countess Joan at Prime in the morning, if you please,' I said.

'Of course, Your Highness. I shall think on it.'

We celebrated Christmas soon after and the year moved into 1197. In July, Joan gave birth to baby Raymond as predicted, one day to be Count Raymond VII, and we settled down to watch the tussle between John and Philip develop. The worst part of it was that the barons and magnates of Plantagenet possessions, both on this side of the narrow sea and in England itself, had split into those in favour of John as the heir to the English throne and those in favour of the ten-year-old Arthur of Brittany. I had been told that Arthur was Richard's nephew, whom Philip had taken into protective custody. Now Philip was plotting to have Arthur sitting beneath the crown of England for his own reasons, while many supported John because they had holdings in England that they believed he would allow them to retain.

We could only watch from a place of safety until the matter was settled.

CHAPTER FIFTEEN

1199

Two years later, we were still waiting. In the year 1198, after Christmas, we moved to Beaufort-en-Vallée for a while. It was due an inspection to check that all was well in its defences, and I wanted to see how the treatment of the sick and poor, which I had instigated during my earlier tenure, was progressing. Richard was many miles to the north, pursuing adventures of his own. I had long given up any hope of an invitation to visit him, nor did I expect him to visit me. As for men, those I had with me who I knew well were Castellan Denis, Father Edwin, Guy de Bernez, my new steward — Oliver — and a hall full of men-at-arms.

In April 1199 the peace that we prayed for daily was shattered by the arrival of visitors.

'A flustered sister nun and a bishop to see you, Your Highness,' announced Oliver.

'Flustered?'

'The sister is red-faced and seemingly unused to wagon-riding. The bishop is better in appearance.'

'Bring them in and make refreshments available for them, Oliver.'

The sister turned out to be no less than Abbess Mathilde of Fontevraud, also Princess Mathilde III of Bohême. My spirits plummeted, and I watched with a sickly feeling as she approached with an expression that held no cheer. She was followed by Bishop Hugh of Lincoln.

'Oh, my dear,' she began with tears in her eyes. 'I'm so sorry. The king is dead.'

My head swam and my stomach churned. 'Where? How?' I stuttered.

'Castle Châlus Chabrol. It was a crossbow bolt. The news has taken a few days to reach us; Queen Eleanor went to his side straight away.'

'Where is Châlus Chabrol?'

'One hundred and twenty miles south of Fontevraud. We heard that he had been wounded, and the queen left immediately, but I fear that he died in her arms on the sixth of April, the evening of the day she arrived. She came back with his body.'

I found a chair and nearly fell into it. 'The burial?'

'It's set for Palm Sunday, the eleventh,' said Bishop Hugh. 'His dying request was that his heart should go to Rouen and his body be interred at the feet of his father in Fontevraud Abbey to atone for rebelling against him. May I offer my sincerest condolences, Your Highness. We have had our differences, the king and I, but that is of no importance now.' He held out a hand, which I grasped in thanks.

So Eleanor had ignored me again to dash to the side of her dying son. That said a lot.

I didn't know what to think. I had not had my husband's company for more than a few hours since we had married, and now it was denied by death.

I felt an arm encircle me. Alazne, dear Alazne. 'Oh, Your Highness, my dear queen, this is so sad.' She took my hand.

'I have not welcomed you, Princess Abbess Mathilde, Bishop Hugh. Please sit with me and tell me as much as you know.'

'I prefer Abbess, Your Highness — too many earthly titles, you know.'

'I do; I also have many and Berengaria will suffice,' I replied lightly, smiling.

'I'm only a bishop,' said Hugh with a chuckle.

As they spoke, I hardly listened. Richard's mother had been summoned to his deathbed, but not his wife.

'You were too far north of Fontevraud,' said Mathilde, 'and we did not know that he had died until his mother returned with his body.'

'Where is Eleanor now?'

'Fontevraud. You are expected, Your Highness,' added Hugh.

'Of course, we'll make arrangements. Please send word to Savery at Poitiers.'

'He will have heard, Your Highness. The cortège will have passed through Poitiers on its way to Fontevraud,' said Hugh.

'Were you there, Bishop Hugh, at the death?'

'No, Your Highness. I was given the news elsewhere and set off for Fontevraud, and I met the abbess on the road. We will leave for the abbey. I am to conduct the service. Will you come as soon as you may?'

'Thank you; we'll prepare.'

I was now surrounded by people all eager to help, but I was alone in my heart. What use was a queen without a king — a widow, a dowager aged thirty-one? What was my future?

Our mood along the road to Fontevraud was, as to be expected, sombre, despite the efforts of the birds in the trees to cheer us. Folk had gathered along the way in villages, but they were eerily quiet, the men doffing their caps as the women curtsied.

The abbey was also quiet, save for a tolling bell. I was taken straight to Eleanor, accompanied by Father Edwin. She was in a chapel, alone at a prie-dieu, save for some ladies hovering behind and her chaplain at the altar.

Unbidden, I knelt at Eleanor's side. She turned a tearstained face towards me. On seeing who I was, she held out a hand, which I took.

'Berengaria, so much was unfinished.'

'I am sorry, madam; there was much done and much to do.'

She called gently to her chaplain standing nearby. 'Will you lead us in prayer, Brother Roger? See if you can find some words of comfort.'

The remainder of the day was spent in the garden in reflection and prayer. The greatest comfort was having Father Edwin, my chaplain and good friend, next to me.

The following day the grounds of the abbey were full, and the church was overflowing with mourners of the highest degree. There were the bishops of Poitiers and Angers and the abbots of Turpenay and Le Mans. The Pope was represented by Cardinal Pietra di Capua, who was conveying the apostolic condolences. Many of Richard's commanders and various civic dignitaries were also present. No king could have had more royal pomp convened to see him off than Richard, as he was lowered into the ground at the feet of his father.

At a loss as to what to do next, I wandered into the gardens with Alazne and my companions.

'We are here for you, Your Highness,' Alazne said. 'Your ladies are here for you.'

'Yes, thank you. It was a grand ceremony. But Richard never did things by halves.'

'No, indeed, Your Highness. That was not his way. What are we to do now?'

'Go back to Beaufort, I suppose. I'm not minded to ride all the way to Poitiers, and Beaufort will be peaceful. There are too many who want to join in with my mourning.'

We stayed for two more days. I sat by Richard's tomb to pray, watching as the crowds of the great gradually faded to go about their business. The remaining gatherings were mostly common folk. Each day Alazne had to persuade me to leave for some refreshment.

On the third day, we bumped into Bishop Hugh as we were making our way back to our quarters to change into riding apparel.

'Your Highness, you are leaving?'

'There's nothing left here, Bishop Hugh. All is done,' I said sadly.

'Where to?'

'Beaufort. I have much to think about.'

'That is on the way to Le Mans. Why not come and stay with us? We'll let you rest and pray and help you to see a way forward.'

This seemed to be a fair offer, so I agreed to consider it, and now that there was no dispute between Richard and Philip, I saw no obstruction to further exploring my various possessions. I prepared to set off, Bishop Hugh opting to stay a few more days with Eleanor and then to follow me.

'Stay at Beaufort for a few days, Your Highness, and I'll catch up with you there. We'll discuss matters further.'

I paid a farewell visit to Eleanor. She was about as much in this world as I, and it was not a memorable moment. I supposed that we would convene at some future date.

At Beaufort my castellan, Denis, was most attentive. We awaited Bishop Hugh to decide if I would travel further on to Le Mans, but the place was eerily quiet, as if the earth was in mourning. On the afternoon of my arrival, as it was turning dark I went straight to my bed, attended by my caring ladies, and tried to sleep as I wept silently. But what was I weeping for, a dead king or a widow's plight?

Time has its own agenda and a habit of handing out surprises, and one of my first visitors was John, once prince and now king.

He arrived in the afternoon, accompanied by Bishop Hugh. Alerted by the shouts of the sentries, I hurried down, pursued by my ladies, into our small bailey in time to see the new King of England gain entry.

'Ha!' the figure on horseback declared. 'Madam, it is easier to gain entry to the Tower of London than this petty castle. I am John, your new king and overlord.'

'Welcome, Your Highness, to my petty castle. I did not see you at my husband's interment; did I miss you?'

'No, madam, I was many miles away in Normandy. But I am here now; should we talk?'

'You are welcome, Your Highness. Bishop Hugh, step down and take some wine. Are you intending to stay?'

John grinned as he slid off his steed, which I thought a little short in the shoulder. The reason became obvious when he was on the ground: he was not much taller than me, with dark red hair and skinny legs topped by a barrel chest.

Coming near, he pulled me into a hug. It went on for too long and became impolite, so I pushed back and pretended to admire him. As he placed his hands on my shoulders, his gaze slipped past me and fell upon my ladies, now lined up behind me. The lechery showed in his eyes, and I decided there and then to keep both myself and my companions well out of his reach.

Hugh glowered but said nothing. Then, taking my hand, he gave it a gentle squeeze.

'This is very sad,' said John. 'Although we did not agree on much, I loved Richard dearly. That must have been your position. May I call you Berengaria?'

'Indeed,' I replied, skirting the truth. 'Have you been to see your mother?'

'Yes, and now northwards we must go, but I needed to become acquainted with Richard's queen, my sister-by-law; we may have things to discuss. Are you staying here, or have you a wish to visit England?'

'Is that an invitation, my lord?'

He laughed. 'Of course; how could you be denied that opportunity? You would have been welcomed as queen, and now you will be welcomed as Richard's dowager.'

'In which case I accept.'

'Excellent. When I am crowned and things settle down, I shall send you a note of free passage; can't do better than that, can I? Now, where's that wine you offered?'

'Inside, my lord; follow me.' Which he did, breathing down my neck and sometimes brushing against me. I wondered how long I could resist slapping him.

Best to stay polite; I will probably need his goodwill in the future, I thought.

Hugh lingered to speak to my ladies and give them a blessing, and then followed us in.

John commandeered the conversation, talking mostly about how eager he was to cross the narrow sea and take full control of England. He also asked some odd questions about my dower lands, including the ones I held in Navarre, gifts from my father. Hugh's eyebrows rose a little, but he kept his counsel.

'Well,' John said eventually, slamming down his emptied goblet, 'things will need to change. We'll need to examine all our holdings, incomes, tithes and the like and see where we are — but not until I am crowned, of course. Perhaps then you can cross the narrow sea and we will discuss my findings. Are all your ladies spoken for?'

'Yes, I'm afraid that you have missed the opportunity.' I was happy to lie; I would sort it out with Father Edwin later. 'And we look forward to paying a visit to England. I would like to see as much of it as possible. My chaplain comes from the north; do you know it?'

'No. But I must be off; I'd like to get to Dives-sur-Mer. That's where my great-grandfather set off from all those years ago. Please excuse me; thanks for the wine.' He tried to plant a kiss, but I stood up, frustrating his aim, and it landed on my shoulder. He laughed. 'Need to practise more. When things are more settled, will you come and visit? I know not where I'll be next, but probably somewhere in my Angevin realm.'

'I'd be pleased to,' I said, although I was already thinking up excuses not to. And off he went. I knew him to be the same age as me, but he had learned no manners in his time.

Hugh lingered and said gently to me, 'I'll go with your new overlord to Dives; he needs watching. Move to Le Mans whenever you wish. We can watch over you there, and you may consider paying Queen Eleanor a visit. Oddly, you may be all that she has left to rely upon.'

Then he too was gone. I looked around to find my ladies watching. Their silence was broken by Alazne.

'He had me undressed in his mind. Isabeau?'

'I was stripped bare. Can we *not* see him again, Your Highness?'

173

'We need his acquiescence in most things. Keep your thoughts to yourself in public but speak openly to me. That's the best I can do until we see how he intends to rule. My fear is that things are about to become worse, my friends.'

'Lord have mercy,' said Father Edwin, crossing himself.

'Bugger,' said Pavot.

'Now what?' asked Bernez. He had been slow to grasp my new position.

'We have a new overlord and your queen is now a dowager,' said Alazne.

Only a day later, near the end of April, my pottage of problems was added to. While I was speaking to my ladies there was a commotion at the gate. A sergeant came running in.

'Your Highness, come quickly. The French are at the gate.'

Picking up my skirts I ran down the stairs, across the bailey and up the ladder to the top of the gatehouse. Castellan Denis was already there, shouting insults at somebody outside.

'There, I told you; she's the Queen of England!' yelled one of the invaders.

'What do they want, Denis?' I asked.

'King John, Your Highness; they want him and think that he is in here.'

Looking through a gap in the wall, I was alarmed to see a troop of horsemen.

'That's Queen Berengaria — I've seen her at Fontevraud!' cried one of them.

Their leader was a fine fellow on a splendid destrier. He remained at a safe distance, but I could see his dress and he was not wearing the emblems of France.

'What emblem is that, Denis?'

'Let me see... It's that of Brittany, Your Highness, not France.'

'What's this, I wonder?' I said, waiting and watching.

The Breton held up a hand and a hush descended, broken only by the tinkling of accoutrements and the shuffling of horses.

They were wary, fearing a bolt from a crossbow, so the leader shouted, 'May I approach, Your Highness? I mean no harm.'

'Tell him that only he and his banner carrier can approach, Denis.'

The message was relayed, and the fellow approached cautiously.

'Madam, I carry the authority of King Philip and I must ask you if Prince John is with you.'

'What should I say, Denis?'

He shrugged. 'Tell them the truth. He was here but has left.'

I leaned over. 'He was here, whoever you are, but King John is long gone. And those are not the banners of France.'

'We are as one with King Philip in the protection of Arthur of Brittany, Your Highness. We fear for his safety.'

I took a chance with my next call. 'You may come in and see, if you wish. You do understand that I am the Queen of England, and that I have been on Crusade?'

'My name is Jolyon, Your Highness. I serve William des Roches and Arthur of Brittany, King Richard's nominated successor, God bless him. But I understand; there is no need to disturb you further. We will catch up with *Prince* John before he reaches Normandy.'

'Why? What do you want with John?'

'He is a false king, self-nominated. Richard chose Arthur, and Arthur it will be. *Au revoir, madame.*'

And with that, he signalled his troop and they galloped off northwards.

'I'd like to be there if they catch the odious turd, begging your pardon, Your Highness,' exclaimed Denis.

'Granted,' I replied. My heart was pounding, and I trembled as I climbed back down the ladder.

Alazne met me at the bottom rung. 'Your Highness, are you upset? What was that all about?' She put an arm around me and helped me into the donjon.

When I was sitting the steward held out a goblet. I could hardly hold it for tremors. 'Your best, I trust?'

'The very best, Your Highness. I keep it in reserve for your use only.'

I looked up at Alazne. 'The French want John. He has a competitor for the position of King of England: Arthur of Brittany. Arthur is the son of Geoffrey of Brittany, my husband's long-deceased brother.'

'Yes, but is Normandy far enough away for John to escape those chasing him, Your Highness? I'd rather not see him again,' said Alazne.

That remark met with a chorus of approval.

Then I remembered something Bishop Hugh had suggested: a visit to Eleanor.

'Who will come with me to Fontevraud? Eleanor must know more about this Arthur.'

Alazne looked at Isabeau and Isabeau looked at Cateline. 'Not our turn,' said Isabeau.

Alazne nodded and said to Pavot, 'Riding clothes, and a gown to change into.' They went off to pack.

I then explained our family relationships to Isabeau and Cateline in fuller detail and tasked Denis with their care while we were away.

The next morning I left with Alazne and Pavot, accompanied by Bernez and his men as escorts. We set off at a gentle amble along the valley of the Loire to arrive at Fontevraud by the following evening.

Unexpected as we were, not having sent any advance notice, we were conducted to guest quarters within Queen Eleanor's royal apartments. The abbess made us welcome.

'She's feeling a bit tired, Your Highness,' she said, pleased to see us back so soon. 'I will inform her of your arrival in the morning so that she may greet you properly. She attends Prime at dawn in her privy chapel.'

Very well organised was Eleanor, even at her age.

I sat down in a privy bedchamber with my two ladies, and we tried to guess Eleanor's frame of mind. Would it be improved by knowing that there were those who would like to see her surviving son out of the equation? It had even crossed my mind that John's beady eye landing on me might have set him thinking, but marriage to another King of England was not an option for me; a return to Navarre as a dowager was infinitely more attractive. Nothing was missed in our conversation, but I supposed that in the end none of our wild theories would be correct. Not many had been in the past few years.

In the morning I awoke to the bustle of a busy abbey as the monks and nuns went about the business of Morning Prayer. Alazne came into my chamber, and we prepared for the day.

Eleanor was already at her prie-dieu and motioned me to join her. I did not recognise the celebrant as he sermonised about the short tenure we had here on earth, and how we should make all efforts to help our fellow man, especially the low-born who had naught. His clothing gave him away as a cardinal and his accent was Italian.

When he had finished, I gave Eleanor an arm to help her to rise as he came to us.

'Thank you, daughter; it is easier kneeling down than standing up,' said Eleanor. 'This is Cardinal Pietro di Capua, who is the papal envoy here.'

'Your Highness,' he responded, 'I have heard much about you from Cardinal Benedetto, one of your admirers.'

'Your Eminence, I'm pleased to meet you. Indeed, Cardinal Benedetto was a saviour and a rock during difficult times. Give him my regards when next you meet.'

'Of course.' He looked at Eleanor. 'The business will be later?'

'Indeed, Your Eminence. Mid-morning in my privy receiving chamber.' Turning to me, she said, 'There are charters for you to witness, dear daughter, if you can attend me there.'

'Of course, Mother.' I was intrigued. I had journeyed here to inform her about John's pursuers, and now she had turned the conversation without asking me why I was here.

'Ah!' she said with a twinkle in her rheumy eye, 'sometimes the young must wait for the old.' And off she swept, still the imperious Eleanor.

'Come on, ladies, let's find something to eat.'

Along the way I reminded my ladies to be discrete when they discussed matters politic, in case their words might be heard in the wrong places and misunderstood.

After breakfast there was time to visit Richard's tomb with Father Edwin. It was a plain thing, and he was in repose at the feet of his father. Whatever had passed between these two in life they were now sharing in death. With my ladies I prayed for peace and reconciliation between them. Then I went to find Eleanor's privy quarters, accompanied by Father Edwin.

Along the way I asked him if he had gathered any information.

'No, I know nothing. I'll listen to the queen with interest.'

'You must; you are my eyes and ears in the Church.'

Chuckling, he walked with me to see what the ageing queen had to say, trailed by my chattering ladies.

Eleanor was found sitting in a throne-like chair at the far end of her solar. She had her own ladies of the bedchamber with her, all seemingly nearer their end than their beginning. I was polite but not deferential, for things had gone too far awry between us.

Cardinal Pietro looked on with a benign expression on his face.

'Berengaria,' said Eleanor, 'I have various charters to sign as a result of Richard's wishes; would you join me as a witness?'

'Of course. What are they for?' I asked as her clerk placed some rolls on a table.

'Gifts to various houses and holy orders, for the benefit of Mother Church.' Here she looked at the papal envoy and smiled. 'I understand that you are busy with charitable works yourself, dear daughter.'

I nodded; she knew perfectly well what I was doing and where I was doing it.

She appended her signature, and I was passed the quill to do likewise. Then Cardinal Pietro signed on behalf of His Holiness. That done, the rolls were taken away, but there was something else in the offing. I waited.

'Do you intend to marry, daughter?'

'No, Mother.'

'What about your sister?'

'Blanca is in Navarre; why do you ask?'

'A marriage might help to heal the rift between ourselves and King Philip.'

'She has avoided marriage for a long while.'

'She is twenty-two years old or so?' Eleanor replied, ignoring my words.

'Yes.'

'And you know of no plans to marry her off?'

'No, Mother.'

She regarded me for a moment. 'What brought you here, before I sent for you?'

'There is something, Mother: we had visitors seeking King John.'

'Who? What did they want?'

'They said they served William des Roches and Arthur of Brittany.'

'Devils, damned devils,' Eleanor spat, throwing down her kerchief. 'Ignore them. They serve a usurper. I am tired now, Abbess Mathilde. I must rest.'

I knew then that my presence was not for approval of anything, Eleanor had already decided what was to be done on behalf of her son. Richard's wife was only there to witness it.

Later, on the way back to Beaufort, I confided in Father Edwin over the matter Eleanor had raised.

'I said I knew naught about the plans for Blanca,' I told him. 'Some time ago Sancho told me that something was in the offing, but I know no details, nor who is involved, apart from Blanca. But where did Eleanor get her suspicions from?'

'Courts leak like raised fishing nets,' said Edwin. 'I shall make some enquiries at the church.'

'And most of it tittle-tattle. Coinage to the mischievous; be discreet, Father.'

'I shall. Fear not, Your Highness.'

For two weeks, when I wasn't working in the town, hospital, church or castle, my mind was occupied by Blanca's future. I had not seen her for years.

I was in my solar, looking at a missive lying on the table, when Father Edwin walked in. The letter was from Sancho judging by the seal, and I was about to open it.

'What's that?' asked Edwin.

'I suspect it might contain a name, Father.'

I waited until Bernez arrived, then broke the seal and began to read.

'Sancho says that Blanca is to be wed,' I said.

'When, Your Highness?' asked Alazne.

'Where?' asked Bernez.

I hushed them and began to pick out the important points from Sancho's letter.

'She will marry Thibaut of Blois, a nephew of King Philip. This is interesting: he is underage but destined to become Count of Champagne when he is old enough.'

'Old enough? Is he still at the breast?' gasped Alazne.

'He's twenty However, you may be interested to know that he is also a grandson from Eleanor's first marriage. He is directly descended from the French kings.'

'Louis — the eighth, as I remember?' said Father Edwin.

'The same.'

'If he is but twenty, that means that...' Bernez began.

'He is too young to inherit his title. Blanca will assume the regency of Champagne under present rules and practice,' I said.

'You knew about this, Your Highness?' asked Alazne, a bit nettled.

'I knew a little, but it has been a delicate negotiation. Think on it; this keeps Navarre at the very centre of things. We are in fashion, courted by the north. Those to our south will be wary of us for a long time,' I replied brightly.

'What next?' asked Isabeau.

'A wedding,' I replied. 'At Chartres next July.'

'It will be good for Aquitaine and Navarre,' said Edwin.

'And it will place ears within the royal house of France,' I responded happily.

CHAPTER SIXTEEN

After some days of thought, I decided to go and occupy the castle of Angers. Beaufort was a bit cramped, and I had been impressed by Angers when we'd attended Joan's wedding.

'Pack your belongings, ladies,' I said to my entourage. 'We're off to Angers, along the valley of the Loire.'

At one point along the route, I called a rest halt on a hill, which gave me the chance to review my cavalcade. It stretched out behind for a good mile.

'Heavens,' said Edwin.

'Aye, Your Highness,' said Bernez. 'It was getting a bit crowded back there. No wonder.'

'We will fit into Angers a lot better. How do they all manage at Beaufort, I wonder?' I asked, quite concerned.

'With not much unnoticed, Your Highness,' said Bernez. 'Nothing much is privy.'

'Oh, I see.'

Château d'Angers, the ancestral home of the Plantagenets, sat high on a rocky outcrop above the river Maine. It was a well-defended site, I remembered as I approached the mighty gates once more. I would be safe in there.

Among the throng inside the bailey was one figure I recognised instantly.

'Robert?' I cried. 'Is that you?'

'Your Highness, it is me, here to see you safely lodged. May I help you down?'

'You may.' We grinned at each other like fools. 'This is big,' I ventured, looking around. 'Are you the castellan now?'

'No, Your Highness, nor the seneschal. I remain *de facto* seneschal of both Anjou and Poitou until King John decides otherwise. I have left de Mauléon in charge of Poitou; we need to see to your requirements above all.'

'Well, I feel safe now that you are here, dear friend. How is Stephen? Have you heard from him?'

'He is safely back with Edeline and their three daughters. I suppose that they are enjoying their life together.'

'Send them my regards when next you write.'

'I will. Let's get you inside,' he said, while waving at my ladies in welcome. He then introduced the next person to stand before me. 'This is Constable Thomas of Fumes, my nephew.'

I nodded. 'I fear that the new king would be hard pressed to rule without you, Robert. How was Yorkshire?'

'Come inside out of view, and I'll tell you.'

Father Edwin had caught the last part of that exchange and scurried in behind us. 'Yorkshire? What about Yorkshire?' he asked.

'Yes,' I joined in. 'What about Yorkshire? Where is it?'

'Father Edwin, by his speech, is from further north in England than even Yorkshire,' Robert replied, 'but my new estate is near Whitby on the coast.'

'I am from Northumbria,' said Edwin. 'Nearly a Scot.' He laughed.

'And you are still caring for our queen, Father?' asked Robert, looking at him admiringly.

'Since Rome. He listens and says naught,' I replied, smiling. 'Are you going to tell me about your wife? Was Isabella difficult to leave?'

'Very. She is like you, Your Highness: a competent woman. And she is comely.'

'Do you not miss her, Robert?' asked Edwin.

'Of course, but here I am — never far away from Queen Berengaria.'

We were in the great hall by now, and after settling my ladies I sat down for supper with Robert to hear his latest gatherings.

'Do you remember the Strait of Messina, when Richard rescued Queen Joan?'

'My best friend — yes, I remember.'

'Did Richard ever mention to you who he had nominated to succeed him?'

'Huh! Richard mentioned little of import to me. I assumed that John was to succeed, but now I have my doubts.'

Robert beckoned me across the table and lowered his voice. 'Then you've heard about his nephew, Arthur of Brittany.'

'We have indeed,' said Edwin, settling at the end of the bench. 'But it's true: Richard did not want John on the throne.'

'We had a visit from a representative of William des Roches when we were at Beaufort; he was looking for John,' I added.

'Really! And John is in Normandy, safe with his barons.'

'Within the family, only John wanted the regency while Richard was away on Crusade,' Robert said, 'and that was taken from him by Eleanor when she returned from Italy, and John went scurrying off to Philip to hide from her ire.'

'Yes, she left us at Messina because she'd heard of his behaviour.'

'There is something else. When John visited and then left you at Beaufort, he went straight to Rouen and was there invested as the duke. I'm sorry, Your Highness.'

That was a blow. Perhaps I should have expected it. How many other titles would I lose now that Richard was gone? Lady of Cyprus, gone, a dowager Queen of England, now not to be the dowager Duchess of Normandy, and I had expected to become the Duchess of Aquitaine when Eleanor departed.

'And this Arthur person?' I asked.

'Arthur of Brittany, Richard's nephew. Philip had him taken into the care of William des Roches, and now Philip has declared he will be the next King of England. Some nobles, led by Arthur's mother Constance, have declared for him. Brittany, Anjou, Maine and Touraine are among them. Eleanor's empire is failing.'

'But how does that affect me, Robert?' I pressed.

'I know not yet, Your Highness, but I feel that I am riding two horses, and that one day I should choose one. What you should do, Your Highness, is stay well back and see what transpires.'

This was food for thought. I needed to keep Eleanor and John sweet, yet not be associated too closely.

'One of the lesser-known items in Richard's negotiations with Tancred of Sicily was Arthur, three years old then,' Robert went on. 'Richard promised him in marriage to Tancred's daughter. Whether he meant it is a moot point, but if Philip ever gets Arthur on to the throne you can expect some winds from the south to blow up.'

'Good Lord,' said Edwin. 'That'll cause much ado in Rome.'

'Aye,' said Robert. 'This is not well known, but Richard sent me on a mission to capture young Arthur, remove him from his mother and ensure his safekeeping in case Richard died.'

'You did not succeed?' I asked.

'No. He is well guarded, as a valuable commodity should be.'

'This mummery grows more horns by the hour,' I said. 'Steward, fill my goblet, please.'

Both England and France had candidates for the English crown, but who would end up with it? Eventually my thoughts led me to an idea that I might have wished away.

'Robert, do you think that they will begin a war over this, John and Philip?'

'A war of Angevin accession, you mean? It has occurred to me. I know that by now Philip despises John. After all his plotting and treachery against Richard, he is likely to react badly if John, sitting in England, crosses the narrow sea to contest Arthur taking control of Angevin holdings here.'

'Are we safe here, in the family home of the Plantagenets?'

'I shall consider it; we may move you. Let us see what transpires first, and then plan for your safety.'

'I need to think about this. Are our quarters ready?'

'Yes.' He waved at the castellan. 'Are you and your ladies ready?'

'Yes,' I said, standing and catching Alazne's eye.

'We're off,' I heard her say to the others. They all came to stand behind me.

'Come with us, Father. I may have missed something.'

'Take Queen Berengaria to her quarters, Thomas,' Robert ordered his nephew. 'We'll see you in the morning, and Thomas, show Father Edwin where the family chapel is along the way.'

'Goodnight, Robert,' I said, and set off behind Thomas. We went across a bailey, up several flights of stairs and along many lengthy corridors before he stopped and pointed to a doorway. A matron stood inside the doorway and bowed as I entered.

'Your Highness, I am Agnes. My girls and I are here to serve you while you are here. Is that priest allowed in?'

That priest was decidedly uncomfortable now he was surrounded by at least ten women and girls.

'Is there a solar, Agnes?'

'Yes, Your Highness.'

'Show me, and we will sit in there for a while. Do not worry about Father Edwin; he is from Northumbria.' This puzzled Agnes, but it stopped her making any further comment, and we were soon sitting comfortably around a table.

'That will do, Agnes. If you wait outside, I will send for you when we are finished, thank you.' When she had left, I looked at Edwin and asked, 'You caught most of the conversation in the hall, Father?'

'I did: most disturbing.'

I went on to explain the situation to my ladies. They digested the information in silence. It was Cateline who spoke first.

'Does that mean that Blanca's marriage is off, Your Highness?'

'It means that peace is off,' said Edwin.

'No, my dear,' I said, 'it means that we stay out of view and go about our daily business unless or until we are affected. When we are settled here, we will go into the town and see what needs to be done for the poor and infirm, as we always do. Won't we, Father?'

'Indeed, Your Highness, as is our duty,' he replied cheerfully.

And that is what we went out to do, although Robert was not happy, so everywhere we ventured we were surrounded by escorting soldiers.

The news came galloping along the many corridors of Angers castle, repeated and embellished until it reached my door, and Alazne burst in to assail my ears with it.

'King John landed at Dieppe on the twenty-third of June, Your Highness. He is in Normandy.'

After we had made our way down the many stairs and along the corridors and across the bailey, we ran into the great hall. It was stuffed full of lords, bishops and soldiers. I spied Robert at the top of the hall, beset by a throng. The hubbub was deafening.

The crowd parted for me as I made my way towards him. Robert saw me and left the table to guide me into a privy chamber at the side of the hall. Then that became crowded as I squeezed in with my chaplain and my women.

'Upon my soul,' said Robert with a grin. 'I've never been squeezed so delightfully. How are you, Father?' he asked Edwin, receiving a grunt in reply. 'Steward!' At Robert's call, a fellow popped his head through the door. 'Arrange this furniture so that we can sit more comfortably.'

In an eye-blink chairs were set around the wall and all superfluous items removed, until we were seated and staring across the chamber at each other, Robert standing by the door.

'Your Highness, ladies, Father Edwin, you will know by now that John was crowned King of England in Westminster on the twenty-seventh day of May,' he began. 'He had already been declared Duke of Normandy, Your Highness.' He looked at me; I sat stony-faced, now used to being stripped of my titles. I nodded and he continued. 'War is near once more; the barons have resumed their hostility towards one another, and we are all caught up in their internecine quarrel.'

'Fomented by the French, no doubt,' said Father Edwin.

'Yes, no doubt,' answered Robert. 'Philip has not got over his spats with Richard, God bless him. But now it has worsened, and lords are taking sides.'

'This has to do with the young Arthur,' I added for the benefit of my ladies.

'Yes,' Robert agreed. 'England and Normandy have sided with John, of course, most of the nobles having holdings in both places, while those on this side of the narrow sea are edging towards Arthur. Brittany is for Arthur, along with various nobles from Maine and Anjou. William des Roches met Philip at Le Mans and they have formed some sort of agreement. The picture is, as you see, quite mixed.'

'And John is in Normandy,' I commented.

'Yes, he went to England to be crowned and to raise an army. They are following him over. For now he is rallying the Norman barons and making defensive preparations at the strongholds in the duchy.'

'Well, there's a pottage, Robert. What are we to do?'

'I'll wait and see. Would you object to going back to Beaufort? Or perhaps Poitiers?'

'We've had quite enough of warfare. We'll get as far away from this madness as possible.'

There was a mumble of agreement from everyone. 'Right,' said Robert. 'That's what we'll do — get you out of the way.'

'We?' I asked.

'I'm not returning to England and leaving you here in this limbo. Have no fear, ladies; I'll be watching and listening on your behalf. You haven't seen the last of me.'

I smiled at his loyalty.

'There'll be a place in heaven for you, Robert. I'll pray for you,' said Father Edwin.

'I'll go back to Beaufort as you suggested and return here as soon as I can,' I said with a dread feeling in my stomach. 'Will you be safe, Robert?'

'Probably. I might be in some in-between place, but hostilities have not been declared. I shall be safe; worry not. After all, I am in a way already in the service of the French king, whose nephew is to be married to the Queen Dowager of England's sister.'

'What?' I muttered, not keeping up.

'As seneschal, as long as you are in my territories I am responsible for your safety, and, by extension, that of your sister, who is to be married to the nephew of King Philip —'

'Stop. Enough, I understand,' I said.

But it did little to stay the feeling that I was cast loose upon an ocean of storms, at the mercy of wind and sea.

Beaufort was as we had left it, small but well-situated, and we settled down to watch John and Philip wrestle for control of the Angevin empire while we prepared for my sister's wedding. In the meantime, John and Philip met at the Normandy border and signed a treaty. How long it would last remained to be seen.

The time sped by as we were occupied in town, helping the Hospitallers to set up new hospitals: one for the sick, one for women and one for Crusaders. Although the prospect of a new war loomed in the background, a peace of sorts prevailed — until, that is, two weeks into September.

News from Fontevraud arrived, brought by a messenger on a lathered horse. This event brought Edwin huffing and puffing up to my solar, causing us to drop our needlework, an occupation in anticipation of my sister's marriage which kept us busy.

Edwin handed me a letter from Eleanor. This was unexpected. My stomach churned as I opened it with trembling fingers and read the message:

Dear daughter,

It is with sorrow that I have to report to you the death of our dear Joan. She was with child once more, but on her way to me after a terrible event in which she was badly burned. But the journey was too much, and she and the child died within the monastery. Will you come for her burial? It will be three days hence, and I will reveal the full dreadful story. God bless Countess Joan.

The vellum dropped from my hand, and I was held up as my legs gave way. Father Edwin took the letter and read it to my ladies. I remembered entering Akko during Richard's Crusade and hearing about the victims of Greek fire. I prayed to God that Joan had not been thus affected.

Father Edwin coughed and made a frustrated sound. 'Your Highness, this is dated three days ago.'

'I will still go,' I replied.

The two-day journey to Fontevraud was not one I wanted to make, and I wondered if I could bring myself to show any sympathy for the grieving Eleanor. It was surely her obsession that had led to the near destruction of her entire family, with only the profligate John left.

Robert was at the head of our sad procession and had sent word ahead so that the abbess was waiting at the gates of Fontevraud to greet me.

'Oh, Your Highness, my dear child,' she said, holding me as I slid off my palfrey. 'I bring you naught but ill tidings. Queen Eleanor is waiting to greet you in her quarters. She is very frail.'

'Come with me, Father, Robert, and you two.' I invited Alazne and Pavot, thinking there might not be many opportunities to see Eleanor. We should make the best of this one.

Frail did not begin to describe the sad echo of a woman sitting in Eleanor's chair. A once vibrant and beautiful creature had been turned into a wizened crone by grief. I stood before her, waiting to be acknowledged.

After a moment she looked up, and when she recognised me she held out a hand, which I took, feeling the very bones of it.

I doubted that she noticed my retinue, so I mentioned them not.

'Berengaria, sweet girl, we are few now. My Joan was my last hope and her little Raymond the only enduring son.'

This was an odd remark; she seemed to have missed out John, so I reminded her. 'What of John, madam? Has he not fruitful loins?'

'Very, but not for spreading the Plantagenet dynasty. He will be fortunate if he hangs on to England, and I doubt that the English crown will retain much land over here.'

'What happened to Countess Joan, madam?' I asked. 'Why did she journey here?'

'Ah, water, sister.' An attending sister poured a small glass of water and Eleanor took a sip before telling the story. 'Did Joan mention that Raymond had enemies in Toulouse?'

'She mentioned some ill will, but I did not make much of it. I was more interested in her new-born.'

'Well, some barons were in revolt and determined to rid Toulouse of Raymond. During an absence, Joan decided to help his cause and set off to besiege a small castle, named Les Cassés, where the leaders, lords of Saint-Felix, were hiding.' Here she paused and took another sip before continuing. 'But she was betrayed by those whom she took with her to the siege; she discovered that they were supplying the castle. When they realised she knew, they set fire to her tent while she slept.'

We were silenced by that. None of us could bring ourselves to speak of such an act of treachery and cruelty.

I thought of something. There was no good in this, and Eleanor deserved my sympathy. 'Joan must have loved Raymond very much, madam,' I said.

She looked up at me through a veil of tears. 'I had not considered that, Berengaria. Thank you.' She was exhausted and I thought that we should withdraw, but she spied my companions. 'Who have you brought, my daughter?'

I explained and she replied, 'I know you, Robert of Turnham; welcome.' She turned her attention back to me. 'Will you call me "Mother", please, Berengaria? I never liked "madam". It makes me sound like a housekeeper.'

I chuckled. 'Mother,' I said, and grasped her hand. There was plenty of wit left in that frail body. Then something occurred to me. 'What has happened to Eirini and Torène?'

'They still have a home with Raymond, and Joan's younger ladies have been found good positions elsewhere. Do not worry,' said Eleanor. 'I'm tired now. Can we meet again in the morning?'

'Of course, Mother.' I kissed her gently on the cheek. She sighed and the nuns made ready to take her into her privy chamber. I motioned to my companions, and we left quietly.

The abbess was waiting for us and asked if we would like to see the tomb site. She explained that it was not finished but could describe how it was intended to look when the stonemasons had completed their work.

Joan had asked to be set at the head of her father's effigy. The abbess showed us a depiction drawn on a board leaning against King Henry's stone. Joan was shown kneeling in prayer with her son in her arms.

The abbess spared no detail as she described Joan's final moments. 'The infant had been cut from her stomach and was baptised Richard before dying too, no doubt in memory of her brother.'

Why did this happen? I thought desperately. But only the Lord knew why.

'Shall we pray, Father Edwin?' the abbess asked.

I went down on my knees on the cold ground and listened as Edwin extolled the virtues of my dead best friend.

We stayed one more night, and I visited Eleanor again as promised. Then, having no inclination nor reason to stay, I asked Father Edwin to take me back to Beaufort. We prepared to move as soon as possible.

CHAPTER SEVENTEEN

When the time came, in order to keep my ladies content, I agreed to take everyone with me to Chartres for my sister's wedding. How we were to be accommodated I could only guess at, so we sent word ahead.

Robert, who seemed to have sprouted wings from his shoes like Hermes, so swift was he about the country, was there to greet us on the road near Chartres.

'Welcome, Your Highness. Allow me to lead you to your accommodation. King Philip has made one of his châteaux available to you; it is fit for a queen, and a surprise awaits you there.' We touched hands and grinned at each other until he turned away and set off along the road, which led us to a grand château in the style of the French. 'Come on in, Your Highness.'

I wandered into the main portico behind him.

'Berengaria,' said a gentle voice from behind a pillar.

'Who's that?' I said as to my delight both my sister Blanca and my brother King Sancho bounced out of cover to envelop me in hugs and kisses. '*Ama santua*, what a fright. Blanca and Sancho, you did not say that you would be here! Shame on you both for frightening a poor widow.'

'Poor indeed!' exclaimed Sancho, picking me up and twirling me around. 'You and your adventures are known throughout Navarre, France and England; you are my heroine.'

'Good Lord.' Father Edwin had caught the unusual sight of a flying queen.

When Sancho had finished throwing me about, I took Blanca into my arms. 'Oh, my dear, see how you've grown. Is it so long since we parted?'

'I thought that you were far too busy to miss me, sister.'

'Not at all; everyone whom I miss I have always thought about ... from time to time.'

We stood and looked at each other until I remembered the queue behind me.

'Meet my retinue. This is Father Edwin, an English priest, given to me in Rome, and I think you know Lord Robert, Sancho? He is my personal shield against the wicked world. And his elder brother, Stephen, brought me back from the Holy Land.'

'I know,' laughed Sancho, then he and Robert grasped each other as old friends.

'What's this; do you know each other?'

'Yes, Robert came to Germany in 1194 with two abbots to try to locate Richard.'

'Aye, with Robert of Boxley and William of Robertsbridge; we found him in the month of March near a town named Ochsenfurt and returned swiftly home before we could be added to the emperor's list of hostages.'

'You are too modest by far, Robert,' said Sancho. 'Later he commanded the ship that carried Eleanor up the Rhine with the ransom money.'

'Heavens above,' said Father Edwin.

'You have kept all that a secret, Robert! Shouldn't I scold you for that?' I was astonished that this had not come up in one of our many conversations. 'Well, you two exchange stories while we women exchange gossip. Blanca, do you remember Alazne? It was she and Arrosa who left Olite all those years ago. Perhaps you were too young when we left.

And this is Pavot; she joined us from my beloved Joan. And this is my French pair: Isabeau and Cateline.'

Chatting and not missing any opportunity to caress me, Blanca led us to our quarters, which were quite nice.

'We'll go up to the solar to talk,' said Blanca.

'Who lives here, Blanca?' I asked.

'We know not, Berengaria; it seems to be a guesthouse of sorts. There were only servants here when we arrived. I asked one girl and she said that it was for "goings-on". Then she fled,' said Blanca from behind a hand. I did not enquire further.

As it transpired, I was allocated a queen's bedchamber with an antechamber, into which I placed Alazne and Pavot, the others being sent to what the seneschal described as women's quarters. I visited them, and it was merely a large hall with a dozen or so cubicles off to one side. I peered into one: lush drapes and a large bed were all the furnishings it contained. My mind raced: 'goings-on' became too graphic to consider.

We were well catered for, staying in this opulent château as guests of King Philip. It was a diplomatic nicety, I knew, as my late husband and Philip had not parted on the best of terms, but nevertheless it was welcome.

Blanca and I chatted until the sun was going down, then a bevy of ladies led by a determined *madame* strode into the solar and reminded Blanca that she needed time to prepare for her big day. After kisses and hugs, it was time for us to part and return to our quarters.

The next morning, with no chance of a long lie-in, I was compelled to join in with the excitement of dressing up for a wedding. I was not down in time to witness Blanca being driven off to the cathedral, but we left in time to allow our carriage to wheel its way through the chattering throngs along the route.

Chartres in July was a fair sight, but it became noisy as we approached the cathedral. Lots of folk had come to see the unusual collection of visitors.

My carriage came to a halt outside the great door, and I was met by Archbishop Renaud de Mouçon. A friendly smile and a welcoming hand put me at ease as he led me along the aisle. The congregation examined me as I made my way through the quire towards the high altar.

It was not my day, though, and I tried to be as insignificant as possible as I took my seat with my ladies standing behind me. Thibaut of Champagne, who looked about eighteen years old, was already there to one side, flanked by his many supporters, all in gaudy dress, the emblems of France and Champagne prominent.

He gave me a shy wave, although we had not met, and I was pleased about that.

The congregation resumed its chatter until a procession of clergy emerged through a side door, accompanied by a trumpet blast as the crowd quietened. I glanced back to see that the great space was now fogged by incense, but from where I was at the front I could see the altar clearly. Brief echoes of my own wedding entered my head, and I felt sad that my dear father was not to witness any of his daughters' weddings.

Blanca entered from the side, followed by her ladies. One or two I remembered, but as most of them were young I knew them not. I noticed a few looking my way and gave them a smile. As Blanca arrived before the altar, Archbishop Renaud emerged from the other side to beckon the couple forward to face him. Thibaut and Blanca's supporters had moved to the sides, save for two; Sancho at Blanca's side and a lord unknown to me by the side of Thibaut. The pair stood together, as they might from now on, and I prayed for them.

A choir began to sing, and when they ended the archbishop began the service proper. Renaud was a close cousin of King Philip. I was not surprised when he avoided the subject of warring kings and the service did not take long to complete, the choir breaking into sung prayer as he finished.

Blanca and Thibaut turned and began their progress towards the exit, Blanca stopping beside me to introduce Thibaut.

'We'll meet later, Your Highness, I'm sure,' was his polite response. He was a handsome lad, and I prayed that he was also a gentle one to my sister.

And then it was a procession out into the sunny air, where there was much cheering and congratulating. For a while I felt happy and optimistic. Sancho found me outside and guided me into his carriage to travel back to the château. There we had a good talk about things, including the question of loyalties. We were betwixt Philip and John, each to whom we were attached. And I shed a tear as I mentioned Father, still in my mind.

'Yes, sister queen, we are in a whirlpool; pray that we can swim,' he said, and hugged me tight.

Time passed as we chatted about lighter matters, then we arrived.

'We are at the château now; I'll help you down.'

'Don't bother; there's a queue for that,' I said, trying to avoid the many helping hands save one pair. 'Robert!' I cried. 'Have you winged ankles?'

'No, Your Highness; a faster horse.'

'Well, come with me and King Sancho; there is much to discuss. You usually know how the wind blows.'

Settling in the solar, Sancho called the steward. 'I trust that this fine château has a fine wine cellar.'

'Indeed, Your Highness, and you shall sample our selection.'
We set about doing so.

'Well, Robert, what news?'

'King Sancho, I'm still a servant of the crown, and you are wearing one.' I laughed; Robert could always find a jest. 'How fare you since you escaped from Germany, Your Highness?'

'Escaped? Let loose, more like. I'm fine, and yourself?'

'Good. I've just given over the castle of Chinon to King John. He wants me to go back to England with him.'

My heart trembled; I did not wish to lose another friend. 'Robert, what am I to do without you?'

'Your Highness, I've given the matter some thought, and there is advantage for you and me in this.'

'What advantage, Robert? I shall find it hard to lose another friend and companion; we have been through much together.'

'Consider your position, Your Highness. Who have you in John's court with your welfare at heart?'

I looked at him for a while before responding. 'Nobody.'

'Then gain somebody,' he said with a serious face.

'You? Will you be in my employ? A spy?'

'I shall be paid by the king, and unpaid to write letters to my friend across the narrow sea — you.'

I stood and wrapped my arms around Robert, planting a kiss upon his forehead as Sancho laughed. 'He will be thinking of his new wife, Sancho,' I said. 'Be not concerned.'

'Oh, you are newly married?' asked my brother.

'Indeed, and that's where we come to the advantage for me,' said Robert. 'All my holdings are in England. I have none over here; if I pick the wrong king, I shall lose it all.'

'I recognise that's how the game is played: who you choose depends on where your holdings are. The idea the Plantagenets might have of where your loyalties lie and why, may be false. That'll discomfort them if they guess wrongly.'

'This is the game they play across Europe, brother,' I reminded Sancho.

'And you, Your Highness, what is your attachment to the Angevins?' asked Robert.

'Much the same as yours, dear friend. Self-preservation, I believe it to be named,' I said, 'and that's it.' Neither man disagreed.

'If you leave to attend to your duties, Robert,' said Sancho, 'perhaps I should put in place some arrangements to protect my sister. Do you agree?'

'Indeed I do. She'll be better served if you put some of your people around her. A captain, and perhaps a treasurer to attend to her money matters. I have been reminded of that by seeing the treasury in Chinon, a gift to John, with a treasurer appointed to care and account for it, but you also have expenditures, Your Highness, and I fear that John's clammy hands will be in the chest before yours can reach in.'

'I know, and my outgoings are certain to increase with war looming. The poor are forgotten, and the wounded need help too.'

'Shall I find you some guardians, sister?' asked Sancho.

'Yes, find someone who can calculate and see if Javier wants a new position, if he is still there, and Arrosa.'

'I'll ask, but neither is in their youth anymore.'

'Neither am I. When will you leave, Sancho?' I asked.

'I suppose that we had better go and find Blanca and her count before they disappear into a bedchamber — say farewell and all that.'

'Yes, let's pray that they find more to talk about than I did with my husband. Robert, what about you?'

'Yes, I'll stay a while and see what gossip I can collect from the French; there's plenty of them about. I'll see you before you leave, Your Highness?'

'Yes, please do.'

'I'll continue to provide an escort, King Sancho, until you send someone to take over.'

'Good. Tread carefully, good friend; the ground is unstable hereabouts.'

'Thank you. We'll stay in touch, Your Highness.' And off Robert went. He was very good at disappearing. It made him a difficult target, I supposed.

The great hall was not very great in this château, but what it lacked in size it compensated for in style. When I walked in arm-in-arm with Sancho, Blanca pushed through the swarm of admirers to bring Thibaut to us.

'Upon my soul, sister, I knew not that we had so many friends,' said Sancho, almost shouting above the din.

Blanca wrapped me in her arms. 'Oh, Berengaria, I am so lucky, and I did not need to suffer as you have. You must, if you want to, tell me all about Outremer. Here is Thibaut.'

Thibaut stepped forward and gave an awkward little bow.

'That's not good enough; come here, brother-in-law,' I said. 'We are family now, and you are going to receive a queen's hug.' Which he did and had the blush to end all blushes.

'Your H-Highness,' he stuttered.

'Berengaria,' cried Blanca. 'You've alarmed my husband.'

'Ha!' guffawed Sancho. 'He'll get over it. Let's find a privy chamber and have a family chat.'

Edwin set off to find a steward and returned with one in tow, and we soon settled into a chamber. There was an overwhelming number of questions and answers to get through, and after about an hour Edwin reappeared to remind us that Blanca had guests. Soon we were back in the thick of it.

'I do believe,' I said quietly to Alazne at one point, 'that I am at a disadvantage here. More people know me, and I hardly know a soul.'

'Never mind, Your Highness; you'll have forgotten most of them by the morning.'

'Can we escape soon? The noise is pounding my head.'

'I'll find Lord Robert and see if he can spirit us away,' said Alazne. 'Go and say farewell to Blanca; they'll be looking for the bedchamber soon, if I read the signals right.'

'Oh, yes, that. I hope that he is gentle.'

'And that she has some patience; the new husband does not seem very, er, experienced.'

'Alazne!' I scolded.

Another day, another farewell, this one less stressful as Blanca and I had a good long hug. Thibaut did not back away this time when my eye fell upon him.

'Take care of my sister, Thibaut, and work together to make a good marriage. Then you shall be blessed.'

'I will try, sister — or should I say Your Highness?'

'Either will do,' I said, laughing. '*Au revoir.*'

Later that week we set off from Chartres for Beaufort — another long journey. The tedium was broken by occasional little gallops to keep the horses interested and occasional visits to the bushes at the side of the road, but most of all by the intrusion of unwelcome thoughts. I could not stop picturing Joan and her fate. It had not fully registered with me at the time, but she must have suffered greatly because of the treachery of those in Toulouse County. I had seen the horrible consequences of fire in the field hospitals: fabric burned onto skin, facial disfigurement and skin scorched off. On top of this she had had her infant torn out of her — death must have been a welcome relief, and I prayed that my beautiful friend and I would be united in heaven one day.

Thoughts of Richard entered my head now and again, to be immediately replaced by thoughts of Eleanor, the spider at the centre of a web in which I was caught. She would not live forever, but how long would it be before her odious son seized the power he sought? I had to plot my own course.

When settled back in Beaufort, I gathered my household together, beginning with a personal statement.

'I had believed that being queen of somewhere, or even duchess, might have been a steady appointment from which I could do something useful, but there are forces at work that are out of my control. Now we are faced with a war between kings. None of this is our doing, but it will affect us all in ways as yet unknown.'

I was at the head of a table in the solar, Father Edwin at the opposite end with Isabeau and Cateline on my right and Alazne and Pavot on my left. Castellan Denis stood by the door, while Steward Oliver hovered near the buffet with two serving girls and Guy de Bernez nearby.

Father Edwin spoke first. 'What did you discover from your new brother and charming sister at Chartres, Your Highness?'

'Lots, and some of it as clear as mud. You see, I am in favour with the French king because my sister has married into the French royal house and is the regent of Champagne. King John, I suppose, would like to see the back of me because I was married to his brother and I have many holdings in three countries, including some of which he now is the overlord, and of which he would like to take control ... especially their treasuries.'

That induced a silence.

'And?' said Alazne eventually.

'And his mother chose me, so he won't annoy her by harming me. I am also much favoured by His Holiness, which is another layer of protection.'

'So we are in the middle?' concluded Alazne.

'Is that not dangerous, Your Highness?' asked Isabeau.

'It would be for most people,' I replied, 'but having a foot on two banks makes it possible to step to either side if necessary.'

'So what are we going to do, Your Highness?' asked Bernez.

'Wait,' I replied. 'Wait and enjoy the sun, which at the moment shines from both east and west.'

From the doorway, Denis burst into laughter. 'Never heard the like,' he spluttered. 'A chit of a queen making fun of two kings at once! Dear Lord, what next?'

'What next, Denis, is that any conversations in this chamber stay in this chamber — understand?'

'You have my word, Your Highness. By my oath, I'll hang on to this story until the matter is all settled and in the past. God bless you; you're worth your weight in gold.'

'Which is not much,' I replied. 'And there will be help coming to me from Navarre, if I ask for it. But I am a pawn in the game betwixt Philip and John at present, and I do not propose to upset either.'

'Think carefully on that, Your Highness,' said Edwin. 'I see no future for you in England. Queen Dowager or not, John is unlikely to enjoy your presence in his realm. You are a reminder of the past, and a queen too many.'

'John doesn't need any help to be upset,' said Isabeau.

Father Edwin had something else to add. 'Perhaps you should keep Rome in mind. They would like to know the situation as you see it, Your Highness. I expect that His

Holiness receives updates, but your views he will find interesting, no doubt.'

'Yes, I had thought of that; to send something to Cardinal Benedetto. He will know how to place it to best effect, and I'll visit Bishop Hugh. Thank you.'

I instructed the steward to serve the wine and food, and the discussion turned to Blanca's marriage, in particular what that château with its sumptuous bedchambers might be used for.

CHAPTER EIGHTEEN

1200

John, during his travels to England, had found a new wife, of the family Taillefer. She was the daughter of Count Aymer of Angoulême, Isabella, and was very young at fourteen. I'd also heard that Isabella was already long betrothed to a Lusignan, and I suspected that would not enhance John's reputation. He seemed to have Raymond of Toulouse's habit of putting aside wives; he had recently had his marriage to Isabella of Gloucester annulled on the grounds of consanguinity, since they were distant cousins. John and his new bride were married on the twenty-fourth of August 1200, in Angoulême cathedral. I did not receive an invitation, which did me no harm.

It was also August when a note from Blanca declared that she was with child. It seemed that the handsome count had more in him than Richard ever had. She was due the following spring, and I wondered if I should go and see her, but John's doings got in the way.

The treaty betwixt John and Philip collapsed and hostilities commenced. Robert sent a note and I read it with Javier, now safely with me. Arrosa was not present, though, as she was with child again.

'It seems that Philip has miscalculated and attempted some advances into Normandy. John's put his army into the field, and William des Roches has become uncertain as to which way he leans.'

'Des Roches, Your Highness?' questioned Javier.

'He was entrusted with the guardianship of Arthur of Brittany. Now young Arthur's future is in doubt.'

'Poor Arthur,' muttered Javier. 'How does he fit into this conundrum?'

'I never quite understood, but it goes back to when we were in Sicily. Richard did not explain it to me, but the future of Arthur was part of the settlement he agreed with the *de facto* ruler of Sicily, Tancred. It transpires that Tancred was cajoled into handing over large bags of silver, some ships and the promise to marry his daughter Marie to Arthur, and Richard then declared Arthur his heir presumptive.'

'Was that likely? There would have been many a hurdle before that came about, I'd have thought.'

'Richard might have meant it to happen at the time, but it was never mentioned in my hearing when he eventually returned home.'

'But Arthur still believes it?'

'Yes. He is thirteen and becoming a dangerous impediment to John, and if des Roches hands him over to John, that's the end of that rivalry.'

'John is in the ascendancy.'

'You have it, Javier. He's free to settle with Philip as he sees fit.'

'I thought that it was complicated in Navarre,' said Javier, 'but this is on a much larger scale, is it not?'

'It is. Are we as secure as we can be?'

'Yes, Your Highness, the castle has as many men as it can accommodate to defend it, and we have the horses and wagons ready to escape to Poitiers, as we decided, if needs be.'

'I will be reluctant to leave. There is much work to do with so many poor, and my new hospital is not yet complete.'

'I worry, Your Highness; have you spent all of the money that your new treasurer Ander brought with him?'

I glanced across the table at Ander, who shook his head. 'We have funds yet, Your Highness — the income from your holdings in Navarre and the castles at St-Jean-Pied-de-Port, Roquebrune and Segreio, for instance.'

'Worry not, Javier. I also have funds from some of my Plantagenet holdings, and I do take a little of the surpluses from my holdings in Navarre, although I'll not take from my homeland funds that are needed there.'

'Have you holdings in England?' asked Javier.

'Coin from England has dried up, Your Highness,' said Ander. 'I suspect that it is being diverted into King John's treasury; he'll need it to take on Philip.'

'How long will it be before the income from the Angevin lands here takes the same course?' said Javier. 'Be careful, Your Highness; do not spend on the basis that your income will remain constant.'

'A worrying thought, Javier. Thank you for that — very cheering.'

I must confess that I had not cast my mind forward to the consequences of a long period of conflict. These warring kings could drain the money from the country, leaving the poor in desperate need. I needed to plan for that possibility.

I also worried about Robert: riding two horses was a precarious position to be put into, I thought. But Robert, astute politician that he was, managed to make something of the situation and was soon firmly in John's camp. We were reconciled by then to watching events from afar. For a while nothing much happened; it was like watching two dogs circling each other, both brimming with hate but neither willing to make the first move. In September, John and Philip met again, only to part without an accord. It also became apparent that John was making slow but sure advances into the Angevin territories which were in dispute, pushing back Philip foot by foot.

Then on the twenty-second of September, things took on a new intensity.

William des Roches was in control of Le Mans when he handed Arthur into John's custody. An act of despicable treachery, I thought, leaving the thirteen-year-old in serious jeopardy.

Then John demonstrated his capacity for spite when he ordered the walls of Le Mans to be reduced. He moved to Castle Chinon, only to learn that Arthur had escaped as soon as John left the resentful town, and the boy had run back to King Philip's protection. That was one of the times when I knew that the power of prayer was real.

It was time for the Church to play a part, and the papal legate brought the pair together to find a solution. Robert came to see me at the end of October.

'Greetings, old friend,' I said, giving him a hug.

'Steady yourself, Your Highness. I've not been that long away from your side.'

'Too long. You old rogue — whose seneschal are you today?'

'Ah! You've heard about my adventures in administration. Not Angers; des Roches occupies that position.'

'Yes, you must tell us about your manoeuvrings. Here is Javier.'

The pair greeted each other, and Javier too wanted the latest news.

'Denis, send for Father Edwin and find my ladies, please. What news of Eleanor, Robert?' I asked, while my household gathered.

'She's in Fontevraud as far as I know. Frail, but watching events.'

'Mmm. Like me, then, though I am not frail.'

'You've got work here, Your Highness. I suspect that it is a lot more rewarding than trying to keep an empire together.'

'Empires, eh? What empires?' Father Edwin had entered and heard the end of Robert's reply. He was closely followed by the women. When they were seated, I let Robert explain the latest news to them while I sat back to think. Then I heard something new: Robert was outlining the changing face of the two alliances.

'The papal legate engineered a truce, supposed to last until Christmas, but it fell apart when the treatment of Arthur surfaced, especially with the barons of Maine and Anjou. Some are taking the cross; I believe they consider that going on Crusade is a much more morally defensible position than imprisoning young boys, and they find crusading a less trying alternative to being caught up in this tangled web.'

'Good Lord, do they not trust John?' asked Father Edwin.

'No. His behaviour while Richard was held by the Germans, his eagerness to ally himself with Philip, his scheming to surrender Richard's holdings to Philip and retire to an easy life in England — this has been met with disgust. No, my friends, no one wants to be the friend of John except those Normans holding on to lands in England. He can count on them. But no one trusts him or his words.'

'You are saying that John's alliances are crumbling?' said Javier.

'By the day. It will not be long before Philip is emboldened to launch a renewed attack.'

'*Ama santua!* The man is done for.'

'Not yet, Javier. If they chase him to the narrow sea, he will cross it and laugh,' said Robert.

'There are more pressing matters, Your Highness,' said Father Edwin. 'The fields have been stripped of young men to provide human sacrifices for the kings' wars. The crops will rot if they are not brought in.'

That was something else to which I had given some thought. Of course, kings needed young men to slaughter each other to satisfy their ambitions, but that would not feed the people during the winter.

'What to do, Robert?' I asked, with only the glimmer of an answer in my head.

'Organise the peasants: those left should be set to work. I must go off and join John; I can't risk being stripped of my holdings. I doubt if things are any better in England, and my wife is well capable of seeing to such things, but we cannot predict the unpredictable as far as John is concerned. And I have not been here.'

'Of course. You've done enough, dear friend; I can't expect any more. Javier, how much of a farmer are you?'

Robert chuckled. 'He doesn't need to be.' Looking at my discomfited soldier, he instructed, 'Let the peasant women tell you what they need — it will be muscle power — then find it, organise it and set it to work. You are well used to organising men; now go and organise one-armed or one-legged or one-eyed men. Old men and your youths, both male and female. Whatever is needed to empty the fields and fill the barns, do it.'

Javier pondered for a few moments. 'Of course, what else is there to do hereabouts? This will keep my men occupied. Thank you, Robert, well said.'

I felt an overwhelming sense of relief. My little hospital had attracted a couple of nuns with two old soldiers to run it, and now this unexpected problem had been solved as soon as it was posed.

The harvest was collected by employing everyone who could help. It was easily explained to them; I went out into the fields and heard Javier's version of encouragement.

'Get that wheat into that wagon else you'll starve before Christmas — and get a move on, the rain threatens.'

And that was to a bevy of maidens. Perhaps they had not worked for a soldier before, but they soon sharpened up. Some lusty soldiers from Javier's men and some from the garrison joined with town lads too young to fight, and soon they were in the fields, pulling the ploughshares with the girls and sowing next year's seed. It was working quite well, I thought.

The air was heavy with the dust of corn cutting drifting up from the fields below as news drifted in week by week.

John's actions in taking Isabella d'Angoulême as his wife had been met with little support on this side of the narrow sea, and indeed, some had suggested that the girl was too young, at only twelve years of age and not the fourteen that John had claimed, but this was set aside as a wicked rumour. The marriage was allowed to stand, as no one could produce the records to test the accusation.

'How will this affect me, Father Walther?' I asked my chaplain as he read my letters.

'Isabella is to be crowned in Westminster next month and will become the Queen of England,' was the unhappy reply.

And that was it. My list of titles was becoming shorter by the week, and there was not much left to do but prepare for the coming winter. Corn was threshed, fruit was stored, and wood was cut. And on the eighth of October, Isabella became the new Queen of England.

In December we were more or less confined to my solar, where we stitched and sewed and prepared for events as yet unknown. The short days did not prevent the passage of couriers, though, and we looked forward to the clatter of hooves approaching the gatehouse, anxious to give our tired eyes a rest from the flickering candlelight.

It was near Christmas when a messenger arrived from Angers. He was brought before me by Denis and announced.

'Humfrey of Angers, from Lord Robert, seeking a privy meeting with Your Highness.'

'Very well. Stay by me, Denis, and send for Father Edwin. I suspect that I'll need some notetaking. Alazne, stay with me. I'll tell the rest of you what I discover in due course.'

As soon as we were settled in my solar, Denis escorted the dusty fellow in. He seemed surprised at the gathering, but soon recovered and gave a little bow.

'Humfrey, welcome. You have come directly from Angers?'

'Indeed, Your Highness — twenty miles or so.'

'Good. Have you been offered refreshment?'

'I have, Your Highness; most welcome.'

I scanned the fellow. He seemed a polite and presentable young man, and I suspected he was a station above a normal messenger — something special was coming.

'How is Lord Robert?'

'Busy, Your Highness. He has given over charge of Angers to Lord des Roches, and he wonders if you could return Guy de Bernez, but only if he is no further use to you; he is needed as a field soldier.'

'Robert is working for King John?'

'Indeed, Your Highness. The kings seem to have reached a new understanding.'

'And what are you about to tell me?'

215

'King John has engineered a peace deal with King Philip, and a new marriage to seal the matter. King Philip's eldest son, Prince Louis, is to marry King John's niece, Blanche of Castile, granddaughter of Queen Eleanor.'

'Castile!' I gasped. 'Eleanor is ambitious; the girl is but eleven in years.'

'Indeed, Your Highness; things are moving apace. Queen Eleanor went to fetch the girl.'

'Good Lord,' said Edwin.

'At her age?' I gasped. 'One needs to admire Eleanor, even if I do not admire her Angevin plotting.'

'Indeed, Your Highness, but the journey proved too much for her. She gave up on the way back and is resting at Bordeaux. A bishop took the intended bride on to Angers.'

'Eleanor!' I spoke harshly. 'Her favourite son and his sister hardly cold in their graves, yet she still plots for what's left of her brood.'

'Indeed, Your Highness. She is a persistent lady,' said Humfrey.

'Is there more?' I asked.

'King John and King Philip intend to meet next month on the border of Normandy to sign a new treaty.'

'I wonder how long that one will last.'

'King John asked for it; he might be struggling.'

'Mmm. I'll need to consider this: there is the sniff of a long plot in it. Has King Philip said anything about my status, Humfrey?'

'You should be assured that the French king holds you in high regard, Your Highness. Your reputation is well known, and he regards relationships with Navarre as important. And it is known that His Holiness looks kindly upon you.'

'Ah!' I said. 'The nub of it.'

Father Edwin expelled a rush of breath and Alazne giggled.

'I am well regarded?'

'Your reputation is much respected, Your Highness.'

'Thank you. What does Lord Robert intend to do next?'

'He will attend this treaty signing. I expect that I may be back later with a report.'

'Good. Give me a moment. Father, give me a quill and a blank vellum, if you please.'

I scribbled something down and passed it back to Edwin. He sealed it and handed it back.

I stood and beckoned Humfrey. 'Give this directly into Lord Robert's hand — no one else may receive it. Do you understand?' I looked him in the eye, trusting him and releasing the document.

'I understand. No other person, Your Highness. On my life.'

'Good. Should we feed you before you leave?'

'No need, Your Highness, but a fresh mount would be appreciated.'

'Of course. Denis!' I called.

He appeared so quickly that I suspected his ear had been very close to the door. 'Your Highness?'

'See to it that Humfrey has a fresh steed, please.'

'Of course, Your Highness. It's already arranged. If you will come with me, Humfrey,' he said, and the pair left the solar.

'What did you write to Lord Robert?' asked Alazne.

'I told him that people who stand on two banks at once often end up in the water. And give me time to make arrangements for Bernez.'

'Oh, I see,' she replied, although I was not sure that she did.

CHAPTER NINETEEN

1201

It was a new year and Philip and John had retired to lick their wounds, or plot against each other, while they proclaimed a new treaty and a new marriage to aid their alliance. John was no doubt impatient for his new wife, Isabella, to be old enough to be declared of beddable age.

I was standing atop the gatehouse with my ladies and Father Edwin. We had a grand view across the treetops and down into the village of Beaufort-en-Vallée.

'Is this how peace feels, Father?' I said.

'I believe it to be so, Your Highness. Do you miss the birds of war circling?'

'Or the kings squabbling and filling graves with Christians? No. Do you think that this new treaty will hold?'

'Perhaps, if John and Philip are weary of war, or have run out of money, or are willing do what Mother Church tells them. I enjoyed Robert's telling of the tale: two kings on one island in the stream.' Edwin chuckled.

'What island? What stream?' Alazne asked.

My chaplain explained. 'On the eighteenth of May last year, after much negotiating by barons and bishops, the two kings met on neutral ground on an island in the middle of the river Seine, known as Le Goulet.'

'"The Gullet?"' queried Isabeau.

'A bottleneck in the stream,' said Father Edwin. 'A good place to open up minds.'

'So what happened?' she asked.

'King John did homage to King Philip for some of his possessions on this side of the narrow sea, effectively admitting that they belonged to France,' I said unhappily. 'Young Arthur paid homage to John for Brittany, and then a granddaughter of Eleanor's, the daughter of another of Richard's sisters — Blanca or Blanche of Castile — married Prince Louis of France.'

'And all is well,' added Father Edwin hopefully.

'Except that John may well spoil things,' I said without hope. 'After that meeting he stomped through the land, upsetting his barons. Maine, Anjou, and Touraine all felt his spite as he took revenge on those who had resisted him.'

'I heard that he is up to his eyes in debt,' said Father Edwin.

'Is that so?' I responded. 'Given his record with promises, the moneylenders might not see any coin back.'

'So what will King John do next?' asked Alazne.

'Try for Aquitaine. His mother sits uneasily on that ducal seat; the barons there have little regard for authority outside their own,' I said. 'That's what Eleanor is doing, trying to hold on to my future duchy.'

Javier had joined us, scrambling up the ladder in time to hear that last remark. 'I shouldn't count on that, Your Highness. John will no doubt find a way to frustrate that ambition.'

'Yes, I am only clinging to a vague hope. I'll probably end up in a nunnery,' I said. 'I wonder what King Sancho will make of all this. Anything else we should hear about, Father, before we begin today's work?'

'No, Your Highness. Let us walk the fields, visit the sick and talk to the priest at the church.'

'Your Highness,' said Javier, 'Arrosa will be giving birth soon, so do you think that I could go home? It seems settled here now.'

'Of course. I'll write some letters, which you can deliver, and the treasurer can find something to aid you and Arrosa. I'll speak to him.'

'You'll be lucky, with that parsimonious old —'

'Alazne, be not so disrespectful of Ander,' I scolded.

Alazne then asked if she and Pavot could go back with Javier for a visit. I readily agreed, as they had not seen their homeland in years.

'We'll manage with Isabeau, I'm sure.'

A little while after Javier had left, I received a note from Sancho confirming the successful delivery of Arrosa's baby and asking if he could change Javier and his men for a new captain and a new detachment to guard us. I agreed, and a new captain named Mendia was sent to me, thus allowing Javier's men to return to their homeland under the command of a sergeant. This allowed me to approach Guy de Bernez with a request.

'Lord Robert, seneschal of various places, has asked if I could release you for warlike purposes,' I said. 'He has need of your talents on the battlefield, it would seem.'

'Instead of guarding several ladies?'

'Is that a problem?'

'Yes, I like it here. But how was the question posed, Your Highness?'

'As if you should have left some time ago.'

'I see. I suppose that I should leave, then.'

'Not my choice, but the request has merit; you are Robert's man, after all.'

'I'll leave on Sunday evening, after Prime.'

'Then we'll have a feast for you on Saturday. You can consider it all day on Sunday and leave on Monday.'

We all gathered to see Bernez off on Monday, as arranged — one more goodbye to add to a lengthening list.

One evening, I noticed Father Edwin standing alone on the battlement. I excused myself and climbed up the ladder to join him.

'Will I disturb you, Father?'

'Of course not, Your Highness. I am contemplating God's good earth, watching and thinking.'

'It is at peace.'

'Indeed, but I am not.'

'Oh! What have I done?'

'No, not you, Your Highness — me. May I speak?'

'We have no secrets, you and I. Tell me what is in your heart.'

The speed of his response told me that he had been thinking of it for a while. 'I want to die in my beloved Northumbria, in the land of Bede and Cuthbert, and of Edward the Confessor.'

'I see. That is your wish?'

'It was another idea in my head when I agreed to serve you in Rome. At that time we both had it in mind that your journey would end in England, and I thought I could continue north.'

'We were both wrong.'

He chuckled. 'We knew what we knew.'

'And now we know different. I don't want to lose you.'

'Aye, but you said yourself that life was a procession of farewells.'

'I want to keep you, but I must send you on your way. Will that be my next farewell?'

'It seems so, if you will allow it, Your Highness.'

'Then so be it. I cannot tear at a man's heartstrings. Who knows: one day I might turn up on your threshold.'

He laughed uncertainly. 'We'll make a nice mead with which to welcome you.'

'Mead?'

'A local delicacy. Monks make it from honey with God's guidance.'

'Then you may return there as soon as you like. You need to find me a replacement chaplain, though.'

'I'll make enquiries, Your Highness. God bless you.'

'And find time to write a letter. You might enjoy this: write to John and send a copy to Cardinal Benedetto. Ask him when — not if — he is going to send me the income from my English dowers, which his brother gifted me.'

I had not heard Edwin laugh so much before, and it took a few moments for him to calm himself. 'This will be the finest letter I have ever composed. Please allow me some latitude in expression, Your Highness. I will leave no meaning unclear.'

'And send a copy to the Archbishop of Angers, if you will.'

Mendia, the new captain of my guard, was a formidable fellow with one eye and a few scars. I believed that he had been sent to us for a rest. His name meant 'mountain' in Basque, which was appropriate because he was huge and darkened the sky when he was near. Still, he was pleasant enough, and joined conversations readily. No one dared to ask how he had lost an eye, but I doubt if the opponent who removed it survived long afterwards. Others arrived to swell my household: there was Paulin Boutier, a knight of distinction who wished to serve me — my reputation was bringing helpers to my door — and two clerks.

'Whence do you come?' I asked when they appeared.

'From King Sancho,' said one. 'We are Simon and Garcia.'

Mendia had brought two sergeants with him, Martin and Pierre, and to complete my list a cantor named Pierre Prévôt was donated from the local church to lead us in song and prayer. Then Father Edwin asked me to meet someone else.

'Your Highness, would you care to meet Father Walther of Perseigne?'

'Is he to be my new chaplain?'

'He might be if he meets with your approval. He has arrived at the village church. Bishop Hugh has sent him from Angers.'

We set off and along the way we stopped to watch the children play.

'Do you regret not having children, Your Highness?'

I might have reacted differently had that question been asked by someone else, but we had been together for a long time now, so it was acceptable.

'Sometimes, when I am thinking about Joan and the child torn from her to die. I wonder if he should have lived for me to care for.'

'Perhaps that was intended by the Lord, but mistakes were made.' Edwin regarded me with kind eyes tinged with pity, I thought. 'Are you reconciled? You affect many around you.'

'I know, it has always been so. Ever since Mother died and I began managing my father's court, I have been at the centre of things. Aren't we always at the centre of our lives, Father? Is that not an arrogance?'

'It may be an accident of birth, Your Highness. Some *are* born to lead; most only follow.'

'Leaders like King John?'

He laughed. 'There are exceptions.'

'Sometimes I am at the centre of things beyond my control, but today, here in this village with my people around me, I am at the centre of our work. Many depend on me.'

'Yes, you are, and with the guidance of God and the teachings of his son, Jesu, you will be your own centre. I pray for it.'

'Then I can be reconciled to the life I lead.'

'Then you are on the path to happiness.'

'Thank you, Father. God bless you. And now it is your turn. Are you content?'

'With life at God's speed? I'd like to slow down, Your Highness.'

Touching hands, we laughed.

Our local priest, Father Pierre, and a stranger were in conversation inside the church and broke off when we entered.

'Your Highness, Father Edwin,' said Father Pierre. 'May I introduce Father Walther?'

'Of course. Father Walther, welcome,' I said.

'Thank you, Your Highness,' he responded.

Father Walther was unlike most priests, being of an athletic stature and military bearing, and although he bowed to me he also engaged me directly with his eyes. There would be no prevaricating with this one, and I challenged him immediately.

'What do you know about me, Father Walther?'

'I know where you come from, and your journeys on Crusade are well known. More than that I do not presume to guess, Your Highness.'

'So, we would make a new beginning, if you decided to join me?'

'If you decided to appoint me, Your Highness.'

'Then know that I am blowing in the winds of fate. Are you prepared to travel? To move about quite a lot? My present position is tenuous.'

'I have had this conversation with Bishop Hugh, Your Highness. These factors have all been taken into consideration, and the result of our deliberations is to let Father Edwin return to his native land when he so desires. Also, I am not without a taste for adventure and have served the wounded and dying on more than one battlefield, including some in Outremer.'

'Really? Then we will have things to talk about, Father Walther. So you are leaving the decision to me?'

'It is your right, Your Highness,' said the dolorous Pierre.

'But we needed to discuss your options,' added my cheery Edwin.

'Thank you, Father Edwin, very thoughtful. Well, we'd better go back and introduce Father Walther to my household.'

Walther's eyebrows went up. 'I'm staying?'

'Yes, if you wish. Thank you, Father Pierre.'

'God bless you, Your Highness. Now, shall we say a prayer?'

'Of course, for a successful future.'

I waited until we were outside before chortling. 'You're a very devious chaplain, Father Edwin.'

'Devious, Your Highness? Deviousness is a fine art in the Church; did you not know that?'

'What news do you bring, Father Walther, fresh from Angers? Where *is* King John? I can't keep up with his perambulations,' I said.

'Last heard of in Lusignan, twenty miles south of Poitiers, seeing to his borders. I believe that Hugh de Lusignan views John's presence with disfavour.'

'Another unruly lord.'

'Quite, and John has plenty of those to keep loyal to him.'

To my surprise, I soon received a letter from John. He was in Chinon. It was witnessed by a William Marshal, who I understood was an important advisor to the king. It listed the funds that would be paid to me and the dates by which they would be paid. This was a surprising turn and I viewed it with suspicion.

'What do you think, Fathers? Should I allocate this money before I receive it?'

Much shaking of heads and tutting gave the answer: no.

'His reputation gives the lie to his promises,' added Walther.

'If King John thinks that he will gain Hugh's loyalty by marrying his betrothed, he will be disappointed.'

'I've heard that she is well advanced in looks and wit,' said Isabeau. 'John may well have met his match.'

'We'll see,' said Walther. 'Perhaps the prospect of a crown turned her head. God is watching. It may take time, but there'll surely be a reckoning.'

Not long after I had agreed to have Walther join my household, Father Edwin came to me with a distressed expression and said, 'Your Highness, if I do not leave soon I may be stuck in Barfleur or some other port, waiting for a ship.'

'Oh, is it time?' I asked. A horrid knot formed in my stomach.

'We agreed, Your Highness.'

'We did. When will you leave?'

'In the morning, or when the next messenger passes through, I'll join him.'

That was a good idea; I did not favour the idea of Edwin wandering around a tense land to reach a port in Normandy. He would be safer in good company.

Two days later, he was mounted up and ready to go.

'I can't reach you up there,' I said through tears. He slid off and we had a most unpriestly hug.

'Sorry, Your Highness. This has been the most interesting time of my life, if unexpected.'

'I'll pray for you and write; that's all I can do. And you must tell me about life in Northumbria.'

'I will. I should send you a bottle of mead.'

'Do. Go now, before I change my mind.'

Our hands slid out of each other's, and he mounted and set off with a wave. Alazne put an arm around me, and we returned to the solar.

CHAPTER TWENTY

Hugh de Lusignan had reacted as predicted to John's abduction of his betrothed, and John's lust-fuelled action was about to rebound upon him with a vengeance. Barons in the south joined with Lusignan, and Eleanor's precious Aquitaine was in peril as the gods of war stirred once more.

'It seems as if Normandy is not to be the next crucible of death, my dear friends,' I said, throwing a letter from Blanca onto the table. 'If John is looking forward to Isabella joining him in his marriage bed, he will soon regret the pleasure of it. His new father-in-law is about to discomfort him.'

'Good,' said Walther.

We also heard that Hugh de Lusignan had been joined by his respected Crusader uncle Geoffrey; Aquitaine was under attack and the nobles of Poitou joined in. John's new queen would soon be abandoned for the heat of war, and it seemed it would only be a matter of time before he was back in Normandy.

It crossed my mind to pay my sister a visit before we became involved in the spring planting. With the excitement over her marriage ceremony long gone and she now expecting a baby, I thought she might like a visit. I sent a letter and received an acceptance.

'Mendia, do you know where Troyes is?' I asked.

That set the giant thinking. 'In Greece?'

'Good try, but not that Troy. Fetch a map and I'll show you.' He brought it and I pointed. 'There.'

'How far is that?' he asked.

'About fifty miles from Paris, a week or so from here. We're going to visit my sister. How soon can you be ready?'

'Tomorrow, Your Highness. Do we have a wagon for you and your ladies?'

'No, we have riding clothes. Choose some horses for us.' I looked at him. 'We rode here from Rome. Did you not know?'

His face brightened. 'I heard rumours, but I thought it a jest. Your horses will be ready when you are, Your Highness.'

Two weeks later we were in Troyes with Blanca, or Blanche, as everyone in France insisted on calling her. She was better placed to receive the most recent intelligences than we had been in Beaufort, and the castle was much bigger too.

Blanca, Thibaut and I were seated in elegant chairs in an opulent chamber facing a fire. My ladies were at the far end of the room, talking to the ladies of Blanca's bedchamber.

'Berengaria, we have concerns for your safety. John is unstable and plots without thought,' said my sister.

'It had occurred to me, too, but I own too much to hand it over to him and his mother without putting up a fight.'

'Good for you, Berengaria,' said Thibaut. 'As my gracious wife has said, John is unpredictable.'

I was sitting between the pair and took a good look at the count of Champagne, something I had not been able to do properly at their wedding. A grandchild of King Louis VIII and Eleanor, from her first marriage, he was younger than Blanca and seemed very much younger in appearance, but I liked him well enough. He was gentle and I thought that they would do well together. Now my sister was the countess of Champagne and married into the house of Blois with a dower of no less than seven castles and their income, how would John react to that? He was faced with two sisters from Navarre: one in the French royal family and one in the house of Plantagenet. I chuckled.

'What amuses you, sister?' Blanca asked.

'John. He is now dealing with two powerful sisters — me a Queen Dowager of England and you a countess of France.'

'And a future something or other in here,' she said, holding her stomach.

'How shall you settle disputes between England and France, ladies?' asked Thibaut.

'We shall have a needlework competition; the winner takes all,' I replied, and we laughed so loud that the ladies at the other end of the chamber stopped their chatter.

'Are you tired, ladies, after our ten days on the road?' I asked.

Alazne nodded, and the others chorused, 'Yes, Your Highness.'

'Yes, me too. Shall we continue in the morning? My eyes are closing,' said Blanca. She looked at Thibaut and some signal passed between them. 'We have a proposition for you, but it can wait until tomorrow. Get some rest; the new day will be here soon enough.' She waved a hand and her ladies stood and prepared to escort us to our bedchambers.

A kiss and an embrace later, we were marching along endless corridors and stairs into bedchambers smothered with so many fabric hangings and floor coverings that all was silent within. I knew then that John, despite the taxes he was wringing England dry with, could never compete with the riches of France. If this was a palace of counts, what must a palace of kings be like? I also saw that any income from my holdings would be difficult to keep from John, despite any promises to the contrary.

The following morning Isabeau, who had been exploring, led us through the palace to the refectory to find the buffet groaning with food and drink.

Blanca and Thibaut were being attended to at a table at the far end of the chamber, and Blanca waved for me to join them.

There was fresh bread, which smelled delicious, a selection of cheeses, some carved meats and chicken legs and a palatable wine.

'Quite a delight,' I remarked, 'after the various places we've stayed in along the way here.'

'Yes, Berengaria. They aren't all palaces,' replied Blanca. 'But the animal life on the palliasses is quite entertaining.'

That amused Thibaut, who asked, 'Is it at cost, staying in these places? I've never asked.'

'There speaks a man who has never seen a coin,' said Blanca, laughing.

At least Thibaut had the decency to blush. My affection for him grew.

'We wanted to ask you something,' said Blanca mysteriously. 'We've heard about your work with the poor and the wounded Crusaders. Can we help?'

I wondered what it was that they'd heard. I decided that I had to be honest. 'I should have sufficient, but all is uncertain. Eleanor occupies my future duchy, and I'm not asking her for money. John is sitting on the income from some of my other holdings in England. I need to write to him again about that, or go and confront him, and he is not paying over any dues owed from Normandy. All I am sure about is the income from Navarre and the little I control from Beaufort.'

'That's what we suspected, Berengaria,' said Thibaut.

'Yes, sister, please let us help. It's our duty,' added Blanca.

'You mean you'll help out with the alms and the hospital? I won't refuse such kindness — thank you.' There was one question I wanted to ask. 'Does King Philip know that I'm here?'

'He does, but he is chasing your brother-in-law around the country. Now, as you've mentioned it, he has asked if you'd accept an invitation to meet him,' said Blanca, smiling.

'The king believes you to be a brave and patient soul, and that you tolerated Richard far longer than he himself could manage,' said Thibaut. 'He is a supporter of your work and prays for you each day.'

I was taken aback by that. 'Blanca?'

'It's true; he admires your patience and your dignity. He prays that I am as faithful to Thibaut as you have been to an intolerable husband.' She watched me as I tried to formulate a response.

'You've heard this?'

'We have friends at court. Give me a hug, sister. We shall support each other so far from home.'

My entourage and I spent a few days exploring Troyes with Thibaut while Blanca stayed behind, resting. He was very interested in how I had gone about organising Poitiers and Beaufort, and he was keen to try the same thing in Champagne.

The time to leave came all too soon. With tearful farewells, we agreed to meet in Orléans after the birth of Blanca's baby, Orléans being roughly halfway between us.

Beaufort was a welcome sight ten days later, but once inside I was reminded how small it was.

Alazne was feeling the difference too. 'I felt lost in Blanca's palace, Your Highness; did you?' she remarked as she unbraided my hair.

'But this is homely, cosy,' said Pavot, laying out my nightgown. 'I wouldn't want to live where everyone can't be found all the time.'

'No,' I responded. 'This is ours, for now.'

I slept well that night and awoke to a bright day. I now felt less alone; although Blanca was several days away, I knew that she was well placed to help us if we needed it.

We gathered later in the morning, and I set out what we had learned at Troyes — mainly about royal support from Philip, and John being at war with the Lusignans. Then I touched on the subject of money.

'Ander,' I said, looking at my treasurer, 'prepare to go to Orléans. There you will meet with my sister's treasurer and receive some coin. Mendia, provide an escort for Ander and see him safely there and back.' I looked at my ladies and Father Walther. 'As for us, we will continue with our alms for the poor and treatment of the ill and wounded.'

'Does this mean that we are working with the approval of the French king?' asked Alazne.

'Yes, at arm's length from the crown. My sister is helping to fund us. As long as John insists on being at war with anyone who upsets him, he sits on income from my dower lands.'

'So he is spending your money on his wars,' said Isabeau.

'You have it, Isabeau, and until things improve he is unlikely to release his grip on my various dower lands in England and Normandy. Thank the Lord for the little coin coming out of Navarre. Now, Father Walther, prepare to write some letters. We shall arrange some dates and send some complaints. John shall receive them, but copies shall go to Cardinal Benedetto and King Philip.'

'I shall enjoy reading what you dictate I write, Your Highness. It's always quite amusing.'

'Thank you. I try.'

Ander went off to Orléans to seek out Blanca's coin courier, and two weeks later he returned with a pair of coin bags slung across his saddle. The presence of four of Mendia's fiercest guards kept him safe.

'Your Highness, we were expected and stayed in a well-guarded safe house.'

'Good, how is my sister?'

'Her courier says that she is well, and here is a letter from her.'

I took the missive gladly and left the bailey to seek the quiet of my solar, where I read Blanca's letter:

Sister mine, we are all well and the child I carry says hello quite often and kicks so. We are so looking forward to his arrival, and it is our fervent wish that you attend us and help me with the birthing in May. I do so wish to talk and scream in our mother tongue when the time arrives; you and Sancho are my only link to our dear departed mother and father. Do say you will come.

All my love,

Blanca.

'Ander, is there more to tell?' I asked.

'No, Your Highness. We have arranged dates for the receiving of coin; all is well in that regard.'

'I will need to attend my sister when she gives birth in May,' I said.

'I'll make sure that we are ready,' said Mendia. 'How many will be going and how long will you stay, Your Highness?'

I knew that it would be a difficult journey. Mendia would need a string of three horses with him that he changed over at regular intervals along the way.

'I'll need my ladies and a good escort,' I said. 'Prepare to stay a month if all goes well.'

Denis looked worried. 'What should I do if the king turns up here, Your Highness?'

'Which one?'

'John.'

'Hide any women, let him in, let manservants attend him and then send him on his way as soon as you can.'

'What about King Philip?'

'He's unlikely to come, but the quarrel is not ours. We'll wait it out and see what transpires before we are forced to reject John, for I'm certain that is what I wish to do. If forced to it, I will choose Philip as my overlord. I will send instructions after I have conferred with my sister. In the meantime, I have every confidence that you will continue to manage the castle and the town in the manner I have ordered it.'

'Thank you, Your Highness. I shall do my best.'

Spring left little time for idle hands and minds as the fields were prepared for planting.

I was often left with Father Walther for company as we penned letters in the candlelight to all we could reach — usually requests for the release of my dues from my dower lands, or messages to those whom I thought could help me in that regard. If John thought that I would disappear, he had miscalculated.

I decided that as we had made good progress in the preparation of our land, I could safely leave in mid-April. So Mendia was summoned, we went through his preparations and, as I expected, I found them not wanting in detail. Sergeants Martin and Pierre would remain here to guard the castle.

After three more days we were back on the road. It was a miserable journey, wet and cold, but at the overnight stay in Orléans we were able to gather more information, with

Mendia's soldiers bringing us gossip they had gathered in the local hostelries. King Philip was watching King John's antics as he sought to keep a grip on things. At present, John was succeeding only in driving a wedge down the centre of his mother's empire, the Angevins split by a choice of John or Arthur.

Our arrival in Troyes had been well anticipated — messengers sent ahead had seen to that — and many citizens braved the wind and damp to see England's Basque queen arrive to take care of her sister. This triumph for Navarre in European politics amused me.

What was not amusing was that I was soaked through. The sheepskin that Mendia had given me was heavy, and as we entered through the town gate I shrugged it off and sat glumly with only my cloak for warmth.

Clattering and squelching, we made our way through the wet but cheering crowds into the château courtyard. I slid off my horse and landed in the arms of Thibaut.

'Your Highness, Berengaria, you are soaked. Come inside quickly; we will find you a hot tub.'

'And tubs for my ladies, and my men, and do not neglect the horses.'

'Of course, of course. I'll attend to everything. Here is Blanche. She has been looking forward to seeing you for weeks.'

Blanca had been sitting in a chair just inside the portico and stood as I entered, waddling towards me.

'Oh, Blanca, do not stand for me,' I said.

'I'm fine, Berengaria, although I do not stand for very long. Holy Mother! You are shivering. Thibaut, get my sister near a fire and then organise some hot tubs for our guests.'

'It's already arranged, my sweet, and there is a fire lit in the small receiving chamber. We'll all fit in there quite cosily,' he said gleefully, beckoning us to follow him. I did, although slowly as I held my sister to support her.

Soon we were next to a monstrous fireplace, and I was conducted to a pair of chairs where Blanca and I could sit next to each other and hold hands. My ladies knelt in front of the flames and soon we were all chatting away, Blanca and I in our mother tongue.

Thibaut, who was chatting with Father Walther, let out a laugh. 'You are steaming, Your Highness,' he said, observing our group. 'Time for your hot tubs.' He waved at someone, and Blanca's ladies appeared and invited us to follow them to the guest chambers.

'We'll talk more later, my sweet,' I said, kissing Blanca on the cheek.

After my bath I was given a dry gown, and I lay on my bed until a gentle hand illuminated by candlelight woke me.

'Isabeau?'

'Your Highness, its suppertime. Are you not hungry?'

'Ravenous. Where is everyone?'

'Waiting outside. We left you as long as we could, but there is an official waiting to take us to the countess's hall.'

'Oh, give me a moment to compose myself, then we'll be off.'

Last to arrive, I had no choice but to make a queenly entrance, saying good morrows to the ladies of the court gathered together. My four were left in an antechamber as I was led into Blanca's privy dining hall.

'Sister,' said Blanca, rising.

'Stay, my sweet,' I responded, putting my hands on her shoulders. 'I am late; I apologise.'

'No need, Your Highnesses,' said Thibaut, who stood respectfully.

'Berengaria, if you please,' I corrected him. 'We are in privy. Come, give your future sister-in-law a hug.'

Thibaut was without doubt a pleasant young man, as befitted a son of Blois. His grasp was firm and friendly, and we were soon seated while a buffet was laid out before us.

'So, dear sister, you are certain that you will give birth next month?' I asked, laughing to see Thibaut blushing and addressing a hunk of bread.

'Thibaut,' Blanca scolded, 'you were there at the beginning; please acknowledge the ending.' She grinned at me from behind her hand. 'Yes, sister, I am sure my son will arrive in May.'

The weeks passed pleasantly enough. Blanca grew no bigger but spent a lot of time sleeping, and I had friendly conversations with Thibaut. The weather had improved, and he took me for walks along the riverbank, where the Seine peacefully glided by.

'It will be very nice when the weather has warmed a little more,' I said to him one afternoon.

'Indeed, and it's very tempting to swim in it, although one does not know what lurks beneath the surface. I prefer a nearby lake, where there is no current.'

'Ah, I see. How do you view King John? What do you hear coming out of Versailles?'

'Not much. Since Blanche has been with child, I have not taken great notice of John's doings, but I have heard that the territories he rules are diminishing by the day.'

One morning, the sky was only just lightening when Isabeau and Alazne woke me ungently.

'Your Highness, come quickly,' said Alazne. 'It's Comte Thibaut; he is not well.'

I began to dress, but they stayed my hands. 'There is no time, Your Highness,' said Isabeau.

The corridor outside Thibaut's chambers was full of anxious-looking courtiers, and I needed to press through the crowd to reach the door. The way was barred by two huge sergeants-at-arms but one, recognising me, tapped on the door and it opened to let me in. My ladies were stopped from entering, but I found myself out of the babble and inside a strangely quiet antechamber.

A very tall and distinguished man popped through a different door and looked me up and down from across the chamber, but he did not come near. He spoke gently.

'The count is very ill, Your Highness.'

'Who are you?' I asked.

'Albert, the court physician, Your Highness.'

'Explain, Albert, if you please.'

'*Le comte* has the sweating and voiding illness.'

'How? He was fine this evening; he went for a walk with his friends.'

'It comes on very quickly from infection, Your Highness. I have seen this before. Where did he walk?'

'As far as I know along the riverbank; it's his favourite area.'

'He must have taken in some water; I believe that to be how the illness enters the body.'

At that there was a terrifying cry from the chamber that Albert had emerged from and a horrid squelching noise — then a nauseating smell.

My eyes opened wide, and my hand went over my mouth. 'Is that...?'

'Thibaut, Your Highness — I'm afraid so.'

'What are you doing?'

'Very little. We are trying to get some boiled water down him, but it comes immediately out again. He is in terrible pain with stomach cramps.'

'Will he...?'

'Die? Yes, I believe so. The priest is with him now.'

'May I see him?'

'If you do so, you cannot return to your sister's side for some time. I believe that the malady is transferable.'

'My God, what can I do?'

'Like all of us, you must wait. He cannot endure this pain much longer.'

'Should I tell Comtesse Blanche?'

'I was hoping that you would, Your Highness. It should be her nearest. But would you wait? If you tell her that he lives, she will surely want to see him, and the child within her...'

'Is at risk. And you are certain, Albert?'

'I am. Some hold different views, but I have witnessed too many such deaths and am certain in my mind. I have also spoken to some eminent physicians who hold similar views. If there was anything that could be done, I would have taken such steps by now.'

At that moment another scream came out of Thibaut's chamber, a sound of such frightening intensity that I nearly fainted, and Albert looked at me from across the antechamber with tears streaming down his cheeks.

Frightened to ask, I merely returned his tear-glazed stare and he nodded. I sat down on a chair, my legs too weak to support me.

'Your Highness, in there,' said Albert, indicating Thibaut's chamber with a nod, 'is the door adjoining the comtesse's chamber. It has been locked. When you are ready to see your sister, take care that you do not allow her to think that she can view the count's body. We must make special arrangements for his interment.'

'And when will that be?'

'As soon as they can make the coffin. It will be at the collegial church of Saint-Etienne nearby.'

'Her confinement is near; she will not be there.'

'Will you attend?'

'I will discuss it with her, be assured.'

'Thank you, Your Highness. Now, there is work to do, if you will excuse me.'

'Certainly, keep me informed.'

He nodded and with a bow backed into the death chamber.

I must have been a picture of misery when I emerged into the crowded corridor and was immediately swamped by my ladies.

'What is wrong, Your Highness?' asked Isabeau.

'Thibaut is no more; a fatal disease has taken him.' This was all the explanation that I could manage to give at that moment.

Father Walther stepped forward and took hold of my hands. I looked into his eyes.

'Tell me more, Your Highness.'

So I burdened him with all the grisly details that I could remember.

'Ah,' he said after a moment. 'Do you know how they will deal with the burial now?'

'Not exactly.'

'Then you should find out, so that you can formulate some responses to your sister's questions. It will not be easy.'

'Can we go outside? Blanca is sleeping but a few feet away.'

'Yes.'

I shuffled outside into a gloomy morning, followed by a crowd of the curious and helped by the caring arm of Walther.

There were some benches arranged outside and Walther led me to one, where we sat in quiet contemplation. Alazne, Pavot, Isabeau and Cateline were standing behind me, sniffling.

'Go and sit over there, ladies. I need to talk with Father Walther.'

I wanted to hear some details before I sifted them for my ladies' ears.

'What will happen?' I asked Father Walther once they had left. 'Have you conducted such a funeral?'

'Yes, Your Highness, all too often. They will not handle the body without the protection of leather gloves and aprons. The coffin will be lead-lined, and when they transfer the body from bed to coffin it will be covered in quicklime. The gloves and aprons are to be deposited into the coffin and the lid sealed. The bedding will be treated with the same care, to be taken outside and burned.'

'That's it — the end of a young life?'

'The grave will be dug especially deep. But you are returned from the Crusade; you have seen that death does not favour only the old.'

'The desert seems a lifetime away now, Father.'

'Would that we could rid ourselves of such memories, Your Highness, keeping only the best, forever.'

I stood. 'Time to see if Blanca is awake. Will you attend me, Father?'

'Yes, Your Highness. Be brave.'

I walked back into the château, and the corridor outside the ducal chambers was as crowded as ever. I spoke to Isabeau. 'Find the seneschal and have him clear the corridor; my sister needs peace, not spectacle.'

CHAPTER TWENTY-ONE

One person stood out in the press of the corridor. Father Walther beckoned me to follow and made straight for a hovering priest.

'Père Bernard, this is Queen Berengaria.'

Bernard bowed and took my hand. I bobbed and smiled at the kind-faced priest. 'I am chaplain to the ducal court, Your Highness,' he introduced himself. 'This is a sad day. If you are going to tell Comtesse Blanche, perhaps now would be best, before rumours begin to penetrate her privy chambers.'

'I'll go in now. If you would both wait outside Blanca's bedchamber, I will ask you in when she is ready.'

'Of course,' said Walther. 'We'll wait in the antechamber and pray for the soul of Thibaut and...'

'...the life of Blanche,' added Père Bernard.

I entered Blanca's bedchamber. The light was muted, with the blinds drawn across the windows. Blanca was sitting up and being fussed over by two matrons. I waved them away and sat on the side of the bed. My face held no secrets, that much I knew.

'Berengaria? What has happened?'

'Thibaut,' I said quietly.

'Is he injured? I told him that new horse was too difficult, but men... What?'

'Not injured, Blanca. It was a disease.'

'He is ill? I must go to him.' Blanca began to throw off her covers, but I stayed her hand. Her eyes opened wide as some realisation hit her and she put her hands over her mouth. 'Tell me, Berengaria! Tell me now!' Her voice rose to fever pitch.

Taking her hands, I looked directly into her eyes. 'The worst, dear sister, the very worst. He died of the flux.'

She fell back against the pillows, and I climbed onto the bed to sit alongside her. Then my dear, precious sister let out a scream.

'No, no, please God, no!'

She turned to me, and we clung together for an age before she began to let out her tears. 'What now?' she gasped. 'I want to see him … what's left of him. Oh, Lord, what has life come to?'

'No, Blanca, for your child's sake, for Thibaut's child's sake, you should not go near him for fear of infection.'

She fell silent for a while as my words sunk in. 'I'll never see him again.'

'Not on this earth,' I said without thinking.

'We should pray,' she said.

I went to the door and beckoned the pair of priests in to do their work.

Eventually Blanca fell asleep. *She must be exhausted*, I thought, as I slipped out of the bed. My ladies and a lot of other people were waiting in the corridor as I emerged, dishevelled and teary.

'How is the comtesse?' asked Alazne.

'Is the baby well?' said Isabeau.

'One is sad beyond measure, and the other is kicking inside her stomach and seems well enough.'

There were more details to impart, although I left out the distressing parts. I needed to explain the arrangements for the body and the funeral, as I was going to be Blanca's representative and they needed to know.

'Are we all to go?' asked Alazne.

'If you wish,' I answered, and they all agreed to attend, which pleased me enormously.

'Now, go and wait in our guest chambers. I will see the seneschal and chamberlain and whoever else is involved and see if they can work out the order of service for the funeral tomorrow. The cause of Thibaut's death means that he must be interred as soon as possible.'

I went along to the great hall and found it packed with strangers. Father Walther spied me, and I went through a round of introductions, most of which I instantly forgot, and eventually I found a chair and left the great and the good of France to get on with it. Father Walther sat with me as the world went by in a whirl.

After a while, Père Bernard came across to join us.

'They have settled on a service. The coffin will be in the centre of the church but will remain shut and will not be taken out when the service has ended. It is feared that the depth of the grave will frighten many, so it will be interred discreetly later. If you, Your Highness, would be at the front of the church?'

I nodded acceptance.

'And at the head of the procession to lead everyone out of the church, you will be joined by some of the Blois family, no doubt, though we do not yet know who will represent them, given the short notice.'

I slept beside Blanca that night; she cried from time to time, and I was restless. I was slow to dress the following morning, even though my ladies had made everything ready for me — a simple gown and headdress was all I needed. I eschewed breakfast and let myself be led out to the waiting carriage, accompanied by my ladies.

The funeral went as planned. I was introduced to only two of the Blois family members, as both Thibaud's parents were dead. A count from Versailles, sent to represent the royal Capetian family, came to commiserate with me, and it was he who stood alongside me in the church. No bishop attended; there were only Fathers Bernard and Walther, with the church priest conducting the service. It did not last long, and soon I was climbing back into my carriage.

Blanca and I shared her bed again that night, two widowed sisters marooned in a foreign land, in the midst of a war and at the mercy of God.

I prayed that God would not test us further that week and that Blanca's delivery would be without complications.

'Thank you for coming, Berengaria,' she said the next morning as she woke. 'No one else can help me, as much as they try. I am over-supported by sympathy from my household. King Philip's mother, Adèle, is coming to see me — did I say?'

'I don't remember; my mind has been in such a whirl.'

Count Thibaut III had died on the twenty-fourth of May 1201; his son Thibaut IV was born on the thirtieth of May. I was there through my sister's pain and joy as she brought him into the world.

'He is beautiful,' said Blanca as she sat in bed, holding her son. 'Think you too, Berengaria?'

'A most lively lad, I can see, Blanca,' I said. 'Father and Mother would have been most proud of you, I am certain.'

'Thank you, sister. Do you want to hold him?'

'Er, yes, of course.'

Taking the proffered bundle and praying that I would not drop it, I sat on a nearby chair. I was about to tell Blanca that we were expecting the dowager queen Adèle the following day, but she was now snoring, so I took the opportunity to hand young Thibaut IV over to his wet nurse and left.

The sixty-year-old French queen, dowager to the long-dead Louis VII, arrived in spritely style. She was tiny with sparkling eyes.

'I doubt that she will miss much, Alazne,' I muttered to my lady as Adèle was handed down from her coach.

'Queen Adèle, we are pleased that you can spend some time with us,' I said.

'Who might you be?' she asked as she peered up into my face.

'I am Berengaria, sister of Blanca.'

'Of course you are, of course. How is the new mother?'

'Sad, *madame*, but comforted by the successful birth.'

'Of course, of course. Let's see the child, Berengaria. Take my arm, if you will.'

She was a chatty dowager, and we had no difficulty as we made our way to Blanca's quarters where she was waiting. I noted that my sister had made every effort to dress as befitted her station, and I was proud of her as she presented the new count to his distant cousin.

'Ah, a well-formed child, Blanche. I have prayed for you both. You are well presented, my child, and in that regard I bring news from King Philip. You are to retain the regency of Champagne until the child is of age — if you want it of course?'

'Oh, *altezza*, I would like that more than anything. I will guard the count with my life until he can assume his full title.'

'Well, there should be no need to give your life; we've had enough death. Just educate the lad and teach him manners.'

'I shall, *altezza*.'

'And there's no need for titles between us. They mean little between friends, and we shall be friends, shan't we?'

'If you wish, *madame*.'

'*Madame*? Makes me feel old, but if you wish. And your sister?' Adèle looked at me.

'My friends and family make do with Berengaria.'

'Berengaria, it sounds like you are waiting to be plucked. How did you get on with Richard, eh?'

'I was unplucked, Adèle, not savoured.'

She cackled. 'So I'd heard. Just checking. Now, where is my bed? I'll manage supper this evening if I have a lie-down now. I'm off to Versailles in the morning.'

'Will your companions require a bed?' I asked, looking at the two middle-aged ladies hovering nearby.

'We're fine,' answered one. 'If someone could show us around the town, perhaps?'

'I'll arrange that,' said Blanca, calling over her chamberlain. 'Now, *madame*, we'll show you to your bedchamber and see to your needs.'

Later that evening, with supper eaten and the baby fed, I flopped onto Blanca's bed for a late-night chat.

'Now the king has confirmed that I am to remain the countess regent of Champagne, Adèle says that I am to pay homage to him, including a pot of coin,' said Blanca. 'My county is secured for Thibaut, since he is count-in-waiting of Champagne now. Things are a bit uncertain regarding money, but I'll send you what I can when I have full control of my finances. Unlike your scheming brother-in-law John, Philip is a man of his word, and honourable.'

'I see that. It was interesting to hear what Adèle had to say about Philip's intentions, wasn't it?'

'He aims to possess all on this side of the narrow sea. If John does not submit to Philip as his overlord, he will be chased back to England.'

'That does not surprise me. John is a rabbit snapping at the heels of a hunting dog,' I responded. 'What about me? Is King Philip likely to want two widowed Basque princesses in his land?'

'I've asked him to confirm that, but you may consider yourself to be under the protection of Philip of France, should you wish to remain in France.'

'That is very kind. Will I meet him?'

'In time, when he has brought John to heel.'

The next morning Blanca stirred first, on hearing the cries of her son. She moaned as she sat up.

'Are you still sore, my sweet?' I asked.

'Sore? Sore does not begin to describe it. My stomach feels empty, and my nipples hurt. I'm certain that young Thibaut has teeth; it is well that I share feeding duties with a wet nurse.'

'Oh, are you not producing milk?'

'Not as much as is required, sister. Let's rise; there are things to do. Acelin and Alaire!' she called, summoning her ladies of the bedchamber.

With Thibaut safely back in the arms of his wet nurse, Elise, the ladies dragged off the bedlinen and swept us off into Blanca's dressing chamber, from which we emerged well washed and dressed in some rather expensive gowns. I felt a little happier, and Blanca was managing better than I had thought.

Sitting in the great hall chewing bread, I watched as my household ladies chattered away with Blanca's ladies at a separate table. Mendia and his men were hosted by men of the Troyes guard in their barracks, and all was well.

'I did not know my husband for long, Berengaria,' said Blanca, shoving some sweetmeats about her platter. 'But he was kind and handsome, and I liked him well enough to see a future together.'

'I know, dear sister. Try to keep the happy times in your thoughts.'

'I will. What are you going to do now?'

'I'll stay with you for as long as you want.'

'Of course, I'd love that. But what about that place you are living in now? How will that fare without you?'

'Well enough. It is in good hands. There are too many places that in theory belong to me but in practice are being fought over by disagreeing kings. I'll wait and see what transpires.'

'Yes, a good plan. Why not move your belongings and your ladies' things up here? I've got some castles to spare and towns to organise. Your reputation for organising things precedes you.'

'Are you offering me paid employment?'

We laughed and I was pleased to see a little joy in her face again.

'If you want it. You can be a great influence, and I want my sister near me.'

We hugged, then I stood and beckoned over my people. When they were gathered, I told them of our decision.

'You now have an opportunity to improve your French; we're staying here for a while, until the land is at peace once more. Alazne, go and tell Mendia and see if some longer-term quarters can be found for him and his men.'

'We'll do that,' Blanca interjected. 'Alaire, find my steward and go with Lady Alazne to arrange things for the Navarrese giant and his men.'

'Father Walther, are you content to remain here for a while?' I asked my chaplain.

'Wherever you are, Your Highness,' he replied happily.

'Do you receive regular news about the situation regarding John?' I asked Blanca.

'We receive messengers every few days, so I can recount what I know. It will keep my mind off things until it's time for Thibaut's next feed. Let's send for the seneschal — he'll know more.'

Hubert, Blanca's seneschal, turned up as bidden and sat us down to recount the latest intelligence he had gathered about King John.

'John and Isabella went on tour to the north of England, so Hugh de Lusignan began to attack John's castles in Aquitaine and Poitou. He was aided by his uncle Geoffrey. Eleanor, in Fontevraud, was of course frightened and sent for John to come back.

'He brought his child bride with him, and when he landed he attacked all and any holdings of the Lusignans in Normandy, including those that had not been involved from the start. King Philip told him to desist, calmed down the Lusignans and demanded that John meet him on the Norman-French border. This happened, and their peace treaty was renewed. John was then entertained by Philip in Paris.'

'That's about as much as we understood in Beaufort. How long do you think this renewed treaty will last?' I asked.

'As long as it takes for John to squeeze more coin out of the English barons and recruit more men,' Blanca responded.

'By Holy Mary, Blanca, you've grown up since I left for Outremer,' I exclaimed. 'You've hardened, I see.'

'This world is tough, Berengaria; you know that to your cost.'

'I do, by my Lord, I do.'

Walther had profited from our stay in Troyes; he now had his own chamber and a family chapel to share with the resident priest, a luxury he was unused to.

'Is it not strange, Father Walther, how sometimes bad events have unexpected outcomes?' I asked him one evening.

'Aye, look at your travels from Outremer to Troyes; that was never on my list of pilgrimages.'

'But here we are, away from the bloody sands of Palestine, only to find ourselves in the ravaged fields of France. We are playthings for addled heads.'

'Be careful where you say that, Your Highness; there are some who resent your position. They'd rather see you married off again to some duke or count or other.'

'I know that. Some men will never accept that I can govern as well, if not better, than they.'

'Yes, their brains hang heavy betwixt their thighs.'

'Father Walther!' I could not imagine Edwin saying such a thing, but Walther often astonished me with the things he uttered.

'It is true.'

'Yes, some of it is true,' I conceded.

He looked at me before chuckling. 'I'm not used to being asked what it is that I want; I go where the good Lord sends me.'

'Or where you're sent by some bishop or other?'

He smiled.

'You must meet the young Thibaut, a count-in-waiting,' I said. 'Come with me.'

'Oh yes, a baby *comte*. I've not had that pleasure.'

As we walked, something occurred to me. 'Was it Archbishop Renaud who sent you to me?'

'You know him?'

'We bump into each other from time to time. Here we are, Father — my sister's privy antechamber. I'll go in if you would wait one moment.'

'Of course,' he replied, and I entered.

Blanca was positively glowing, I was pleased to see. 'Have you come to hold him?'

'I have.'

She gave him to me. Strange feelings immediately surfaced, and I took fright.

'I've got my chaplain outside,' I said. 'He would like to offer Thibaut a blessing.'

'Bring him in.' I gave the infant to Elise and called Father Walther.

'Ah,' he said. 'I see your eyes in him, Comtesse.'

'Thank you, Father. Is he not beautiful?' said Blanca.

'Very,' he replied, looking at the tiny creature. 'He has been baptised?'

'By the Bishop of Chartres, Father,' said Blanca. 'The one who married Thibaut and I.'

'Comtesse Blanca,' said Walther, 'I'm sorry that our first meeting should be in such sad circumstances.'

'Worry not, Father; we're making the best of it. I understand that you are my sister's rock. She speaks highly of you.'

'I'm not Saint Peter, but I do my best, Comtesse. May I bless your son?'

'Please do; he'll need all the help he can get.'

Walther's eyes lit up and he laughed. 'I believe that you understand the way of things, Comtesse Blanca. You shall do well, I'm certain.'

He pulled out a small phial from his garments and, dripping some water from it, he sprinkled it upon baby Thibaut's head and said a few words in Latin.

'There,' he said. 'That's my small gift to the child. Now, with your permission, Your Highness, I shall go and find your garrison chaplain and see how we can cooperate for the use of his chapel.'

We smiled at each other. The infant had inspired something strong within me. I thought that I might enjoy being here, witnessing the development of my new nephew — things were brightening up.

CHAPTER TWENTY-TWO

1202

John continued his reckless pursuit of the Lusignans until he was slowed by Philip.

'He is hell-bent, Your Highness; he has a chance but chooses to continue with his vendetta against Philip's relatives,' said Father Walther in a family conference at Troyes.

'Philip insisted that he bring the matter to court for a settlement,' added Blanca.

'But John prevaricates and has not yet agreed a date,' I said.

'How long will Philip wait for an answer, Comtesse?' Father Walther asked Blanca. 'As you are closer to him than any.'

'Not long. He has waited beyond Christmas and into spring. I fear I have heard rumours of an army being prepared.'

'That means a spring offensive. We are in March of 1202 now; there cannot be long to wait,' I said glumly.

'Your forecasts dismay me, if I may say so, Your Highness,' said Father Walther.

'They frighten me, too,' added Blanca. 'But what other conclusion can we come to?'

'Prepare your castle guards and close up your town defences. We must warn my castellan at Beaufort; the tides of war can surge wildly.'

It did not take long to draft a quick note to Denis and Paulin. Most of the French counties were swinging between John and Philip, or Arthur in reality, depending, it seemed, on the time of day. Eleanor still clung to life, brooding in Fontevraud, her dynasty fading before her eyes with my duchy still under her control.

On the twenty-fifth of March, both kings agreed to a conference, but neither would face the other, so it was held with proxy go-betweens.

The pace of our days varied a lot. I, and to my surprise Alazne and Pavot, turned quite maternal, and poor Elise had to prise little Thibaut out of their clutches. I suspected Blanca was quietly pleased, because the business of managing her county was quite demanding.

The regular news was not at all encouraging. Philip, being John's overlord, had summoned him to court in Paris to answer for his disobedience. John declined to appear, so he was tried in absentia and named 'a contumacious vassal', and his lands were declared forfeit.

'Philip has had enough and invaded Normandy, my sweet,' said Blanca. 'And he's going to knight young Arthur, betroth him to his daughter Marie and invest him with John's forfeit lands of Anjou, Maine, Touraine and Aquitaine, in which you have an interest, Berengaria. I am sorry. It gets worse: Philip has declared that he intends to keep Normandy for himself.'

I looked at Alazne; I could see that she now understood why we were still here in the Blois holdings. All my domains were but pieces in Philip and John's game of chess.

'I have been loath to forewarn you that this might be the outcome, Alazne. There was always a chance that some of my holdings might not survive John's misadventures,' I said.

'I'm sorry too, Your Highness,' she said, her eyes brimming with tears. 'You will always be my queen.'

'Oh, well, I feel a lot taller without the weight of all these duchies and counties on my shoulders,' I said, smiling weakly.

The time had now come for us to discuss my return to my duties in Beaufort. It was Blanca who broached the subject as we sat outside in the weak spring sun.

'What news from Beaufort, sister? They must be planting by now. Shouldn't you be there?'

'You've had enough of me?'

'No, but things need to be done, and I am well enough to act the comtesse now.'

'You are right. I need to leave for home one day, and it might as well be now if you're content.'

'I'll manage. You need to sit in your domain in case John decides to occupy it in this war of changing possessions.'

Two days later, I was hugged breathless as we made ready to mount up. Eventually I climbed onto my beast's back and, reluctantly letting go of Blanca's hand, I dug my heels in and we set off on the long journey to the valley of the Loire.

Ten days later, we were in Tours and dismounting in the bailey of a local lord's chateau when Mendia was approached by a messenger. He was clad in a tabard, which signified that he was travelling on behalf of someone important.

After a conversation Mendia came over to me and my ladies. 'That fellow yonder,' he said, 'is from King John. He reckons that he has been sent by the king to see Your Highness and has stopped off for the night in that hostelry across the road.'

'I suppose that we should see what he wants. Stay near, Mendia — does he pose a threat?'

'No, I'll squash him before he gets near you, Your Highness.'

Knowing that to be probable, I said, 'Summon him, if you please.'

'Over here!' Mendia shouted, beckoning the fellow towards us.

He seemed gentle enough and smiled as he approached. 'Queen Berengaria?' he asked.

'I am,' I replied.

'I am Peter of Canterbury. My lord King John has sent me with an invitation, Your Highness.'

He produced a scroll from within his tabard and offered it to me. The seal I recognised; it was John's and had previously appeared on letters containing many broken promises.

'Ladies, gather round. Father Walther, Mendia, we'll enjoy the words of the King of England together.' I perused the vellum, and as the words registered I exclaimed, 'Holy Mother!'

'What?' said Alazne.

'It's an invitation to meet him and his new queen at Chinon, where they are lodged for now.'

'Where is Chinon?' asked Isabeau.

'It's a diversion north — about the same distance as Beaufort,' answered Father Walther.

'Is it a trap?' asked Mendia.

'I understand that His Highness would like to discuss Aquitaine, Your Highness,' said Peter of Canterbury.

'His mother is not yet in her grave, and he is *discussing* her most precious holding,' growled my good priest.

'Then we shall divert and listen. Besides, I want to meet this queen of his.'

The following morning, we changed direction and headed for the town of Chinon.

Mendia exclaimed in Basque when the outline of castle Chinon came into view. I too gazed in surprise at the mighty citadel atop its ridge above the town.

'We'll not enter there without an invitation, Your Highness,' added Father Walther.

'We'll not get out without one either,' said Alazne.

'Oh well, trust in God. Off we go,' I said, with more confidence than I felt.

The climb up to the ridge would have been defence enough, but we also needed to cross dry moats and retractable bridges to gain access to the inner sanctum — wherein stood John and his queen, waiting for us to appear.

Using the dismounting platform provided, I crossed to the stairway to be met by John at the foot. Isabella held back at the top, seemingly uncertain.

'Berengaria, we are pleased that you could come. My commiserations for your sister's loss.'

'Thank you, John. You are most kind. I shall relay that to Blanca.' I glanced over his shoulder. Isabella did indeed seem very young and very beautiful, with startling blue eyes and golden hair, her slim body clothed in white with gold trim.

John turned and beckoned Isabella down, and as she descended the last step I saw that she was taller than I. She curtsied before me, and I noticed that she was also taller than John.

'Madam,' she said, 'welcome to Chinon.'

'Queen Isabella. No need for the "madam"; Berengaria will suffice. Thank you for the invitation.'

'You have the freedom of both the castle and town for as long as you wish. My brother liked it here,' John said.

'I've heard it mentioned. Thank you, King John and Queen Isabella. We have much to talk about.'

'Thank you ... Berengaria.' She hesitated as she tested the protocol, then held out a hand. I took it and found that her grasp was warm, and close up with a smile on her face she was even more beautiful than from a distance.

John waved at his seneschal, bowed and directed us to follow him. I walked up the steps side by side with Isabella, closely followed by my entourage.

'Your quarters are ready, Berengaria. How many are in your retinue? They shall be made comfortable for as long as you wish to stay.'

I directed my reply to the seneschal marching into the great hall before us, surprised by the warmth of John and Isabella's reception.

I didn't need to wait long for John's intentions to reveal themselves. The questioning started at breakfast the following day. His early morning conversation revolved around the French court and King Philip. It was all nicely disguised, but I could tell that he was intelligence-gathering.

As soon as I left John's privy hall, I gathered my court around me. The place was big enough to find a quiet part of a courtyard, so we huddled together and I began to question them.

Were questions being asked about Philip? Everyone confirmed that this was the case. We were involuntary recruits to John's cause.

'Should we leave now, Your Highness?' asked Mendia, not pleased at being used as a spy.

'No,' I replied. 'I have given it some thought: we can turn this to our advantage and do some intelligence-collecting of our own.'

'My word, Your Highness,' chuckled Alazne, 'you have learned a lot since we returned from Outremer. You are a player in a big game — in the lists of diplomatic jousting.'

'The Plantagenet ways have sharpened my skills. Listen and smile but reveal naught. You know nothing of value. Only concern yourselves with women's things: that's all you are interested in when you talk with the ladies of Isabella's court. Mendia, ensure that your men understand.'

'How long shall we stay, Your Highness?' asked Pavot.

'That depends. Father Walther, write to Beaufort and enquire each week about the planting, and ask how the alms houses and the hospital are managing. I will work on the Queen of England; I want to know what the King of England talks about in the bedchamber.'

As it transpired Isabella was an empty vessel when it came to politics, though she gladly listened to tales of babies and childbirth. She seemed to echo John's view of the Lusignans, which was not complimentary.

Letters from Beaufort told of planting completed, hospitals managing, and no hostilities in the area. Since I wanted to watch John close up, we remained at the castle.

My people soon became irritated by John's never-ending complaints about treachery and how much wars cost. I resolved to be on the road as soon as possible, but my hand was played for me.

One morning, John was absent at Prime.

'He's gone north to see to the defence of some castles in Normandy. King Philip has demanded that they are handed over to him,' said a dishevelled Isabella, evidently straight out of bed.

'I thought that all of Normandy had fallen to Philip,' I replied.

'John has had some success; he only needs money from England to push Philip back.'

My money, I thought, *or some of it*. At least the girl understood something of the conundrum of strife: no money, no war.

'Did he say when he would return, Isabella?'

'He didn't discuss it. He just comes and goes when he chooses.'

'Has he taken his soldiers with him?'

'I don't know. Why?'

'It would be useful to know if we are vulnerable to attack by the Lusignans, dear Isabella.'

'Oh, I suppose I could go and ask.'

'Ask whom?'

Isabella looked at me vacantly; this was too complicated for so young a queen.

'Steward,' I called across the hall, 'send for Captain Mendia.'

'Your Highness,' he replied as Mendia stomped in unbidden.

'Your Highness, the castle is nearly empty. The garrison has mostly left. There's a sergeant and about twenty men; we can only man the main gate.'

'John said something about leaving but I was nearly asleep. Do you think that we will be attacked?' Isabella, it seemed, had finally recognised our position.

'Get that sergeant over here, Mendia. There's some organising to do.'

Sergeant Mathew of London, when he appeared, was fierce enough and seemed competent. He too was surprised that I had not been briefed before John left.

'What were your orders, Sergeant?' I asked.

'To keep Her Highness safe... Your Highness. Are you in command, or is Queen Isabella?'

I looked across at Isabella, who was standing open-mouthed and wringing her hands. 'Whom would you prefer?' I asked.

'Er, what are your orders, Your Highness?'

'Listen to Captain Mendia and work together. Do you know where King John is?'

'He's gone north to Normandy. That's all I know.'

'Are you in communication?'

'He said that a messenger would be sent now and again.'

'I see. When the first one arrives, I'll be sending the king a message of my own. Captain Mendia, come and see me when your arrangements are agreed. I'll be in the king's hall.'

As I gathered my people in the hall for something to eat, it gradually dawned on me what John had left behind for me to sort out — the safety of his queen. I had become her protector.

'Dear Lord, the man's an idiot,' I gasped as I slammed down a knife I had been cutting into my bread with.

'Your Highness?' Father Walther sat up straight and my ladies stopped eating.

I looked at Isabella. 'When will your husband return, Isabella?'

Poking at a piece of cheese, she found it hard to meet my gaze and then burst into tears.

Isabeau put an arm around her shoulders to comfort her.

'Are you thinking what I am thinking, Your Highness?' asked Father Walther.

'Probably. Where is Mendia?'

'Give him time; he'll be a while. There is much to do.'

Then the air was rent by screeches of anger: Isabella was on her feet, and the platter in front of her went flying as she screamed her displeasure.

'That man, he only wants me for one thing! I'm supposed to sit here while he cavorts around the land, and I'd wager he has company in his bed every night while I lie alone. And as for being the queen, there are two of them ahead of me before I'll ever see any domains to my name!' Here she glared at me before stomping out of the hall, her companions galloping after her. She just avoided the towering figure of Mendia as he appeared in the doorway.

'What in God's name?' he asked as Isabella dashed past him.

'You have just missed the Queen of England, Captain Mendia,' said Alazne, laughing.

'What shall we do?' asked Isabeau.

'Nothing,' I said. 'Father Walther, can you go to her when she has calmed down and remind her of the public view that a queen must present. Then I will reason with the girl — she is very young.'

He nodded, 'God has authority in the presence of His priests. She will listen to reason, Your Highness.'

'She will, or she will find herself alone in this cold castle. Mendia, what have you to tell me?' I motioned for him to sit and had a goblet of wine offered to him.

'Your Highness, we have around thirty fit men-at-arms between ourselves and Sergeant Mathew's men. I have split them into three parts and each part shall take one watch throughout the dark hours and one watch during the day. We have no hope of manning the whole perimeter as it is too long; however, as we are on a ridge, the side and rear walls are fairly secure. The main gate will be our focus and the drawbridge and portcullis will be closed at all times, unless we have authorised visitors. The watch will send out patrols along the battlements at regular intervals. We cannot do much more.'

'Right, good. Can we women do ought to help?'

'Aye, I have borrowed some of the kitchen servants from the steward to help on the walls, and the steward was not best pleased. So he would welcome assistance in the kitchens, and the guards on the wall will need food and water taken to them at intervals.'

'I will see to it. Anything else?'

'Yes, Your Highness.' He looked at Father Walther. 'Pray. Pray for us, Father, that we receive no unwelcome visitors.'

So that was it: thirty men and a dozen women were to defend a stronghold as big as a town. *Would that God hears our prayers*, I thought.

CHAPTER TWENTY-THREE

On the third day of John's absence, the prayed-against visitors presented themselves before the secured gate.

A soldier came running into the hall, calling out as he saw me and heading in my direction. My ladies stood up in alarm and Isabella's face paled.

'Visitors, Your Highness. The captain asks if you can attend him.'

'Yes. Stay here, Isabella, until I find out who calls on us.'

'This is my castle, Berengaria. I will go and see.' And with those unwise words, she trotted off in the direction of the gate.

'She will have some difficulty in convincing any Lusignan that she is not here,' said Father Walther.

'Quite. I will go. Stay here, ladies,' I commanded. No one moved, so I left in the company of the startled man-at-arms.

There was an internal stairway winding up to the battlement of the tower, and it took a while to climb. I emerged to find Mendia and Isabella locked in angry confrontation.

'Don't show yourself. It will not be safe,' growled Mendia.

'I am the queen! Stand aside, lump.'

'You're not my queen. Get back inside. Berengaria, get this girl out of my way.'

The conversations with Isabella that Father Walther and I had attempted only three days ago had come to naught. She understood nothing of her own safety. If the Lusignans discovered that she was in this castle almost unprotected, they would turn up at the gate in great numbers — and I would become a second valuable hostage.

Reaching up to place my hands on her shoulders, I fixed my gaze on the wilful girl. Then, speaking slowly and without passion, I put it to her in simple terms.

'Do you want to be entertained by the Lusignans? Old Hugh will be very pleased to see you in his great hall. There you will be encouraged to explain in public why you broke your betrothal to his son. Is that the fate you seek?'

Her eyes began to lose their wildness and I felt her relax as my words took hold.

'How do you know who is there?' she asked, nodding towards the parapet. Although we could not be seen through the crenels unless we looked over, I did not want anyone on the ground to catch a glimpse of us.

'I don't know, but it is not John, that's for sure. Mendia,' I said quietly, 'call down and see what they want. I'll listen from here.'

He grunted and crossed the battlement to thrust his head into the gap between the merlons. 'What?' he called.

'Hospitality and some food, if you please,' came the response from the ground.

'Who are you?'

'A patrol of Ralph de Lusignan's.'

'We're full. Go away.'

'That's rude. Why are you full?'

'King John is in residence. Away with you.'

There was a silence, and I heard muttering. Then the voice replied, 'John is in Normandy.'

'He's back.'

'Liar. Is Isabella in there?'

'I know of no Isabellas.'

'What's your name?'

'Captain No-man.'

'You talk oddly. Are you foreign?'

'Not as foreign as you. Now leave.'

I looked along the gate battlements. Every man we had was lined up with a weapon pointed outward. It occurred to me that this was what Richard had faced when that well-aimed crossbow bolt had ended his life, so it was rather comforting to be on this side of the hostilities.

'I think that you may be from the south, Captain No-man. We'll find somewhere else for the night, but we may return. *Au revoir, Kapitaina Ez.*'

My stomach churned as the man on the ground addressed Mendia in Basque; it seemed he had recognised my captain's accent. If he knew there was a Basque captain in here, it would not take him long to work out who was being protected.

I put a warning hand over Isabella's mouth and shoved her towards the stairs. This time she cooperated. This castle was now a cage.

To add to the gloom we felt, it had begun to rain. I entered the stairway behind Isabella, and Mendia stomped behind us until we reached the guard chamber at the bottom.

'They know that we are here, Mendia.'

'Yes, Your Highness. They've cleared off now — probably gone for reinforcements.'

'We should leave immediately — go back to Beaufort before they return.'

'Agreed. I'll get our men ready if you will prepare the ladies. We should let Sergeant Mathew choose his action.'

'His duty is to guard this castle.'

'The queen, more like.'

'Then let him choose. The castle is an empty shell without people in it,' I said.

I was fuming. John had dumped the well-being of his queen onto me, and I could not leave her to become a bargaining tool for the Lusignans.

Mendia was working on a plan. 'I'll send some scouts into the town to make certain that Ralph has left no soldiers behind,' he said.

'Good. We need to travel light. Hear that, Isabella? No pack horses — take only what you need and can be carried on your horse.'

Isabella nodded. She was clearly frightened now and ready to do as I ordered.

The hall fell silent as I entered. My frustrations must have shown, but I had no time for detailed explanations. Isabella went to sit with her ladies. I hoped she would be silent.

'We are leaving tonight in the dark. Make your clothing fit for the thirty-five-mile ride along the valley to Beaufort, and take no possessions that you cannot carry on your horse. Questions?'

'Why, Your Highness?' asked Isabeau.

'We believe that the Lusignans have discovered that John has left his queen here. She is in danger.'

Mendia entered and spoke quietly to me. 'The steward has informed me that there is a track along the foot of the castle's rear wall then through the woods, so that we need not go near the town. If it continues to rain it will aid us, as any patrols will be unsighted and the noise of the rain will mask our progress, and that path will point us in the direction of Beaufort.'

'Very well. We will eat at dusk and then depart. Alazne and Pavot, show the royal ladies how to pull up their gowns between their legs and be ready to ride swiftly should it become necessary.'

Alazne and Pavot giggled and Isabeau looked askance. During our crusading journeys, we had become used to dressing in pants and short kirtles, something not at all usual for women of the courts in Europe. The trick to wearing gowns astride a horse was to reach through the legs and grasp the bottom of the kirtle, pull it through and secure the top into a belt, turning the skirt into pantaloons and making it possible to ride without fear of falling off. The ladies could amuse themselves practising that while I went into detailed discussions with Father Walther, Sergeant Mathew and Captain Mendia.

When we were certain that all aspects of our projected journey were complete, I asked Father Walter to write to John. I was going to tell him exactly what I thought of being a nurse to his queen, who was his responsibility, not mine. And I'd let him know that if he wanted her back, he could come and reclaim her from Beaufort.

'Is this strong enough, Your Highness?' asked Walther, reading through the script. 'He may not understand the meaning,' he added with a gleam in his eye.

'It'll do. Get it sent with one of Sergeant Mathew's messengers once they know where he is.'

It had been dark for a while when we gathered in the inner bailey, lit by the battlement braziers. All was to appear normal from outside.

'Gather round,' said Mendia quietly, and we all crowded near him. 'It is time. You have been briefed, so remember your part. My scouts will go first, then six of my men and then the main body, Their Highnesses, their ladies and Father Walther. Finally, bringing up the rear, there will be six more of my soldiers. We will lead the horses until we're down on the track, where we will mount and make haste to Beaufort.'

He waited for a moment then gave the order quietly for his scouts to move out, and I took a firm grasp on my mount's reins and followed along as ordered.

It rained steadily, but the scratches of the horses' hooves on the stony ground along the tower walls, the rustle of clothing and the splodges of boots in the mud all sounded as if they would be heard a mile away — and not everyone could resist a cough or a curse as they slipped on the treacherous ground.

I was relieved to reach the bottom of the gradient and firm ground. I tried to hold the reins and pull up my skirt without success, as the palfrey was skittish, but a firm man's hand came out of the dark and took the reins from my grasp as I struggled with my kirtle. I was soon ready and tried to mount, but the beast was too high. The same hand came out of the dark once more, and I was propelled upwards into the saddle. We were soon trotting off into the dark and away from Castle Chinon.

For the rest of the night we ambled in woodland along the riverbank until daybreak, then broke into a trot now and again to ward off the cold and wetness. Relief came as the sun rose and we began to steam. We watched the fields and vineyards begin to fill with peasants and returned their waves. Our procession stopped at an occasional hostelry for wine or beer, then regretted it a few miles later as bushes were sought to ease the discomfort. Mendia had his usual string of mounts and changed them at regular intervals, the poor beasts suffering under his weight, and we arrived at Beaufort in the middle of the afternoon.

'It's the queen!' called out the sentry atop the gatehouse. 'Open the gates. Sergeant Martin, the queen is back.'

The castle had been well guarded, and the sentries were alert; I thought to reward them when we had settled in. But now I needed to pay attention to the outpouring of my household staff from the great hall and other doorways to greet me.

'Your Highness, welcome back.' It was Castellan Denis, all of a flutter.

'Denis, we ladies need a soft bed and a flagon of wine. And see to Captain Mendia's men and horses. If we sleep past dusk, make a noise and we'll come down for supper — which your cooks will have prepared, I am thinking.'

'My very thoughts, Your Highness. Steward Oliver is working on it as we speak. Who's that?' He had caught sight of the delectable Isabella.

'That, Denis, is the latest addition to the list of Queens of England. Her name is Isabella, and she is married to King John and shall be treated as such.'

'Oh! And a privy chamber?'

'Just so. Do your best.'

'Is she going to dismount?'

Looking across I could see her sitting tight, inspecting my tiny bailey.

'Come inside, Isabella. We're here,' I called.

Her reply was a sniff and an order to one of her ladies to get her down.

'I want to know everything about the activities in my domain since my absence,' I said to Denis.

'Let's to the hall, Your Highness. I'll find Ander, Oliver, and the sergeants of the guard. Your questions shall be answered.'

'Good. Captain Mendia, when you've finished with the men and horses, come and join me.'

He waved acknowledgement, so I set off up the steps.

Isabella came in and sat apart with her ladies to watch as I took a goblet of wine and got ready to listen to my household reports.

They were interesting at first and told a tale of competent management of accounts, fields, hospital, and security. But the wine and the long day of travel brought weariness, until Alazne whispered in my ear, 'Your eyes are closing, Your Highness. Time to retire.'

Not objecting, I managed to say to Denis, 'That'll do for now. Wake me for supper, if you please.' Then, led by Alazne, I climbed up the stairs to my bedchamber, where she insisted I remove my damp clothing before I climbed into bed.

I awoke with my head full of tasks and began searching for dry clothing.

Isabeau ambled in. 'Can I help, Your Highness?' she asked sleepily. 'We took your clothing down to the kitchen to dry. I'll go and fetch it.'

'Don't bother,' I said. 'My clothes chests are in the next chamber. Dig something out for me — heaven knows there's enough.'

Soon I was clothed and surrounded by my ladies, ready for Prime. Father Walther was up and waiting in my chapel. Isabella was not, so I sent Alazne to search her out. She did not appear until mid-morning, when I was in the hall receiving requests and issuing instructions — she did not look happy.

'Isabella, good morrow,' I said.

'*Madame.* How long are we staying in this...?' She gazed around my hall.

'Until it is safe for you to return to Chinon, or until your husband sends for you.'

'I'm hungry.'

I motioned for Steward Oliver to attend to her and resumed my discussions.

'Right,' I said to the local leaders, 'as soon as the ground dries out, we'll set seed and the like. How many of my men could you use to help?'

My clerks, Simon and Garcia, scribbled down my words and the responses.

John's letter came a few weeks later, instructing me to send Isabella to Caen. Caen was in Normandy and John must have had it secure, else he would not have wanted her there. It was close by the sea; perhaps he was going to flee across to England and there play the king. I cared not and sent for Mendia.

'Would you care to visit Normandy, Captain Mendia? You can take the Queen of England with you and hand her over to her king.'

A great guffaw shook the ceiling of my solar. 'Gladly, Your Highness. That'll make a lot more space around here, and it'll be a lot quieter.'

After two days he was ready, and Isabella was on her horse with forty men surrounding her. I waved goodbye to her and returned to my business of the day.

Our peace ended in late July. Father Walther dashed into my solar with an announcement.

'Your Highness, there are scouts from King John's army. One is in the great hall, waiting to see you.'

All needles and wool dropped, my ladies and I hurried down the stairs and across the courtyard to find the hall full of curious folk. A way was cleared for us, and we sat down in a semi-circle of chairs facing a rather harassed-looking and dusty rider. He was in the colours of England, so it must have been important.

He introduced himself as Alfred of Winchester.

'Speak, Alfred. Is King John near?'

'Yes, Your Highness. I am but three miles before him.'

'To where is he bound?'

'South, towards Poitiers. Queen Eleanor is in trouble.'

'Good Lord, at her age. Steward Oliver, some wine for Alfred.'

'I have two companions outside, Your Highness.'

'I'll see to it, Your Highness,' called Oliver on his way out.

Soon Alfred had by him a flagon of wine and a goblet, from which he took a sip before relating his tale.

'Your Highness, I am to inform you of the following events. It concerns Arthur of Brittany and the Lusignans. As you are aware, several lands to the south are rightfully Arthur's, as decreed by King Philip. Queen Eleanor had heard that Arthur, aided by the Lusignans, was going to seize the Angevin holdings in Poitou, and she set off from Fontevraud to frustrate him. Arthur is now a fifteen-year-old knight and, encouraged by the gift of two hundred cavalry from Philip, he set off to capture the queen on the road between Fontevraud and Poitiers.'

I was shocked. 'But Eleanor is his grandmother.'

'Indeed, Your Highness. The queen was able to take refuge in a ruined castle named Mirebeau, near Poitiers. My king will ride there to rescue her.' Alfred paused as we heard a tumult in the yard. 'John is here, Your Highness,' he said, plonking his goblet on the table as he quickly bowed and left. I followed, pulling up my skirts as we all rushed to see John.

'Berengaria!' called the sweat-drenched king as he slid off his mount. 'You've heard?'

'I have. What possessed young Arthur to hunt for his grandmother?'

'Philip, always Philip — no loyalty to his servants.'

I thought that remark a bit odd coming from John, himself a traitor to his brother and full of devious doings. *Reap as you sow* crossed my mind, but I stayed silent.

'With your permission, Berengaria, we'll rest the horses and my men and soon be on our way.'

'Of course. How many are you?'

'About fifty. We're short of horses, so that's all I could muster.'

'And you set off from…?'

'Le Mans, with nearly one hundred miles to cover.'

'But you are only halfway there.' I was amazed; they must have been flogging their horses. 'Mendia, can we swap some horses for the king?'

'Aye, Your Highness, but not fifty.'

'See what you can do.'

After an hour, John's sweating and tired steeds had been swapped with those in my stables and he was ready to get off once more.

'I forgot to say, Berengaria: thank you for looking after Isabella,' he said. 'We are most grateful.'

'My pleasure,' I lied, and waved him goodbye.

'Ah, those poor horses,' said Isabeau.

'You could go to the stables and help feed and water them,' I said.

She was quickly followed by my other companions, which gave me time to think.

'Father Walther, what should I do? I feel helpless here. What if Eleanor is harmed? There'll be the devil to pay.'

'If I'm following this properly, Eleanor is in danger from her own grandson and John is off to rescue the lady. What could transpire?'

'Those who support the Lusignans might not like John, but they will not tolerate any harm to Eleanor, and neither will King Philip. He actually admires her, although her son is a different creature.'

'Mmm. Do you think that Mother Church should intervene?'

'I think that the Holy Father should take an interest. But how?'

'Let's go to Fontevraud. It's closer to Poitiers and the abbess will have a view.'

'I agree. I'll see if Mendia can make ready some of John's horses, and we'll be off in the morning.'

CHAPTER TWENTY-FOUR

We arrived in Fontevraud to find a turbulent scene. The first things we saw were the banners of England: John's army was there.

'Have they not rescued Eleanor?' I gasped as we stopped to take in the view.

'We'll know soon enough,' said Mendia, closing in on me as two riders galloped towards us.

'Halt!' they shouted. 'Who are you?'

'Queen Dowager of England, Berengaria.'

'There's two of them here now,' said one of the riders.

'We should tell the king,' said the other, and they turned and galloped back to their lines.

'I think that they forgot to say "Welcome, Your Highness", Your Highness,' said Father Walther.

'At least we know where Queen Eleanor is. Should we move in further, Your Highness?' asked Mendia.

'Yes; Queens of England should stick together. Let's go and find the other one; she must have a tale to tell.'

We entered the abbey grounds and were conducted to the cloister where Abbess Mathilde was sitting quietly. She rose as I approached with my ladies, my men having been left outside.

'Berengaria, welcome.'

'Mathilde, thank you. Sad times.'

'Sad indeed when a grandson attacks his grandmother. Sit and I'll tell you what I know.'

'Where is Eleanor?'

'Sleeping. I fear that such misadventures are beyond endurance for one of such an age.'

'I see. What can you tell us?'

We settled down and Mathilde began Eleanor's tale.

'Eleanor had received word that the Lusignans, together with young Arthur, were plotting to seize Poitiers and the county of Poitou, and she thought that if she sat in Poitiers it would deter them. Unfortunately that treacherous grandson of hers came across her as she rode towards the town, and she took refuge in the ruins of Mirebeau castle, resisting arrest. One messenger escaped and found King John in Le Mans. Yesterday, the king arrived before daybreak and so surprised Arthur and the Lusignans that they were overwhelmed at breakfast, and many were killed or taken prisoner.

'The attack was led by William des Roches. He caught Arthur, who was then legitimately William's hostage, but he wanted some assurances from John that the lad would not be harmed if he handed him over.'

'A King John promise?' I asked sceptically.

'Indeed. It included young Arthur and the Lusignans, Hugh and Geoffrey. Eleanor was freed unharmed.'

There were some sympathetic murmurings for Eleanor, now eighty years old. But not many expressed pleasure at the outcome. This was indeed a success for John and a disaster for Philip.

'So what about Arthur, Richard's nominee to succeed him?' I mused.

'With John's talons about his neck, what are the odds that Arthur will survive?' added Alazne.

'The Church and all of Europe is watching,' said Mathilde uneasily.

'That means naught to a tyrant, dear Abbess. We must pray for Arthur and hope that Philip can prise him out of John's grasp. May we wait to see Eleanor?' I asked.

'Of course. I'll arrange it for when she has recovered. You may bump into John if you venture outside.'

'I'm anticipating that. I have some thoughts to share with the king.'

She laughed. 'It's a pity that Isabella is not here; a trinity of queens would be a rare sight.'

'Yes, and two too many for John, I'll wager.'

Abbess Mathilde came to me the following day, after I'd spent the night in a chilly and empty nun's cell, and conducted me to where Eleanor was resting in her privy quarters.

I was shocked. The most powerful woman in Europe had been reduced to a wrinkled shell.

'Madam,' I said, 'I hear that you have been out adventuring.'

'Oh, Berengaria,' she croaked, 'I fear that it might have been my final sally forth.'

'Ah well, you're safe now.'

'Thanks to John. You've heard about John's bravery?'

I had heard no such thing, but I nodded anyway. 'I've met Isabella, you know. She stayed with me at Beaufort.'

'Ah, Isabella. Every inch a queen, wouldn't you say, Berengaria? Such a pity my Richard got himself killed, else that would have been you.'

I did not know how to answer, so I decided it was time to leave. I looked at Mathilde for support, and she gave it immediately.

'Do not task Her Highness with too much chatter now, Berengaria. It's time for her to take a little rest.'

I agreed. I took Eleanor's wrinkled hand and kissed it. 'Goodbye, Mother.'

Mathilde and I walked to the gate.

'That may well be the last time I see her,' I said.

'Do not despair, Berengaria. I've seen worse recover, with the right amount of care and prayer.'

We embraced and I left the abbey.

John was waiting outside the wall and seemed somewhat distracted. 'You've seen Mother,' he said. 'We're leaving now.'

'We are too. Write to me now and then, and keep that beautiful queen of yours safe. Do not let her suffer the same fate as your mother, John.'

'No, quite.' He needed a discreet shove from one of his men to climb into his horse's saddle, and he waved me goodbye from his precarious position.

'Mendia!' I called and turned to find myself staring up at him. 'Let's return to Beaufort, Captain.'

Expectations that John would soon be forced back to England proved over-optimistic. The most important lords and men whom he had captured at Mirebeau were treated as prisoners and scattered around in chains to various castles, with some sent over to England to await their fate. William des Roches appealed to John to let him keep hold of Arthur, but even though John agreed he never did let go of Richard's nominated successor, and the lad ended up in Falaise Castle in Normandy — most of which county John had reclaimed.

John's victory over the Lusignans gave a new impetus to his supporters, and it seemed it was Philip who would have to concede ground. Then it became a game of rapidly changing fortunes on the battlefields of France. As far as England was concerned it was the purse whence the wealth to wage war came from. Any notion that I entertained of John sending me my portion of that wealth was dashed when he set about scraping yet more money from his barons to fund his efforts to recover the lands he'd lost to Philip.

The loss of Aquitaine, his mother's personal possession, or Normandy — which was most precious to his barons, who had many holdings there — would be most egregious if Philip were to seize them.

I decided to go once more to Troyes to see how Blanca was managing her county.

Since she had been receiving reports, she already knew of my problems.

'You'll not be receiving any money from John, not while his pleas for coin to pay for another war are falling on deaf ears, Berengaria.'

'No, of that I am sure. This new treaty they have signed is set for two years, is it not?'

'Or until John finds the money — Philip knows that. Two years of peace are the most he expects.'

'I won't write again to John,' I said. 'As things are, it would be a waste of time and I will risk annoying him for when the time is right to try and recover my lost income.'

'Stay here with me; you can be my mentor in the organising of things.'

I agreed, and we both looked forward to a bit of peace.

In September, Father Walther came to me with some news.

'I believe that you know of someone named the Cypriot princess, Your Highness.'

'Eirini — what now?' I asked. I had heard that a little while after Joan's death, Eirini had become Raymond of Toulouse's fifth wife. 'I thought we'd finished with that preening beauty.'

'Count Raymond has. She's run off with a young nobleman, Thierry of Flanders, and they headed off to Cyprus. She intended to claim back the island but received no support, and they continued to Armenia. She has family connections there, I believe.'

'Cyprus? Armenia? Holy Mother!' I thought for a moment before it came to me. 'She tried to reclaim her father's kingdom?'

'Of course,' said Father Walther.

'Ah, it is difficult to feel any sympathy for old Raymond. He used a few women in his life, but to be outdone by one so young? He must feel bitter.'

The days went by pleasantly enough. Letters from Beaufort told of a successful harvest, but as always funds for the hospital were tight, and I mentioned the fact in passing to Blanca. She was, of course, fully engaged with the welfare of young Thibaut, now eighteen months old and exercising his lungs at all hours of the day and night.

'You should tell me about these things, sister,' scolded Blanca one day as I studied Ander's accounts. 'We need to talk. I have been asked to see what your intentions are.'

'Who is interested?'

'Philip. He admires you greatly, as we all do — the one shining star in the Plantagenet sky.'

'The Plantagenet sky seems to consist mostly of thunderclouds.'

'Quite. Your work in Poitiers and Beaufort is much admired, and there are those who wonder which side of the narrow sea you see your future in.'

'I have no intention of getting my feet wet. England does not need me, and there is work to do here. Is Philip going to send me away?'

Blanca put her arms around me and planted a kiss on my cheek. 'Silly sister, quite the reverse. He wants to keep you and help with your work.'

'And annoy John, I suppose.'

She laughed.

'I expect that it would sit well in Rome, Philip giving me what John has not.'

'Yes, but would it sit well with you, Berengaria?'

'Would it be selfish of me to consider it?'

'My advice? Consider it — you deserve more than has been given.'

Did I want to leave this tangled mess and return home to Navarre rejected, or was there merit in continuing my work for the unprivileged and wounded Christians here in Philip's realm?

'I'll give it some thought,' I replied eventually.

Somewhat settled, before the end of the year I managed a visit to Beaufort to deliver funds from Blanca. With Ander's help, I set the accounts for the following year, then travelled back to Troyes for Christmas.

A messenger arrived early in December with news of John's latest attempts at diplomacy. He'd had Hugh de Lusignan brought to him at Caen to see if some form of peace could be negotiated, although the Bretons were still angry at the imprisonment of Arthur. John also had Isabella brought back to Chinon, a risky indulgence as again it left his queen vulnerable to capture.

'It seems that Isabella's obvious attractions are more important to John than her safety,' I said.

'I think we have had enough of John's exploits, Berengaria,' said Blanca, slapping the table. 'Let's forget about your troublesome brother-in-law and concentrate on the good Jesus.'

CHAPTER TWENTY-FIVE

1204

Important news came in March of 1204, while I was with Blanca.

'King Philip would like to see you, sister.'

'At last. What does he want?'

'He says to meet him in Le Mans, and he will tell you.'

'Really, Le Mans?' I began to hope; I had wanted to go there for a while, but John had always been in the way. Now, with Rouen, the most important city in all of Normandy threatened, the way was clear for me to test how far I could go in claiming some of my dower lands. The county of Maine seemed a good place to begin. William the Conqueror must have been turning in his grave at such an egregious blow to Norman pride as John's losses mounted.

'Come on, Blanca — you must know more.'

'The king wants you to be secure and happy, and I know that you wanted to be in Maine one day, and...'

'And?'

'And he thinks that having you installed in one of your rightful counties — though he will be your overlord, of course — will further establish his superiority over John. Quite amusing, don't you think, the former Queen of England in France's care? You don't have to go, but it would be nice. You can move in if you sign a disclaimer.'

'A what?'

'He knows that you have been looking around for somewhere to settle, including Angevin Loches, but he has plans there. So if you would sign a document stating that Loches is not in your plans, it would please him greatly ... and it would aid your purpose if you wanted to move to Le Mans.'

'I see. I knew not that I had anything with which to bargain.'

'You might have more to bargain with than you think.' Blanca embraced me and added quietly, 'I am but a messenger, sent to test your reaction. You should think it through. It may be your only opportunity to repair some of the damage done by John — to move a dowager queen of the English into Le Mans.'

The two hundred miles to Le Mans from Troyes passed quickly enough. I only took certain people, my household now being too big for a foray into the unknown.

With the knight Paulin leading, followed by his squire flying the banner of Navarre, Mendia was immediately to my left. Alazne and Pavot were behind, flanked by Sergeants Martin and Pierre flying the banners of Poitou and Maine. They were followed by a wagon containing some of my most precious gowns, which was guarded by Isabeau and Cateline. We were all trailed by a troop of a dozen horsemen. I felt quite closeted by them as we rode towards the old Roman walls of Le Mans. My escort rode much closer here than on the rest of the journey, but I supposed they wanted to show that their landless queen was as well protected as any other.

A pair of horsemen galloped out from the main gate, looked at us and then returned. Soon, figures began to line the walls and gatehouse.

'We are expected, Your Highness.' Mendia turned and called back, 'Smarten up, men! We shall own this place before long.'

Two columns of men, one on either side of the road, ran out from under the gatehouse and lined up, ready to receive us as we entered the city.

Inside the gate a trio of horsemen were waiting, horses all fully caparisoned in the emblems of France and Le Mans. They led us towards a palatial building, and outside more troops were drawn up. We came to a halt beside a box that had been put out to help me dismount. Whoever had arranged this was well organised.

An aged churchman shuffled forward. 'Your Highness,' he croaked, holding out a hand while supported by two priests, 'I am Hamelin, Bishop of Le Mans. Welcome, Your Highness.'

'Your Eminence,' I said gently, and brushed my lips on his ring.

His supporters held him firmly and one explained, 'His Eminence rarely emerges from his cathedral, but he did so want to greet you himself. It is not often one meets a Queen of England.' Looking down at Hamelin, he said loudly into his ear, 'Her Highness thanks you, Your Eminence. Shall we retire now?'

The bishop nodded, waved a hand in my direction and was led off into the throng of clergy, who were there to support him and take a look at me, I supposed.

Someone else appeared before me, bowing. 'I am Herbert de Tucé, Your Highness. On behalf of our citizens, may I welcome you to Le Mans?'

'Monsieur de Tucé,' I responded, a bit puzzled. 'Thank you.' I looked him over: he was well dressed and well built — probably a merchant with money. As a local, he might be useful. 'How does it come about that it is you who welcomes me?'

'Oh, I received a letter from Her Grace the Comtesse de Champagne, inviting me to put myself forward. I am in some respects a citizen of standing in Le Mans.'

'I see. She said nothing to me. But sisters…'

'Can be jesters?' he proposed.

'*Are* jesters,' I answered. I liked this fellow immediately.

We stood for a moment, surrounded by an expectant crowd. Someone needed to speak. I looked up at the grand building before me.

'This is…?' I said, waving a hand at the edifice.

'The palace of the Plantagenets — home of the counts of Maine and Anjou since before the time of Geoffrey the Fair and Empress Matilda, the parents of King Henry II of England. Henry II, the father of King Richard, was born here.'

'So this is the genesis of that brood?'

'Indeed, Your Highness, the very place. Shall we enter? You'll find it quite acceptable.'

'Yes, let's. Is King Philip here?'

'He is expected in the morning.'

'Good. There is a wagon with my apparel in it. Would you have it unloaded?'

'Consider it done. I'll instruct the steward, and all will be brought to your chambers. There are privy quarters for a king and a queen.'

'Thank you, Monsieur de Tucé. I've not met King Philip, although we may have passed each other somewhere in the bloody dust of Palestine.'

'Herbert, please. Of course, you were on the Crusade. Perhaps you can tell me about that.'

'Perhaps. Although the memories of it are not always welcome.'

'Your Highness, forgive me.'

'Don't concern yourself. Now, where are the queen's quarters? My men will be seen to, Herbert?'

'Of course; soldiers have very fine barracks here and their commander shall have his own accommodation. Duke William, before he became King of England, was very careful to treat his soldiers well.'

'Did you see my commander, Mendia?'

'Was he sitting on a very tiny horse?'

I laughed. 'No, the horse was quite big, but Mendia is bigger.'

'I'll get the steward to shore his bed up.' He laughed with me. This was hopeful.

We soon settled in. Our gowns had been delivered and Alazne was working on them with a damp cloth, trying to remove the creases. When she had finished and laid out all our embellishments, she suggested I examine them. One item remained on the bed, hidden in a satin bag.

'What's that?' I asked once I'd sorted through the clothing.

'Your crown — the one they used in Cyprus, Your Highness.'

'Mmm.' I was not certain this was suitable anymore; I had been widowed before I could be crowned in England.

Alazne watched me struggle and then made a suggestion. 'I have a golden circlet in that box in the corner.'

I brightened up. 'Let's see.'

In the box was all my Basque princess regalia — some in silver, some in gold.

Looking up at Alazne, I remarked, 'It seems that we were looking forward to a promotion at one time, dear friend.'

'Yes — full of hope and expectations, as I remember. But you are still a Queen of England, and a princess. Wear something.'

She held my gaze for a moment before I moved towards her. We hugged, tears flowing, and then began to laugh together.

As we separated, she said, 'Give no thought to anyone else. Let's be happy for a change.'

I could think of nothing better, so I agreed. 'When I meet Philip, I shall do my best to wrest something useful from him. Then we will settle here and enjoy life.'

We embraced once more, and then Alazne made a suggestion. 'Should we go for a walk around the city? It seems to be quite a peaceful place.'

So we did, chaperoned by our own escort. We found the Cathedral of Saint-Julien of Le Mans, within which we prayed for a better future.

I awoke early the next morning and spent some time soaking in a large tub in an antechamber. Alazne added some oils and unguents to the water, and I almost went back to sleep until she insisted that I emerge to get dressed.

'Your knight Paulin has been up to see us. The king arrived during the night and has invited you to partake of breakfast with him, Your Highness.'

'Oh well, Alazne; here we go. If this is successful, I will be regarded as a princess once more and live in Le Mans.'

'Your Highness will always be a queen.'

We emerged from our quarters to find the corridor full of people. Three stepped forward.

'Good morrow, Your Highness. I am Chancellor Alibert, this is Madame Marguerite, the housekeeper, and here is Castellan Guy, who is responsible for your safety. We will conduct you to King Philip Augustus.'

I looked at Alazne and shrugged; we'd have a whole new household if we stayed here.

'Stay close, Father Walther, if you will.' He shuffled near, and I was ready.

Alibert shooed off Castellan Guy, and he and Marguerite led us through the myriad corridors and into a privy chamber, wherein we found the King of France.

Philip Augustus was sitting at the centre of a large table, surrounded by food and wine of all descriptions.

'Ah,' he declared, rising, 'the Queen Dowager of England; at last we meet.' He came round the table and took my hands in his. He was very tall and wore no cap, revealing his bald head. He looked solid, as befitted a king, and addressed me with a smile, although I'd been told he did not do that very often. 'May I call you Berengaria?'

'Please do ... Philip?'

'Of course. We were very near each other in Akko, I believe.'

'I think so. You left before we met.'

'Indeed. An illness, you understand?'

'I understand. We are all afflicted from time to time.' I allowed him that comfort, although I knew that he had left after a great argument with Richard.

'Please sit.' He guided me into a chair opposite his. I noticed that my chair was unusually high so that when he took his place opposite, our heads were level. How very kind. I began to feel more relaxed as Alazne was invited to sit with Marguerite, and Father Walther was conducted to a desk and introduced to a clerk. I suspected that our business for the day lay there.

'Well, Berengaria, you must tell us about your time in Rome. You are friends with His Holiness, I hear.'

'So it seems, Philip.'

We continued to talk as we ate. After a few glugs of wine, he leaned forward and came to the point.

'I would like an agreeable end to all this conflict. Your brother-in-law finds it difficult to understand that agreements and treaties are to be kept — kept, that is, by honourable men or women.'

'I agree. John's approach is altogether too confusing for me.' I smiled and he chuckled.

'What do you desire, Berengaria? How should this end?'

'I want somewhere to settle and be useful.'

'I've heard of your work and your piety. Need I remind you that John did some damage to the walls of Le Mans? They have stood since Roman times, but he interrupted their grandeur. They have been repaired, but some in the city may resent an English queen ruling over them.'

'I am queen by marriage, yet Basque by birth. If I take up my dower, I shall do my very best to serve the city to the best of my abilities.'

'You have properties in Navarre and are entitled to a dowager's pension from England?'

'Yes. Promised but not yet delivered.'

'By John. But your dowers in France now belong to me,' Philip went on.

'I accept that. They were mine as long as Richard lived — and until Eleanor dies.'

'Eleanor's Aquitaine, perhaps. A tenuous position, Berengaria.'

'I've grown used to that.'

He smiled again. 'A pragmatist. Would you like an end to uncertainty in exchange for certain responsibility?'

'I would like an end to uncertainty, yes, but I would like to choose my own responsibilities.'

'I'll cut to the position that I would like to reach; time is pressing, and the tumult grows outside these doors. Give me the dowers in France, and I will give you Le Mans and one thousand in coin. What do you think?'

'I've heard that you want Loches?'

'I'm going to build a royal palace and citadel there, in the very heart of the Plantagenet lands.'

'That will hurt John. Five thousand, and my own seneschal.'

'You have someone in mind?'

'I have.' I thought of Robert of Turnham.

'Three thousand, and your own seneschal for Le Mans. William des Roches remains seneschal for the County of Maine and retains his castle of du Loir.'

'You've not mentioned Aquitaine.' I looked at him across the table and searched for any signs of duplicity.

'You may question my motives, Berengaria, but I suspect there will be some pleasure for you in this. Am I right?'

'Perhaps, but I believe that you were not the first to be wronged by the Plantagenets.'

He laughed. 'A thought has occurred to me: how long would it have been before you and Richard had a clash of wills?'

'You think that I would have been what Eleanor was to her husband Henry?'

'I can see it. Tell me, was Richard really going to sacrifice his sister to Saladin's brother?'

'Yes.' My eyes welled up; that awful vision of Joan, with her flesh burned off her bones, kept repeating.

'I'm sorry, my dear. I did not mean to upset you. Forgive me.'

'Do not concern yourself, Philip. Eleanor sacrificed dear Joan to secure her southern border.'

'I know. I believe that we will be the better for ridding the earth of this scourge named Plantagenet. I worry for England

— perhaps one day you will be clear to go to England and be of use to your realm.'

'I will not be obsessed by that. Who knows what damage John will do if England becomes his only amusement?'

'Ha! *Amusement*: that describes it well. You were Duchess designate for Aquitaine; have you received any coin from there?'

'Not while Eleanor lives.'

'I hear that you have met Isabella. How do you view her?'

I pondered before answering. 'I believe that she values a queen's crown over any love for a king.'

He guffawed. 'I have heard she is something of a firebrand.'

'I've seen signs of that, yes. John may find her … difficult.'

'Mmm.' Drumming his fingers on the table, he regarded me for a while. I did not flinch. 'John will inherit Aquitaine when Eleanor departs the world.'

'Yes — no income from there.'

'If we can make an agreement, I will have two prominent Basque royals within my realm,' he said.

'And your southern border will be secured.'

'As secure as any border can be. How about four thousand in coin and five hundred per year, as well as your own seneschal?'

That was as much as I was likely to get, and more than I'd expected.

'Do we have a deal that suits you, Berengaria?'

I nodded. I'd achieved all I could hope for in the circumstances.

Philip smiled. 'Clerk,' he called, 'read out the list of the queen's dower lands she is relinquishing.'

'Your Highness, they are Falaise, Domfront and Bonneville-sur-Touques, in Normandy.'

'When I rid it of John,' interjected Philip.

The clerk continued. 'We have already mentioned du Loir in Maine, and the counties of Maine, Anjou and Touraine. The queen gets the city of Le Mans, its twenty-seven suburbs, its income and four thousand marks of silver immediately, plus five hundred per annum.'

This didn't take much consideration. I stood up and stretched across the table to offer my hand. Philip stood and he too stretched across the remains of breakfast.

'Agreed?' he asked.

'Agreed,' I responded. 'But no more titles; they are too easily lost.'

'But you have acquired Damsel of Le Mans to add to Queen Dowager of England, Princess of Navarre, and — the best of all — "Brave Berengaria", a credit to womanhood. God bless you.' He laughed. 'John will not like a Queen of England lurking in my France. Help me; be a pest and a thorn in his side. You are owed a large chunk of England's coin, if my intelligencers have it right.'

'Of course. Thank you, Philip. I shall give that some thought. And you have acquired a Queen of England at little cost.'

Chancellor Alibert poked his head round the door.

'Good timing, Alibert; the matter is settled. The clerk has it all. Let us sign; you can witness it.' He looked across at Father Walther. 'Father, will you also witness this, please?'

'Of course, Your Highness.'

He and Philip's scrivener crossed the chamber and placed two documents before us.

'So,' said Philip, signing first his copy, then mine. Alibert did likewise.

'Done,' I said, signing and handing the quill to Walther, who signed the two vellums.

'I am off now, Berengaria. I have a kingdom to rule, else I would enjoy more time with you, but no doubt we shall meet again soon.'

'I look forward to that. One question puzzles me, Philip: where is Arthur? He was in your charge at one time.'

'Caen, I think, but ask John. Only he knows for certain.'

'I see. Has the lad been seen lately?'

'It seems not. I do not expect him to reappear, somehow.'

'That is my fear too. *Au revoir*, Philip. Take care of yourself.'

'Goodbye, Berengaria. God bless.' He waved at Alibert. 'See Queen Berengaria safely back to her quarters and wait for her instructions.'

'A city and a seneschal, Alazne; what about that?' I whispered as we followed Alibert.

'A good outcome. How many chambers does this rambling maze have?'

We laughed. 'Alibert, is there a throne room here?' I asked.

'Indeed, Your Highness. This is where Henry II of England was born. His parents, Geoffrey and Matilda, were not shy of grand gestures. I'll take you to the audience chamber now, if you wish.'

'Note that, Alazne, Father Walther. The Queen Dowager of England will occupy the throne of the former King and Queen of England, and there's naught that the present King of England can do about it.'

They both smiled and Alazne pressed my hand.

'Father Walther, find yourself a suitable chamber. We are about to fill the world with notes of complaint and news of our business here.'

'Certainly, Your Highness, and who will be receiving these notes?'

'Firstly, my brother, King Sancho. We will give him early news before rumours reach his ears and ask his opinion. Then the usual list: the Archbishop of Canterbury, the bishops of England, some cardinals in Rome, and you might send greetings to His Holiness. Then ask the Archbishop of Le Mans for a meeting; there is much to discuss.'

'What about King John?'

'He can find out by whatever means he may.'

'Mendia, tour the walls and inspect the guard. Alazne, find the mistress of the wardrobe. Alibert, send me the head cook and larderer; they will learn new skills, including feeding the poor and injured.'

Not many tears were shed when the next messenger arrived in the second week of April.

'Queen Eleanor is dead, Your Highness,' the dusty fellow declared.

'When?' I asked.

'Where?' added Alazne.

'Fontevraud, on the first of the month, Your Highness,' he answered.

'Some days ago,' I said. 'Where is John?'

'I know not, Your Highness.'

'Thank you. Are you returning to the abbey?'

'Yes, Your Highness, forthwith.'

'Take a message for me to the abbess, if you will. Father Walther, we will compose a letter of condolence to the blessed abbess.'

'Very well, Your Highness. You are not going?'

'I think not. I have had little love from that family, but we shall pray for her.'

'As you wish, Your Highness.'

'That changes the game, Alazne. Only John left.'

'One is enough, Your Highness.'

'Of course. I am not entirely at ease, but we shall continue with our works here.'

After some pondering, Father Walther put forward a ridiculous proposition.

'Did King Philip mention England, Your Highness?' he asked.

'Not directly — why?'

'If John flees across the narrow sea, Philip might be inclined to follow him. Then you could visit, too.'

'What a mischievous thought, Father. Can you finish those letters and get them off, please?'

Leaving him to complete his tasks, I went outside to think. Was invading England such a preposterous idea? What if the English barons were to encourage Philip? I pondered for a while longer and then went back in to sign off my deluge of letters.

My brother replied quickly:

Well done, sister. Keep King Philip near and those certain trusted friends about you. Keep good relations with all, save John; he is not to be trusted. As for England, put that to one side and we will see what transpires.

It was sound advice. One day, perhaps I would see the country of which I once wore the crown.

A NOTE TO THE READER

Dear Reader,

Berengaria was indeed the winner in this messy affair; she survived a vicious holy war, an indifferent husband, a mother-in-law obsessed with dynasty, and chaotic European politics in a dangerous world. Berengaria was content with her lot in Le Mans and worked tirelessly to aid the sick and wounded, she founded Le Pau abbey, which is where she is buried, and became in her time known as, 'The Lady of Le Mans.'

After King John died relationship's with England improved and her incomes were re-instated by John's successor, Henry III, with whom she became friends.

Reviews are the author's lifeblood, so I would be very grateful if you manage to find time to leave a review on **Amazon** or **Goodreads**.

More details about my writing can be found on my website: **www.history-reimagined.co.uk**

Thank you.

Austin Hernon

Sapere Books is an exciting new publisher of brilliant fiction and popular history.

To find out more about our latest releases and our monthly bargain books visit our website: **saperebooks.com**